No Substitute for Motives

Carolyn J. Rose

2016

Thanks to Cheese Puff's many fans
for encouraging me to continue this series

Chapter 1

Motives.

They're not just for criminals or investigators, prosecutors or defense attorneys, politicians or protesters. If you don't believe me, check the Internet for answers to the question: "Why did the chicken cross the road?" You'll see motives ranging from "to get to the other side" all the way to "for some fowl reason."

Whether we realize it or not, most of us have motives for plenty of things we do.

Motives don't have to be of the complex, multi-step, take-over-the-world variety. They can be simple, straightforward, and relatively insignificant.

Maybe you drive a little over the limit because you want to get to work on time. Maybe you don't tell your boss what you think because you want to keep the job you sped up to get to. Or maybe you *do* speak out because you're sick of the job and ready to climb out of your rut in the rat race.

Motives can be obvious or obscured. And having a motive for doing something doesn't mean you'll do it. Even if it's a strong motive. Even if you have means and opportunity.

For example, last year Reckless River Police Detective Charles Atwell believed I had a motive for killing history teacher Henry Stoddard. In fact, I did. Stoddard was a bully. He treated me and other substitute teachers at Captain Meriwether High School like we were substandard, brainless, and generally in his way. But, much as I feared and loathed Stoddard, and much as I fantasized about the improved quality of subbing life without him, I wasn't the one who twisted his tie around his neck and left him to assume room temperature. The deed was done by a woman with a different motive, a motive far loftier than mine.

Cowering at the top of Atwell's suspect list made me more aware of motives—my own and those of others. And, since a drug dealer used my car as a drop, a politician's wife tried to kill me to save her husband's career, and my incarcerated ex-husband started a blog that put me and my dog in danger, I spend more time considering what people might *really* be up to, and why.

It doesn't always make me popular.

My neighbor, Muriel Ballantine, claims I'm suspicious of everyone. But *she* was never suspected of murder. And *she* was never married to Jake. To call him a philandering con man is like calling the Grand Canyon a pothole.

Drug cop Dave Martin, my live-in boyfriend, believes I have a tendency to be paranoid. "Barbara," he'll say, "you're as jumpy as some of the tweakers I arrest."

Dave's teenage daughter Allison claims I don't give her an ounce of credit for good intentions. She insists she's not scheming up ways to bend, break, or skirt the rules 24/7.

(For the record, I give her credit for not scheming during the eight hours she's asleep. Then I knock off an hour because I have a hunch she's dreaming about scheming.)

And then there's my sister. Indigo Zephyr, known as Iz, believes I should suspect everyone's motives—except hers. Iz stepped in to raise me when my parents checked out emotionally after my brother's death, so I owe her a debt that's tough to repay. She knows that, and uses emotional leverage to manipulate me.

If I point out what she's up to, she questions—in a booming voice—*my* motives for questioning *her* motives. Arguing with someone who loves to argue gets me nowhere, so I'm perfecting the fine art of deflection. I've even managed some manipulation of my own.

Sneaky? Slimy? Spineless?

Call it what you will, the result is my sister no longer views my condo as her personal guest house, and doesn't treat my scrawny bank account as if her name is on it. She still lectures me on what she sees as my inability to function without a man at my side, but I treat her comments like background noise.

Still, I'm relieved when she directs her sermon at someone else—especially when she's foolhardy enough to target Mrs. Ballantine.

After my unemployed sister managed the task of gutting the former Krammee's Restaurant with only minor collateral damage—mostly to her thumbs and toes—Mrs. B hired her to clean out a second bedroom so it could become a mini dance studio. The process involved transferring the more elegant and exotic articles of Mrs. B's late husband's wardrobe to the costume racks of a local theater company. Marco Ballantine had been noted for his flashy style, donning opera capes and ruffled shirts and velvet smoking jackets. When Mrs. B asked if thespians could find a use for such things, the director gushed her appreciation. When a substantial monetary donation accompanied the clothing, the director's gushing gave way to shrieks of joy.

So, while Mrs. B sorted out more commonplace shirts, slacks, jackets, and sweaters, and set them aside for a homeless shelter, Iz transferred boxes of showy outfits to the truck borrowed from her partner Penelope. For the first few hours, my sister demonstrated remarkable restraint and withheld comments. I know because my condo is right next door, my windows were open, and I was listening. Hard.

Well aware of how difficult it was for Iz to contain her opinions, Dave and I had set up a pool, dividing the day by 15-minute increments. A quarter bought a square, so winning was less about money than about bragging rights. A side bet covered the nature of the first opinion Iz expressed. Dave thought she'd refer to Marco's wardrobe as ostentatious, or a waste of money. I contended Iz was insensitive, but not stupid enough to malign the love of Mrs. B's life. I bet she'd go for the reason behind the remodeling—Mrs. B intended to use the space to rehearse her dance routine for *Still Got That Strut*, a reality show based in Las Vegas.

Back in the day—which specific day in which specific year she never says—Mrs. B was showgirl royalty in Lost Wages. Long-legged, graceful, and flat-out gorgeous, she wore feathers, furs, and frippery like no one else. On top of that, she was intelligent, witty, and kind. Marco, one of many suitors, beat out the others with suave style and a call to adventure spiced by a dash of danger. Pretending to be on the run from the mob, he carried her away from Las Vegas and around the world.

Marco's death left her reeling for years. When we met, she was living in the past, surrounded by thousands of photographs and hundreds of articles of his clothing. I like to think I helped her get unstuck, but most of the credit goes to Cheese Puff. The scruffy ten-pound orange mutt I discovered shivering beneath a rain-drenched shrub won her heart. Concerned about the hours he spent alone while I subbed, she formed the Cheese Puff Care and Comfort Committee. Committee members, all retired residents of my condo complex, are ready at the drop of a hat—or any other object—to mix a drink or mix into someone else's business.

Except for a few glitches and hiccups, the Committee's system mostly works. On the plus side, I have peace of mind and can concentrate on surviving as a substitute teacher. On the minus side, as walking and feeding expanded to become over-the-top pampering, Cheese Puff expected to be treated like royalty 24/7. On the plus side again, the Committee accepted my sister and welcomed Dave and Allison when they moved in a few months ago.

But more about that later.

After a few hours of sorting and packing, Mrs. B called me over to have a look. I hadn't been inside the space for almost a year and what I remembered was a stuffed closet, stacks of boxes, clothing racks, and shelves laden with photograph albums and souvenirs. Now I saw only indentations in the cream-colored carpet and a few scuffs on the beige walls.

"Wow! I forgot this room had a window."

"Yes. It lets in more light than I remembered." Mrs. B raised the blind and gave us a view of the condo parking lot and the maple trees and hedges bordering it. The hedges were slowly recovering from the devastation wrought by my ex-husband during the few weeks he'd faked his way through duties as a handyman and groundskeeper. The maples were sporting tints of yellow, orange, and red. The last day of September already.

"Of course I knew I couldn't keep Marco with me by storing every little memento of our life together." Mrs. B slipped her arm through mine. "But somehow I couldn't let go of a single thing until lately." She turned me toward the open closet. "Everything from in there is in tubs in the corner of my bedroom. I'll have shelves built for the scrapbooks and memorabilia I can't part with. And I'll hang a few of my favorite photos once the walls are painted."

I kissed her cheek. "What's your plan for the studio? Besides a hardwood floor?"

Mrs. B smiled, her sapphire eyes twinkling. "Two walls of mirrors. And a ballet barre so I can practice my kicks without falling. According to the date on the calendar, I'm not as young as I used to be."

And that comment opened the door for my sister.

Chapter 2

"Exactly the point I'm obligated to make." Iz straightened her broad shoulders and flicked dust from a XL T-shirt with a message suggesting men should climb down the evolutionary ladder and start over. "When you were young, women didn't have the options and opportunities they do now. They didn't have as much awareness of their rights and abilities. They were forced to take demeaning jobs."

"That's a history lesson." I checked my watch, wondering if my initials were on this 15-minute square. "What's your point?"

Iz scowled and did a twitchy thing with her eyes signifying she'd speak to me later, then turned to face Mrs. B. "The point is, you didn't know better then, but you do now. You should inform Dario O'Brien you won't take part in this sleazy and degrading program. Tell him you won't wear revealing costumes, parade in front of shallow minor celebrities, or be judged according to standards established by men."

Wow.

Way to insult Mrs. B in the past *and* the present. My sister was as sensitive as the average chunk of granite.

The twinkle in Mrs. B's eyes sharpened to a glitter and she fingered her pearl necklace—a single short strand worn with a pink shirt that had once belonged to Marco. "You've never been hungry, have you, Iz?"

I could have fielded that question with a resounding "No." But I kept my lips zipped and my gaze directed at the floor. Iz might grow peckish—say, on a long flight with limited food service, or at a convention where she was forced to prove sisterhood by waiting in line at the lunch buffet with other women. But true hunger? Never. As long as they sold cargo pants and she continued to stuff the pockets with granola bars, crackers, nuts, chocolates, and bottles of juice, she was mere seconds from a snack.

Iz tugged her T-shirt over the bulge of her stomach. "I—"

"I mean *really* hungry," Mrs. B continued. "So hungry it feels like teeth gnawing at your stomach. So hungry all you have the strength to do is cry."

Iz tugged her shirt again. "Uh . . ."

"Pride can be a terrible thing." Mrs. B's voice softened. "After Aunt Tildy died, my family went off the rails. She was the one who kept my father thinking straight and looking to the future instead of to the past and the horrors of war. She was practical, realistic. She did what had to be done to provide food and shelter, and she didn't give a fig what people thought. But after she was gone, my parents wouldn't take charity, even when all we had was dry beans and the last potatoes from the garden. They wouldn't tolerate the shame of asking for help, or the disgrace of accepting it."

She caught her lower lip between her teeth and closed her eyes for a second. "My father was a man filled with fury waiting for an opportunity to burst forth, so I never told him I got lunch and breakfast at school. I never said a word about the times friends invited me to their tables. Those meals kept me walking. But dreams let me run."

I'd guessed Mrs. B's childhood had been hard, but I never heard the details. I was mesmerized. Iz, however, narrowed her eyes in a skeptical way.

Mrs. B gripped our shoulders. "You girls have dreams. You know dreams have power."

I nodded. My dreams were sweet and simple—visions of being happy, loving and being loved, and helping others in small ways. Iz's dreams were bigger and broader. They were about fame and adulation. Lately I felt my dreams coming true. And I felt hers slipping away.

"Well," Mrs. B went on, "a friend took dancing lessons and taught me what she learned. And sometimes I visited friends with TV sets and watched variety shows. When I got older and brave enough, I dressed like a boy, walked to the highway, and stuck out my thumb. I had two dollars to my name when I got to Las Vegas, but I knew how to be hungry, and I knew I couldn't afford to be proud. I bought apples and a sack of peanuts, and I made up my mind I'd walk down every street and knock on every door where I might find work."

"I bet you didn't have to knock on many," I said.

"You'd lose the bet, dear." Mrs. B released her grip on my shoulder. "A lot of young women were knocking on the same doors. I was lucky to get on as a waitress at a diner—luckier because I got the overnight shift."

Iz stepped back, breaking Mrs. B's hold. "How is that lucky?"

"It meant I got plenty to eat. We had the strongest coffee around, we served good food at reasonable prices, and at night we never rushed anyone, especially those doing business in the corner booths. So I met all kinds of people, and overheard conversations about all kinds of, well, let's call them 'activities.'"

Iz rolled her eyes. "I can make a guess about some of those activities."

"I'm sure you'd be right." Mrs. B shot me a wink.

"Prostitutes and pimps," Iz muttered. "Mobsters."

"Perhaps. My boss told me to treat them like other customers—take their orders, keep their cups filled, and never ask about their business."

"But you knew," I suggested.

"Of course, dear. Everyone knew."

"You're making my point," Iz said. "You should have walked away when you realized your boss turned a blind eye to what was illegal or immoral."

I turned on my sister. "How moral is letting a child go hungry because of stubborn pride? How legal? If we walked away every time something wasn't squeaky clean, we'd be walking most of the time."

Mrs. B chuckled and patted my arm. "Thank you, dear. So much of what goes on in this world isn't all black or white, is it? And, as you well know, it's easier to walk away when you have a place to walk *to*. And a walking-away fund."

Iz scowled. If she'd ever had a walking-away fund, my guess was it hadn't been enough to walk more than a few blocks and crash on a friend's sofa.

"I was naïve." Mrs. B blinked the far-away look from her eyes. "But I soon saw what happened to girls who got entangled with some of the men I waited on. I realized I had to stay in control. So I never drank or took pills, I never accepted a favor with strings attached, and I never went where I wasn't safe."

She clapped her hands. "But enough. I soon landed a job where I was treated like a queen. I met a wonderful man. And now I intend to honor his memory and the courage of that determined girl who hitchhiked to Las Vegas and lived on peanuts. I intend to appear on *Still Got That Strut*."

10

Iz tightened her lips and narrowed her eyes, but I hugged Mrs. B. "I'm dying to see your routine."

"And I'd love to show you, but I want to keep it secret until the last minute."

"Then I'll be surprised with everyone else."

Mrs. B smiled, turned her sapphire gaze on my scowling sister, and cut the legs out from under her objections. "Clearly, I don't need the prize money, Iz. If I win, I intend to donate it to women's programs. And I'll want you to help me decide which ones."

"I love the days you don't sub and get bored enough to cook." Dave cut a huge slice of meat loaf, scooped mashed potatoes from the bowl, built a spud mountain on his plate, and planted it with broccoli trees. "It seems like weeks since we had anything besides pizza, take-out Chinese, and salads."

"You could have cooked," Allison pointed out, earning points with me. "We did dial-and-dine stuff because Barbara was subbing in middle school."

She said "middle school" the same way some people say "hazardous waste," or "flesh-eating bacteria." In other words, pretty much the way I said it. Some teachers enjoy the noise and pace and drama of middle school. I admire their attitude and fortitude—from a distance whenever possible.

"And before that," Allison went on, "she subbed at the juvenile jail and found out who stole the pedigreed cat and got threatened because of the blog Jake wrote for Cheese Puff."

At the sound of his name, Cheese Puff sat up and pawed at my knee, making it clear he wanted meat loaf, and wanted it now. Playing the pity-me card, he cocked his head from side to side, showing off patches of stubble where his hair had been shaved and his cuts treated after a losing battle with a duck. "Later," I told him. "You can have a tiny piece later."

Cheese Puff snorted his disgust and stalked over to sit beside Lola, the drug-sniffing Golden Retriever partnered with Dave. Well-mannered and well-trained, she'd remained flopped beside the sofa, raising her head only to scent the air and make with pleading eyes when I took the meat loaf from the oven.

"I wasn't saying Barbara should have cooked more often," Dave protested. "And I've been busy, too. I had those joint drug sweeps over in Portland. And endless shopping trips with my daughter."

Allison rolled her eyes, but didn't pursue the attack. Truthfully, Dave helped out a lot in the dinner department, although mostly by picking up take-out meals and carrying garbage to the trash bins at the far end of the parking lot. He made a killer loaf of garlic bread and could grill burgers or chicken or chops with the best of them. But when it came to the rest of what made up a meal—veggies and fruit and whatnot—he floundered.

"There may be more full-meal deals in your future," I told him. "Big Chill shot me an e-mail this afternoon. I'll be in the pottery lab at the high school for a week."

"I thought you hated pottery," Allison said.

"I don't hate it. I find it stressful. And scary."

And it was. Kids were always tempted to toss lumps of clay or poke each other with shaping tools. And then there was the kiln. But a week of pay was, well, a week of pay. Another sub would snap up the assignment if I didn't.

"Anyway, it means I'll be home earlier." I tapped Dave's wrist with my index finger. "And if certain people are especially nice to me, I might manage to assemble a meal or two."

He shot me a wicked grin. "Exactly how nice do I have to be?"

"We can negotiate that later."

12

"She probably wants you to wash her car," Allison said. "Or mop the floor."

"I'm willing to start on the floor." Dave leered. "If I can work my way up to furniture. My back isn't what it used to be, and the floor is, um, hard."

I felt myself flush and avoided glancing at Allison. She was closing in on 16 and, thanks to TV, movies, and social media, probably knew far more about sex than I did at her age. But Dave and I limited public displays of affection to hand holding and the occasional kiss. And, although Dave did a lot of alluding and I contributed my fair share, we never talked in specific terms when she was listening.

Dave cleared his throat and returned to an earlier discussion. "Sounds like Mrs. Ballantine took the wind out of your sister's sails with her promise to donate to women's programs."

"Temporarily at least."

"Iz never backs off for long." Allison jabbed a broccoli spear with her fork. "It's gonna be so great to go to Las Vegas and see all the casinos and meet Glorree Morning."

Chapter 3

"Who?" Dave and I asked in unison.

Allison shot us the smug smile of a teen in possession of knowledge adults don't have. "The showgirl who was always competing with Mrs. B. For the best dance numbers and costumes. And boyfriends. Even Marco."

"Glorree Morning?" Dave asked. "That was her name?"

"Her stage name. I can't remember what he real name was. She picked Glorree Morning 'cause she had really blue eyes— almost as blue as Mrs. B's. And she did this twiny viny dance." Allison demonstrated by raising her arms, wiggling her fingers, and rubbing her hands together. "And when she did it, she wore a veil over her nose and mouth and puffy see-through pants and bangles and stuff."

Mrs. B had a rival. On the stage and in the realm of romance. Why hadn't I heard?

"She always tells me I ask too many questions about back then, when I should be asking about right now or what's ahead," Allison went on. "But lots of times, like when we're shopping, and something reminds her of when she was all famous, she gets misty."

"Misty?" Dave asked.

"Like maybe she might cry." Allison mimed wiping her eyes. "But she never does. Just sniffles a little and then tells me a story. Except I guess they're not stories if they're true."

Dave shrugged and shot a glance that signaled the answer was on me. "We could call them bits of history," I said. "But with a personal spin."

Allison pointed a fork loaded with mashed potatoes at my nose. "And *that* means?"

"Memories can be influenced by the power of an experience, how it affects someone, and how that person filters it. Right?"

Allison considered, holding the fork upright and licking mashed potatoes like ice cream. "I guess."

Her tone said she didn't care, but I was on a roll. "Remember the food fight in the cafeteria before school let out?"

"Yeah." She grinned. "Food went up to the skylights. It was awesome."

Dave growled. "I bet the custodians didn't use the word 'awesome' when they had to clean it up."

(For the record, they used several words I won't print here. Not that I can't spell them or have never used them, but I prefer not to see or hear them.)

Allison's grin faded a few degrees. I waited a moment, letting her consider the ramifications of the food fight. "How did the fight start?"

"Uh, Doug said Mick squashed his burger on someone's head. But Josh said he saw two girls throwing raisins. And Lily swore she saw Dane dump his milk on Derek, and—"

"Exactly my point. Everybody had a different view because of where they were sitting. And their memories are colored by what they heard about the fight later, and by how they feel about the people involved."

15

"Or which kids they want to pin the blame on," Dave added.

"I bet some kids who say they saw the whole thing weren't even there," I said.

Allison stirred her pile of mashed potatoes. "So what Mrs. B tells me about her past might not be the truth? She might be lying?"

"I doubt she's lying," Dave said. "But it's *her* truth. It might not match up to what Glorree Morning remembers."

"How come you always say confusing stuff and make me feel stupid?" Allison pointed an accusing finger. "You do that all the time."

Dave's gripped the edge of the table, a sign the end of his rope was in view. The twitch at the corners of Allison's lips indicated she was baiting him. Since Dave had decided we should eat as a family and in the old-fashioned way—without cellphones at the table and with the TV off—baiting had become a form of entertainment.

"It means," I said as I laid a hand on Dave's arm, "if Mrs. B didn't care much for Glorree Morning, her feelings could influence her memories."

"You mean she'd only remember the bad stuff? Can you do that? Just tell your brain to forget."

"From the state of your grades," Dave muttered, "that's what you do."

I gave his arm a vicious squeeze. "I think you can convince yourself some memories are more important or meaningful than others. And if she didn't like Glorree Morning right from the start, she'd slant incidents and conversations."

"Like if Glorree Morning asked how she was, Mrs. B would remember it like Glorree was asking only because she hoped Mrs. B was sick?"

"Sure."

Allison smashed a broccoli spear into her potatoes. "How do we know if Mrs. B's memories are true to the way it was?"

"I guess you'd have to find Glorree Morning," Dave said, "and ask her about her memories of Mrs. Ballantine."

"And if she says everything all opposite? If she says Mrs. B was a total witch?"

"Then you'll have to decide whether her memories are false, or whether the truth is somewhere in the middle."

"You mean, be like a jury in a trial?"

"Pretty much," Dave agreed.

Allison nodded and ate the mashed broccoli spear. "I'll ask her when we get to Las Vegas."

I blinked. "It's been a long time. Glorree Morning might not be in Las Vegas. She might live on the other side of the world."

"Maybe. But she'll be there for the show. She's the other one."

"Other one what?" Dave asked.

"The other showgirl on Mrs. B's episode of *Still Got That Strut*." Allison sighed in a way that implied Dave was too stupid to live. "Every show has two. They compete against each other and judges grade their performances."

And Glorree Morning, Mrs. B's rival from back in the day, would be out to upstage her.

Forget talk about competing for the hungry girl she once was and the memory of the man she loved. Muriel Ballantine, it seemed, had a more powerful motive for returning to Las Vegas.

Sunday evening, Mrs. B dropped in while I was selecting outfits for a week of subbing in pottery. The process involved picking anything that matched gray clay or would stand up to a dousing of stain remover and at least one trip through the wash on the heavy-duty setting. Making a little tutting sound, she ran her fingers over my picks. "What about those blouses and slacks I bought at the August sale?"

"They'd be ruined in a day."

She tutted once more and cradled Cheese Puff against her shoulder. "I suppose you know best, dear. But these jeans are wearing thin at the knees. And the T-shirts are fading."

"So if they don't make it through the week, it's no loss."

"That's the only point in their favor." She flicked through the rest of my outfits—mostly variations on the jeans and T-shirt theme. "I wish you'd let me treat you to a major shopping excursion."

Translation: My outfits didn't twitch the needle on the "glamorous" dial.

Mrs. B, as Dave often said, was a force of nature. We couldn't change her course; we could only reckon with her. So I didn't argue. I deflected. "Let's wait until I get a teaching position. We can shop and celebrate at the same time."

"That's a wonderful idea. And we'll buy posters and shelves for your classroom. And potted plants."

Ha!

The average potted plant in a high school classroom had a life expectancy somewhere between that of Mayflies and brine shrimp. When the time came, I'd steer her toward plants of the plastic variety.

I moved the first of five outfits to a hook in the bathroom and crossed to the bureau in search of socks and underwear. I wasn't at my best at 5:30 when I hauled myself out of bed for the washing-dressing-eating rush designed to get me to school at 6:55. Seconds lost deciding what to wear, or searching for a missing shoe, added up. And if the engine in my aging car took its usual notion to cough, sputter, and die before kicking over, those seconds became minutes.

18

Now, you might wonder why I don't get up 10 or 15 minutes earlier. Well, I have. Several times. The result is pretty much the same. The more time I allocate, the more the dogs dawdle through their morning duties, the hair dryer overheats, or the toaster goes rogue and singes my bread. So, 5:30 it is.

Mrs. B rubbed her nose against Cheese Puff's, made kissy sounds, and set him on the bed. "Can you spare the little prince for a few days?"

"The little prince" was one of her pet names for my entitled mutt. Asking if I could "spare" him was her way of assuring me she knew he was my dog, no matter how much time he spent snoozing on her lap or sitting at her feet and begging for the designer dog treats she stocked.

"You'll be subbing all week, Allison will be out with Josh after school, and Dave and Lola will be away for special training." Mrs. B straightened my sock drawer, lining up pairs according to the colors of the rainbow, anchored on one end by black and gray socks and on the other by beige and white. "The little prince will be all alone."

I groaned—silently. With Mrs. B and other members of the CPCCC dropping in to coddle him, or taking him out on excursions that made me simmer with envy, Cheese Puff would be "all alone" for about two hours a day. He'd spend the time napping in his favorite spot between the cushion and arm of "his" chair in the living room.

But I didn't mention any of that. First, because it was obvious Mrs. B had a plan, and second, because a few days without feeding, walking, and other dog-related chores would be relaxing. "What did you have in mind?"

"I'd like to take him along to the resort."

Before I could say anything, she rushed on. "He's had such a tough time since he fought that dreadful duck—stitches, pills, wearing a cone for a week. And now . . . well, I'm certain he's stressed about his hair."

Stifling a laugh, I bent low and dug through the bottom drawer in search of an ancient gray sweater with sagging pockets and sleeves long enough for an orangutan. At the best of times, "scruffy" or "scraggly" were words I used to describe Cheese Puff's orange hair. Having portions shaved and dabbed with a blue-green antibiotic salve hadn't done all that much damage.

I tossed the sweater on the bed. If it didn't survive the week, I wouldn't be heartbroken. "You're going to a resort? Like a spa?"

"Oh, no, dear. It's hardly a spa. I called it a resort because it once was." She dabbed the corner of one eye with her fingertip. "When life was lived at a slower pace and people took time to savor sunsets, it was a destination. Now it's a tired little hotel, and never more than a quarter full."

That didn't sound like Mrs. B's kind of place. "Where is this hotel?"

"North and east about 25 miles or so." She tapped the last pair of socks into place and closed the drawer. "Way up at the head of Lost Canyon Creek. It's called the River Rise Inn, although I don't know how the person who did the naming mistook a creek for a river."

An inn at the head of a canyon sounded remote. Remote was fine if she and Dario were aiming to get away from it all. But why take Cheese Puff? And—

Wait. Dario returned to Las Vegas this afternoon.

"Workmen will be in and out all week putting down the floor, painting, and installing the mirrors and barre," Mrs. B said. "How can I focus on my routine?"

A question she didn't give me time to answer.

"I asked Jim to keep an eye on the workmen while I'm away."

"What about renovation work at Krammee's? Isn't Jim tied up with that?"

"Lana Dylan probably knows more about what should be done than Jim and Verna." Mrs. B put a finger to her lips. "Don't tell them I said that."

I'd helped Lana Dylan's son when he was framed for kidnapping a pedigreed cat. Mrs. B had, in turn, helped Lana with a job managing the restaurant that would soon open in the former Krammee's building. Lana had been a waitress most of her life and was no stranger to hard work, long hours, and people who couldn't make up their minds in a timely manner.

"My lips, as usual, are zipped. How's the renaming coming along."

"Slowly. Everyone has an opinion."

Everyone included three of my neighbors—Jim, Verna, and Sybil—who were also founding members of the Cheese Puff Care and Comfort Committee. All retired, they had lots of time on their hands and relished "a project." Penelope, an electrician, and my friend Paulette, an interior decorator, had also been pressed into service. And so had Josh, Allison's boyfriend. He'd worked at Krammee's flipping burgers before Woodrow Krammer was murdered—a crime that significantly raised the restaurant health-rating average in Reckless River.

"I bet they're poles apart. And I bet no one wants to compromise."

"Naturally. Poor Paulette is about to pull her hair out."

Paulette was in charge of color scheme, furnishings, logo, and signs for what would become a gourmet grilled cheese sandwich shop. She'd already pushed back her deadline twice. One more push meant last-minute-rush prices, something

Verna, in charge of accounting and budgeting, insisted they avoid.

"Will you have to step in?"

Mrs. B winced. "I hope it won't come to that. I think they'll get there. Probably in the nick of time." She twinkled a faint smile my way as if to say that time-nicking was usual for the group. "At any rate, Jim said he'd watch over my place as long as I toted my jewelry to the safe deposit box at the bank."

And there was a lot to tote. Mrs. B had quite a collection of pearl necklaces. Not to mention diamonds, rubies, emeralds, and other precious gems. "Good suggestion."

"Yes, Jim takes crime prevention seriously. Although at times I think he's a tad paranoid."

Balancing her tendency to be a tad trusting.

"Anyway, the River Rise Inn has a wonderful ballroom and stage. It's just about the size I'll be on for the show. And the owner—he's an old acquaintance of Dario's, by the way—said he'd be delighted to have me make use of it."

If the hotel was never more than a quarter full, he'd probably also be delighted to charge her for the privilege. But I didn't mention that. While extra fees crimp my budget, Mrs. B would barely glance at the bill when she handed over her credit card.

"I've booked a ground-floor suite to make it easy for the little prince should he need to go during the night."

"You don't think he'll be a distraction while you're working? He's been especially needy since you got chummy with the cat next door."

"A little jealousy is natural." Mrs. B brushed that objection aside. "He realizes he owes Apricot for saving him from that horrible duck. They're becoming great friends. They play together all the time."

If you interpreted Cheese Puff's attempts to chase the cat away as playing.

"I'll bring a special cushion for him to snooze on while I'm practicing. And several new types of treats."

"Okay, but you know he's all about demonstrating his displeasure if he doesn't get what he wants when he wants it."

Cheese Puff glared at me and raised his upper lip, displaying tiny canine teeth. I lifted my lip in response. Since his ignominious duel with the duck, he'd been even more of a "little prince" than usual—snubbing food, fighting attempts to get him into his harness, and refusing to walk more than a few yards without sitting and whining. He'd also increased his efforts to abandon me at every opportunity, zip out the door to the deck, and scamper along to Mrs. B's unit. I couldn't blame him. Mrs. B had high-quality snacks and excelled at pampering, coddling, and offering unconditional love.

"Now, dear, let's not characterize with negative terms. I prefer to take the view that Cheese Puff has very clear preferences and expresses them in no uncertain terms."

Said the woman who, despite an opinion from the vet, wouldn't believe Cheese Puff was fine and milking us for sympathy.

"But, that being said, I understand your concerns. We'll share together time whenever I need to rest." She fluffed her silvery hair. "And, I confess, that is far more often than I hoped. We'll go for a short ramble every morning, and I've arranged for the chef's daughter to take him on a longer walk after school."

In other words, asking me if I could "spare" Cheese Puff had been asking me to rubber stamp a plan already made. See what I mean about the force of nature thing? "Sounds like you're all set. Shall I pack his harness?"

"No need. I bought a new one after I dropped Dario at the airport. It's bright blue with built-in lights that flash so I can see him in the dark. It also has an alarm I can trigger with a remote."

"An alarm?"

"There are creatures in those woods—cougars and coyotes and bears. The alarm is quite shrill."

And would probably frighten Cheese Puff more than any predator.

I kissed her cheek, inhaling the light scent of lemon soap and a perfume that made me think of a tropical garden. "Then go for it."

"Thank you, dear. I'll let myself in and pick him up in the morning." With a last glance at my wardrobe selections for the week and a final soft tut of dismay, she headed for the door. "Don't worry about either of us. We'll have a wonderful time."

Famous last words right up there with those of Union General John Sedgwick who, moments before he was shot, told his men: "They couldn't hit an elephant at this distance."

Chapter 4

Monday morning in the pottery lab passed without incident. Well, without *major* incident. No fingers were sliced off, and only a few drops of blood were shed in an attempt to trash a broken mug before I noticed. Recalling my training in dealing with bodily fluids, I handed the kid a wad of tissue to hold against his cut, sent him to the nurse's office, and called a custodian to collect shards and clean up droplets.

Little did the wounded sophomore know I was delighted to see that particular mug shattered. Egged on by advanced students, I'd made it last spring when I filled in for a few days. Plenty of solid advice hadn't balanced my lack of artistic talent, and no step in the process had gone well. The mug was lopsided, the handle hung at an angle, the blue and green stripes turned muddy where they overlapped, and the uneven glaze didn't help a bit. To say it was ugly was like saying the Mariana Trench is deep.

Suspecting it would look worse when it emerged from the kiln, I'd etched a set of fake initials on the base. X and Y, my old friends from algebra.

After one glance at the fired mug, I "forgot" to take it home. I'd anticipated the mug would be tossed in a box with other unclaimed projects and consigned to a closet, but it became a teaching tool, an example of what not to do. It even had a place of honor in the center of a shelf loaded with other rejects.

When the bell rang for lunch, I shucked my sweater and headed for the teachers' room where, during my first week at Captain Meriwether, I'd been invited to hang out. Crammed with desks and shelves, it had space for only six chairs at the table. One had been unused since December when Susan Mitchell was charged with murdering history teacher Henry Stoddard. Several claims on the seat had been thwarted in the months since, and the empty chair offered mute testimony to how deeply she was missed.

Doug Whitman grinned when I opened the door. "I thought that was your lunch sack in the refrigerator, but I checked the sandwich to be sure."

Peanut butter and strawberry jam on artisan bread—one of my go-to lunches. It required little effort, but delivered the comfort-food taste and texture I craved after three tough periods.

History teacher Aston Marsden, who often ate in character as a mountain man from the 1800s, glanced up from carving slivers of meat off a gnarly bone, possibly a ham hock. "If the sandwich looked edible, you knew it wasn't Brenda's."

Sounded like their off-again-on-again relationship was in the off mode. Forcing myself not to glance at Brenda Waring, I skirted the end of the table and opened the tiny refrigerator. It hadn't smelled like a garden in bloom at 7:00 when I wedged my lunch sack inside, but now the odor was reminiscent of a garbage dump on a scorching day. Brenda's lunch? Or festering remnants of Aston's meals from weeks past? Hard to tell.

When Susan was with us, she'd tossed items on the way to science-experiment status, wiped spills and smears, and placed a fresh bowl of baking soda on the shelves each week. Since she went to jail, no one had stepped up.

I couldn't blame them. With changes in lesson planning, curriculum, and reporting, food spoilage was the least of teachers' worries. I, however, didn't have those demands on my time or energy. When the final bell rang, I walked to my car without lugging a computer and a load of papers to grade. Cleaning the refrigerator was a nasty job, but they'd taken me in and made me feel welcome. Aston gave me a ride when my car broke down. Counselor Gertrude Suttle provided a wealth of information about how to handle kids acting out because of problems at home. English teacher Doug Whitman found me a summer job. And Brenda . . . Well, never mind. This was my tribe.

"I'm free fifth period," I volunteered. "I'll clean the refrigerator if you all go through it before then and toss anything that smells suspicious."

Brenda pointed a knife at Aston. "Don't say a word. I bet nothing I have in there is worse than your leftovers."

Aston remained silent, but his body language—mock gagging, and nose holding—spoke volumes.

Brenda shook the knife and beige glops spattered on the tattered red tablecloth Susan brought in ten months ago. Doug eased his chair another inch from the table and stared at the substance as if he expected it to eat through the plastic. I made a mental note to buy a table cover, then added napkins and pepper and salt shakers to the list.

"I think we can manage a simple task like sorting through our leftovers," Gertrude said in a tone that implied it was time to adult-up. "I have a bit of cheese on the top shelf. And a tiny jar of mayo in the rack on the door."

Doug tapped a container of spaghetti and meatballs. "This is all I had in there. And I intend to finish it and take the bowl home."

I popped my cola, unfolded the plastic wrap shielding my sandwich, and dropped into the chair between Doug and the place where Susan once sat.

"I probably have the most." Brenda used her knife to transfer the beige substance from a plastic tub to a slice of bread mottled brown and rusty red. "Since I'm the only member of this group pursuing cutting-edge cuisine."

"Speaking of cutting," Aston said, "that bread resembles a hunk of old bandage from a Civil War battlefield."

"I'll have you know this 'hunk of old bandage' is beet and whole wheat bread. I made it myself."

"Because no one else would?" Aston sniped.

Doug ducked his head and stifled a laugh. I bit off enough of my sandwich to keep my mouth engaged. Gertrude sighed and massaged her temples.

"I hate to think about what you have in that refrigerator." Brenda went on the attack, aiming her knife at Aston. "Wolverine jerky? Sautéed snake? Biscuits made with gopher fat strained through the hair on your chin?"

Aston combed his shaggy beard with his fingers and tipped his head as if considering the merits of all she mentioned.

"You have a lot of nerve complaining about what I eat." Brenda waved the knife, sending another beige glop flying.

Doug ducked lower.

"Good reflexes," Aston said. "Missed you by half an inch."

Doug glanced over his shoulder. "What is it?"

"Goose liver with garlic," Brenda said. "An excellent source of protein. Good for your blood and lungs."

"I'll pass." Aston pointed to a rectangular container beside the tub of goose liver. "What's for dessert?"

"Not that you care, but I brought chocolate-covered asparagus. There's plenty for everyone."

Urk!

What a waste of chocolate.

I don't hate asparagus, but a little goes a long way with me. I prefer it chilled and used as a tool to convey dip to my mouth. I couldn't imagine how it would taste covered with chocolate. I didn't *want* to imagine.

I tried to swallow, but the bite of sandwich I'd been chewing seemed glued to the roof of my mouth, defying my tongue's valiant efforts to scrape it loose. I sipped cola and swished the way you do when a dentist stops drilling for a few seconds and the assistant squirts just enough water in your mouth to make you wonder if there's a rationing program you weren't aware of.

"Enough!" Gertrude smacked her spoon on the table. "Barbara, if you find anything that smells like toxic waste, don't think twice, just toss it. If anyone has the gall to complain, I'll deal with it."

She fixed Aston with a stare a basilisk might envy. He glared in return, but only for a moment. Then he dropped his gaze and devoted his attention to the pig's knee or elbow or whatever. Brenda didn't attempt a return stare when her turn came. She made a great production of opening the asparagus container and defiantly biting a stalk. Had the stalk been crisp, that might have gone better. As it was, the asparagus was tough. She tore at it with her teeth, leaving smears of chocolate in the corners of her mouth.

"All right," Gertrude said, "now let's talk about something else. Any idea who's been stealing food and clothing from the Family Support Room?"

"Why steal?" Doug raised his hands in disbelief. "All kids have to do is ask for what they need. You give it to them if you have it, or try to round it up if you don't."

"That's the policy," Brenda agreed. "No forms, no strings, and darn few questions. I know you weren't happy to have another job dumped in your lap last year, Gertrude, but you were the obvious choice. You know most of the kids in this school. And you've done a great job."

"You don't mess with success," Aston said. "You keep it simple, fast, and easy. Donations in, supplies out to any kid enrolled in the school."

Gertrude beamed at the praise.

"How much is missing?" Doug asked.

"That's a good question." Gertrude pinched her chin. "Like Aston said, donations come in and supplies go out. Sometimes the same day. I have more than 400 kids assigned to me, so my counseling schedule is packed. Fortunately, the custodians bring up donations left in the front office."

And it was a long hike from her counseling office to the Family Support Room near Assistant Principal Tremaine Scott's office on the upper level of the school. Two lengthy hallways and a staircase lay between.

"I'm the one who hands things out, but I have no time to take inventory," she went on. "So I'm going by what I've noticed isn't there and should be because I didn't hand it out. There was a quilt with a design of trees and ferns, a case of chicken noodle soup, another of tuna, six pairs of new socks, and a set of bright green rubber boots. And probably a whole lot more."

"Is there a pattern to when things disappear?" I asked.

Gertrude considered for a few seconds. "I have a feeling things go missing at the start of the week."

"Who else has a key to the room?"

"The administrators. The custodians. And Big Chill."

"I bet she took those boots," Doug said with a grin. "For wading through BS from the central office."

I chuckled at the mental image of the tiny head secretary, usually shod in fashionable high heels, tromping around in rubber boots. No way. And no way would she steal anything. Tremaine Scott surely hadn't taken the tuna—I knew he couldn't stand the smell. But beyond that, he'd known poverty as a child and wouldn't deprive anyone of a meal. As for Principal Jerome Morrow, well, he seldom left his office. He might not be aware the Family Support Room existed. "I think we can rule out the Chillster and the administrators."

"I agree." Gertrude sighed. "And probably the custodians. If they wanted to steal supplies, it would be far easier to divert items before they got to the Family Support Room."

"If someone's stealing, he's hurting everyone." Aston whittled off another shred of meat. "It's a crying shame people go hungry in this country. And lawmakers don't give a hoot."

"How about the challenger in the state senate race?" Brenda said. "She says she'll do more for education and programs for at-risk kids."

"Buffalo chips." Aston snorted. "Doesn't matter who we elect, they're all talk. Might as well put on a blindfold before you vote, for all the difference it makes."

"He has a point." Doug wound spaghetti around his fork. "I haven't been voting all that long, but I'm already fed up. I hear promises, but I don't hear concrete plans. And I don't see much performance."

"And the mud-slinging campaigns go on longer than some marriages," I added. "I get so sick of the candidates it's hard to care who wins."

"And even if we elect people with solid plans," Brenda said, "they face opposition from those who have no vision of their own beyond getting in the way or saying 'No way.' The frustrated folks with ideas might as well hold a match to a glacier and hope to melt a path through it."

"Too many been camping in DC and state capitals for too long. Don't take risks. Don't want to lose their paychecks." Aston thumped the ham hock on the table. "Reminds me of McClellan's army. We need run-and-gun cavalry."

"Like the 7th?" Doug shot me a wink.

Aston snarled. "Leave Custer out of this. You know what I'm saying. We need men of action."

"Not women?" Brenda asked.

"You bet. Women too. Anyone who won't sugarcoat what needs to be done or double-talk the issues. Candidates who aren't soft and wishy-washy."

"Hmmm." I made a frame with my fingers and peered through it at Aston. "Sounds like a description of you."

"Yeah," Doug agreed. "Maybe you should run for something."

"Like what?" Brenda giggled. "Varmint control officer?"

Gertrude shushed her with a wave of her hand. "You'd certainly make a race more interesting, Aston. But it's too late to get on the ballot."

"It might not be too late to be a write-in candidate," Doug suggested.

Brenda's eyes widened. "Don't give him ideas."

Too late. The gleam in Aston's eyes told me he was considering tossing his hat—perhaps the grease-stained leather model he wore when he portrayed a fur trapper at living history encampments—into the political ring.

Chapter 5

When the final bell rang and kids crammed through the exits in a headlong dash to escape the halls of learning, I worked the kinks out of my shoulders and surveyed the long pottery room for tasks left undone. Thanks to daily assignments that contributed to their grades, most students pitched in to wipe tables and counters, clean sinks, and put tools where they belonged. Naturally there were always a few slackers—but that was my experience with the world outside of high school as well.

As I noted goof-offs' names to pass along, Allison and Josh trudged in lugging their backpacks. Josh, being a senior and dedicated to getting the best grades he could, carried more than 20 pounds of books. Allison, being a junior and dedicated to clothing, makeup, movies, and Josh, had only a few notebooks, a couple of sparkly pens, and a stash of lipstick, blush, and mascara. Five pounds, tops.

Josh had filled out over the summer and built muscle in his arms and chest. He could no longer be described as gangly or weedy. He'd also gained confidence, and now stood straight, shoulders squared. That put him at the six-foot mark.

For the first time, I saw him not so much as a boy, but as a young man. And a handsome young man. The shoulder-length brown hair that once fell across his face was trimmed and styled, and the hoodie replaced by a pale blue button-down shirt tucked into a pair of almost-new jeans.

"Josh is gonna give me a driving lesson," Allison burbled as she fluffed her hair, this week a coppery blond. The fluffing revealed a streak of green and another of blue. Marker pen, I guessed. The streaks hadn't been there this morning.

"I'll only do it if it's okay with you and Mr. Martin." Josh didn't press his hands together in prayer, but his tone indicated he hoped it wouldn't be.

"Did you ask your father?" I grilled Allison.

"I tried, but he's not answering. Or calling back."

"There might not be cell service up there," Josh said.

"Up there" was somewhere on the slopes of Mt. St. Helens. To broaden his experience, and see what Lola could do, Dave had taken vacation time to take part in a search and rescue training course. What he didn't mention, to anyone except me, was that Lola's allergies were getting worse. He was concerned her days as his drug-sniffing partner were numbered. She could "retire" and live out her life with us, but Dave felt she needed fulfilling work, needed to be needed. He thought she'd be bored and listless if her law enforcement career came to an end.

I wasn't so sure.

When she wasn't working with Dave, Lola seemed content to hang out and ride herd on Cheese Puff. She had strong protective instincts and, when we walked on the trail along the bank of the Columbia River, put herself between us and anything her canine brain identified as suspicious. I expected she'd find a second career escorting condo residents who wanted to walk or jog, but worried about being out alone. Given her size, she'd also provide stability for those less steady on their feet.

Dave, I suspected, was less concerned about how Lola would adapt to retirement than about how he'd adapt to a new partner. He probably also worried about how Lola would accept another dog taking her job.

My biggest concern had to do with living arrangements. Since condo rules limited the number of pets allowed in each unit, we'd have to move if Dave got another canine partner. Or come up with a creative solution, like listing Mrs. B as Cheese Puff's official owner. Not, as I've said before, that anyone actually *owns* my entitled pooch.

"Dad always says it's okay if *you* think it is," Allison wheedled. "And we don't have to tell him."

I made an umpire's you're-out motion. "Wrong."

"Yeah," Josh agreed. "Ever since that crazy woman tried to run you over on Spruce Ridge, your dad wants to know about anything outside the normal routine."

Allison turned away from him, locking her gaze on me. "Well, I *normally* drive with Dario. But he's way too busy in Las Vegas. Especially because he has an assistant—Jackie Whatever-She's-Called. She's all pushy-pushy and trying to change stuff and making new rules and schedules. So, anyway, if Josh takes his place, that would be the *new* normal."

Josh inched behind her, shaking his head and waving me off. He wore the panicked expression of a gerbil stuck in a toilet bowl.

Refusing Allison outright—even for a good reason— sometimes led to hours of cajoling, soft-soaping, hard-soaping, pouting, and sulking. Having other plans for my evening, I passed the buck to the state of Washington. "Are there rules about who can supervise a driver in training?"

The fear in Josh's eyes faded. He whipped out his phone.

"I don't know," Allison answered.

"Well, maybe we should check before you take off."

Allison huffed out a sigh. "That will take like for-ev-er. And Josh has to meet Jim at the restaurant pretty soon. And if there *are* rules, I bet they're stupid."

Exactly what she said about the questions on the safe-driving test she'd now failed twice in an effort to get a permit.

"Stupid or not, if you break state rules about driving before you take the driver's test, it may be a long time before the folks who made those rules decide to allow you on the road."

Josh tapped his phone, drew his finger down the screen, and grinned. "I have to have my license a lot more years before I can teach you."

"That's dumb." Allison wheeled to face him. "You got your license a whole year ago. And—"

"And I don't know why we're even having this discussion," I interrupted. "You don't have your learner's permit."

"That won't matter if we go where Dario and I go."

Meaning the site of a development on hold.

Josh's jaw went slack.

"Technically, you shouldn't drive anywhere until you have your learner's permit."

"Then why does Dad let me go with Dario?"

Crud. A curve ball.

The quick and easy answer was Dave shouldn't. But Dario was the kind of man who inspired fear or confidence—sometimes both at the same time. When he and Allison took off for a lesson, we knew she wouldn't come to any harm. No matter how many times she turned the wheel too fast, backed up without looking, or stomped the gas instead of the brake, Dario would bring them home without injury. As long as you didn't count his frazzled nerves.

To end the discussion, I passed the buck to Dave. "Ask your father when he returns your call. In the meantime, no driving lessons. If you want to review the driver's manual, I'm sure Josh would quiz you."

Allison groaned. "Forget it. Just forget it." She snatched the strap to her backpack and stalked to the door. "I need ice cream."

Josh tucked his phone in his pocket. "Thanks," he whispered. "I tried to tell her it was a bad idea, but—"

"She wouldn't listen. I understand. Been there, done that." I dug in my briefcase and handed him a few bills. "Ice cream money."

Josh shook his head. "I can't take money from you."

"I'll get it back from Dave, so think of it as money for him. You'll earn it. She'll try to talk you around, no matter what I said."

"Yeah." Josh stuffed the bills in the watch pocket of his jeans. "She doesn't give up without an argument—or three." He glanced over his shoulder at Allison who stood in the doorway, hip cocked, gesturing for him to hurry. "Dario says he's never seen a worse driver."

"Dario's not the type to exaggerate."

Josh winced. "That's what I thought. And I'm not so sure she wants to learn to drive. If she did, she would have studied and passed the permit test."

"Interesting point. Maybe she thinks if she gets a license, you won't spend as much time with her."

Time together had been the issue that led to a dramatic break up a few days before school started. Allison subscribed to the be-with-me-every-minute concept of a relationship, while Josh needed space to pursue other interests—music, the reconstruction of Krammee's, and his education.

37

"Come on," Allison called. "We'll wait in line forever if we don't hurry."

Josh grabbed his backpack and jogged to the door.

I scraped a wad of gum from the back of a chair and wondered if Josh and Allison would make it through the school year together. If they did, how would she do after he graduated? Not that he planned to go far at first—only to the community college down the road—but that distance would seem huge. For the good of all of us, Allison had to let go of a ton of her neediness and demands. And get her license so she'd be more independent. Sooner would be better than later.

After a stop at the library to pick up a couple of British mysteries, I hit the drug store for feminine products, a fresh tube of mascara, and a bag of new and improved cheese crackers.

(For the record, I'm willing to admit that cheesy snacks are my guilty little secret. But what's the point? First, by now you're well aware it's no secret. And, second, generally I feel no guilt.)

Anyway, when I reached the condo complex around 3:00, I spotted Bernina Burke going door to door slipping bright red papers in the boxes reserved for condo business. As condo manager, Bernina saw it as her calling to never leave well enough alone. Not a month went by when she didn't propose at least one new rule for the board's consideration. When she wasn't dreaming up fresh rules, Bernina enforced existing ones. Each day she marched around the perimeter of the complex with a clipboard and a pen, noting infractions as she went.

Several recent rules had been aimed at my household and members of the Cheese Puff Care and Comfort Committee. They included limits on pets, regulations about appropriate attire to be worn in the pool area, and restrictions on feeding birds and other wildlife. I wasn't her target because I'm the type who flaunts rules or demonstrates lack of good sense—at least not consistently. No, Bernina's motive was jealousy. She'd fallen hard for my ex-husband, Jake Stranahan. And, despite all evidence to the contrary, she believed I wanted him back.

What Bernina didn't see—or refused to recognize—was that Jake was as shallow as he was insensitive. The qualities he looked for in a woman were money, physical beauty, and the firm conviction that he was phenomenal and deserved to have his ego fed daily. Bernina had little spare cash. What she did have was spare poundage. Jake wouldn't see her as arm candy. To be blunt, Bernina was more like arm pot roast.

Spare poundage is something I understand all too well. With my extra ten, I may not be arm pot roast, but I'm definitely arm pasta.

Bernina, in fact, recently demonstrated more willpower than I have, shedding a significant chunk of herself. The loss, I well knew, wasn't enough to meet Jake's standards. During our brief marriage I trimmed off seven pounds at his "suggestion." Every ounce returned within a month, thanks to stress eating brought on by the discovery that Jake had siphoned my bank account to fund his affairs and bogus investments.

Bernina chose to believe I was at fault for Jake's roving eyes, hands, and other body parts. She contended he was misunderstood. Even during the brief time Jake was out of jail and worked here as a handyman/groundskeeper, the devastation he wrought hadn't been enough to make Bernina jettison all dreams of their future. And his weekly requests for deposits to his jail account hadn't made her see how bleak the financial part of that future would be.

I'd hoped she'd transfer her feelings to one of the feline-loving bikers who turned up last month threatening violence over the cat-bashing blog Jake started in Cheese Puff's name. But apparently nothing had come of their encounter, and

Bernina was still at the top of the list of character witnesses for Jake's defense. I wondered how she'd spin his job performance at the condo when she took the stand. Those attending the trial—and everyone on the CPCCC was planning to be there—would erupt in gales of derisive laughter if Bernina attempted to paint his workmanship as any better than shoddy.

Mrs. B believed Jake was working on being a better person. Her proof? When one of his investments came through in a big way, he'd paid back what he pilfered from me along with a ton of interest. I believed repayment was a means to an end—possibly to get me to testify in his defense. Jake's core character was set in concrete. It would take a megaton life-altering blast to shatter it.

But, moving right along. When I pulled Bernina's red-paper notice from my box, I saw these words: "Let's Win the Reckless River Holiday Decorating Competition."

"Let's not."

I crumpled the notice without reading more. I'm all for holiday decorating, but in a sane and simplistic way. And with a unifying theme. What I'm not for is tossing everything you have on the roof and lawn. Mix huge inflatable cartoon characters with tiny wicker deer and I can't drive past your house fast enough. The gag-inducing garish display that won the award last year proved plenty of folks love the more-is-more approach.

While residents were free to decorate at will inside their units, exterior holiday displays were forbidden except as approved by the condo board. Last year, Mrs. B bankrolled fresh lights and ornaments for the tree by the condo complex sign, and paid for professionals with a lift truck to decorate it. The result had been tasteful and plenty for me.

I let myself in to my empty condo, pondering the potential expense of the extreme effort Bernina would have to mount to win the competition. I also pondered her motive. When it came to taking on extra duties and additional work, Bernina wasn't the type to raise her hand. In fact, she was the type to sidle off and avoid the assignment, or attempt to delegate. So what was up?

I tossed the notice, changed to a pair of shorts and a tank top, and got busy dozing on a lounge chair on the deck, collecting Vitamin D from sunlight. At the sound of shuffling footsteps, I opened my eyes to see Jim, one of the founding members of the CPCCC and the only male in the group, chugging up the path through the strip of rose garden abutting the riverfront trail. His breath came in short bursts, his shirt was damp with sweat, his cheeks were cherry red, and the state of his Santa Claus beard indicated he'd been tugging at it—a sign he was upset or angry.

I pointed to the glider swing. Covered by a small awning, it offered a patch of shaded shelter. "Sit. I'll get a glass of water."

"Thanks." Jim flopped on the swing and fanned himself with his hands. "Bernina's latest scheme has my blood pressure spiking."

I hustled to provide water and a damp towel, and then rounded up a bottle of beer, a can of sweet and salty nuts, and a refill on my lemonade. If the topic was Bernina Burke, this conversation wouldn't be short.

C h a p t e r 6

Jim accepted my offerings with a grunt of thanks, drank half the water, chomped a few nuts, and twisted the cap off the beer. "I shouldn't let her get my goat."

I toasted him with my lemonade. "Same goes for me."

"I've got enough to worry about with the renovation at Krammee's and those guys painting upstairs." He cocked his head toward Mrs. B's condo. "I've seen garden slugs move faster."

Since Jim was a hurry-up-and-get-it-done guy, I took that negative comment with more than a single grain of salt.

"I can't believe the board gave Bernina a two-year contract." He sloshed the rest of the water on his neck and chest, set the glass aside, and went for the beer. "If I'd known the pool of applicants for the manager's job was so shallow, I would have applied. Heck, I would have filled out an application for Sybil."

I chuckled. Sybil, another member of the CPCCC, was a sweetheart and a loyal friend, but her mental porch light was seldom illuminated. When it was, it tended to flicker. On the plus side, Sybil's air-headed ideas were usually amusing. And easily set aside.

"Did you read that bulletin?"

"No. I tossed it."

"Forewarned is forearmed." Jim gulped beer. "You better read it. Learn Bernina's plan."

"I will. But I'm less interested in what she's doing than why."

"Motive's clear to me. She's after another job."

"Great!" I toasted him again. "What job? Where?"

"Shoalwater Bend."

"Those expensive condos up the river? The ones with the indoor pool and on-site restaurant?" And a sauna and hot tub, workout room, underground parking, and landscaping that didn't look like it was kept up by a flock of sheep.

"Exactly. Rumor has it their manager is leaving at the end of the year."

I mulled that for a minute. "What do holiday decorations have to do with Bernina getting the job?"

"The manager at Shoalwater Bend has been there since the place was built five years ago. So have almost all the residents. Change will worry them. They'll look for a manager who has plenty of experience, good rapport with residents, and strong leadership skills."

That pretty much ruled out Bernina. She was experienced, all right, experienced at being annoying. Rapport implied harmonious relationships instead of antagonistic tussles. And leadership implied residents viewed her as someone they'd at least consider following.

Residents of Number 90 Columbia Lane—notice my complex doesn't have a fancy name, only a number—were a different breed. With the exception of Mrs. Ballantine, most of us couldn't afford even the smallest units at Shoalwater Bend. And only a few of our owners had been in residence for five years. In fact, several units at Number 90 passed to new owners each year. Several others were rented out. Turnover and absentee owners made us a less cohesive group.

"We're between a rock and another rock." Jim blew across the top of his bottle, making a sound like a foghorn. "If we don't get behind the decorating project, there's absolutely no chance she'll be considered for the job. She'll be with us for another 23 months. And she'll spend the time making our lives miserable."

"But if we go along with the project, we'll be out a lot of money."

"And even if she's considered, there's no guarantee she'll get the job."

I pondered that. "How much money are we talking about? Is there enough in the board's discretionary fund for lights and decorations?"

"Hardly. My guess is we'd be looking at a special assessment."

Meaning all the owners would have to kick in. "That would be as popular as the plague."

"You might be surprised." Jim tugged at his beard. "A lot of residents go all out for holidays. And there are a few on the board with competitive streaks."

Not what I wanted to hear. "Maybe we can knock Bernina out of the running before she even gets in."

Jim sucked at his beer, a dubious expression on his face. "How do we do that?"

"Get Shoalwater Bend board members to drive by here. From the state of the grounds they'll see Bernina is a crap manager. All the decorations in the city can't disguise dying shrubs, hedges Jake mutilated, and grass high enough to hide a stalking lion."

Jim's expression brightened. "I hear she ran off another landscaping service last week."

"That's four services since Jake quit and returned to jail. Don't you think word about her lack of people skills has reached Shoalwater Bend?"

"If it hasn't, it should." Jim drained his beer. "But we have to be careful about who carries the news. If it's one of us . . ."

We'd pay if she found out. Bernina had ways of making residents suffer. Some were subtle, some not. You might get a blizzard of memos or find your car blocked by a yard cart or, in my case, get a letter from the folks at animal control about dogs barking too much.

"Maybe we should call a meeting of the Committee and others who have their fill of Bernina," I suggested. "When Mrs. B gets back."

"Have to be a secret meeting. Away from here."

"How about the rec center?"

Jim gave me a high five. "Yeah. Bernina avoids exercise equipment the way we all try to avoid her."

As I was throwing together a tuna and pasta salad, Penelope called. Skipping past the greeting, she got right to the point. "You may be seeing more of your sister over the next few weeks."

"Why?" I braced myself against the counter and set aside the knife I'd been using to chop a red onion. Having a sharp object in my grip when discussing my sister could be hazardous to my health. "What's going on? Did you break up?"

"No. I'm taking a job out of town. Starting in the morning."

"What? Why? I thought you had more work than you had time for."

"I do, but this is a rush job in Olympia. The pay is astronomical."

Astronomical pay was nothing to sneeze at—unless the work was of the you-may-not-come-back-alive variety. "My sister isn't going with you?"

"I'll be working ten hours a day, at least. All day Saturday, too."

Factor in sleeping and eating, showering, and getting to the job, and they'd have almost no time together.

"It will be good for us to be apart for a while," Penelope said with hesitation, skepticism, and a dash of hopefulness.

"So it's not just about astronomical pay?"

Penelope made a noise that was more crying than laughing. "You see right through me, Barbara. No, Iz needs space. She's depressed and floundering. She needs to make decisions about her future—and how *her* future affects *our* future."

All things I'd noticed. Some people, as Thoreau said, lived lives of quiet desperation. Iz's desperation had volume. Lately it was cranked to the max.

"When you say I might see more of her, what does that mean? Exactly?"

Penelope made that little noise again. "I'm riding up with another electrician, so she'll have my truck. She might want company. Might drop by."

Memo to self: Plan to be out—often. Turn off cellphone. Don't answer door.

"I know she makes you crazy," Penelope said. "Sometimes she can be critical and opinionated."

Sometimes?

More like, all the time.

"And she doesn't always recognize the impact of what she says."

Doesn't always?

More like, never.

"But deep down I think she respects you."

46

Really?

"How deep down? You don't have to be exact. Round off in millimeters."

"Well . . ."

"Has she ever actually *said* she respects me?"

"Um, no," Penelope admitted. "But I have a feeling she does."

And *I* had a feeling Penelope was so far off base she was in the nosebleed section of the ballpark bleachers. But that was her choice. As long as I didn't have to sit with her. Or my sister.

"Anyway," Penelope went on with a note of pleading, "I'd appreciate anything you and Dave can do to help her move through this."

Dave's idea of helping Iz move would involve a boot to the rear, but I didn't mention that. And I didn't actually agree to help. I wished Penelope a safe drive and got off the phone.

Appetite shot, I consumed only a tiny bowl of tuna salad—enough to fuel me through a water aerobics class. With Iz in crisis, Bernina promoting a self-serving project, Aston getting into politics, and four more days in pottery looming, I needed to work the kinks out of my neck and shoulders. If I didn't, I'd find myself in an emergency room pleading for something along the lines of a horse tranquilizer.

As I hoped, when I reached the rec center I found Paulette in the far corner of the locker room. She wore green-and-yellow flip-flops, a bright yellow bathing suit, and a green band in her bronze-red hair. She also wore a frown.

I dropped my swim bag on one of the wooden benches. "What's wrong? A problem with the décor for Krammee's?"

Paulette shook her head. "No. Everything's on order or on schedule. Except anything that needs to have a logo on it."

"Are they any closer to deciding on a name?"

"I wish. Sybil and Verna bicker about everything. Lana says she shouldn't offer an opinion because she's more of an employee than a member of the Krammee's Reconstruction Committee. Jim refuses to mediate because Verna and Sybil turned on him last time he tried. And Josh says if Jim's scared to get in the middle, then he's definitely not going there."

Paulette draped a green towel over her shoulder and slammed her locker. "I keep hoping Mrs. Ballantine will jump in and make a decision, but when she said she was stepping aside to practice her routine, she meant it. I called her last week and she said it would all work out eventually, and in the meantime everyone would learn lessons about working and playing together."

Spoken like a woman who didn't have to worry about money and therefore didn't care when the restaurant reopened.

"And now she's out of town until the weekend." I kicked off a pair of orange flip-flops Allison had discarded, shucked a gray sweatshirt and worn jeans, and revealed my end-of-summer-bargain swimsuit.

Paulette choked and covered her eyes.

"I don't like this suit, either," I told her. "But for 60% off, I can forgive purple and red paisley."

"If you say so." Paulette's tone implied she couldn't forgive either pattern or color, even if the designer threw in a cruise.

I pinned my car key to the shoulder strap. "In a few months the chemicals in the water will chew up the elastic and it will go in the trash."

Promise?"

"Promise."

"And you swear you won't wear a T-shirt or a pair of jogging shorts over it to put off buying a new one."

That wasn't an outlandish suggestion. Plenty of women did that if a suit blew out before they bought a replacement. This was a community rec center, not a country club.

"I swear I won't. I bought a spare when I got this one."

"Tell me it's not paisley."

"Nope. A floral print." I spread my hands wide. "Big flowers. Orange and pink. I'll look like a sofa upholstered in the 70s."

"I can hardly wait." Paulette groaned and headed for the shower area. "Well, let's get this hour of torture over with."

An odd attitude for someone who was usually first in the water and last out. "Are you feeling okay?"

"I'm fine." She glanced over her shoulder at a cluster of women on the other side of the locker room and lowered her voice. "I'm dreading this. Margie's off for two weeks."

Margie was our regular instructor. She had a voice like a military drill instructor and was all about doing the exercises the right way so we built muscle and improved flexibility while avoiding injury. She offered individual advice and explained the benefits of new moves when she integrated them into the routine. "Who's filling in?"

"Cheryl. You won't like her."

Meaning Paulette didn't like her and expected me, as her friend, to feel the same. I was all for friendship and loyalty, but I was also all for knowing what I was being loyal to. "What's wrong with her?"

"She doesn't allow talking."

Ah. While Margie didn't encourage a lot of chatter, she was okay with occasional comments or jokes or even a quick exchange of ideas about the best happy hour snacks in town. "That's it?"

"If *you* talk, she tells you to leave. But *she* talks all the time. Doesn't explain the point of the moves or suggest how you might modify an exercise if you have pain. Never realizes that she can do it faster because we're working against the water." Paulette hung her towel on a hook jutting from the beige-tiled wall and stepped through the doorway and along to the third showerhead, her favorite. "She repeats instructions endlessly and tells us to power it up. In a loud and screechy voice."

Not good. I liked time to think about instructions and feel my body working. And I came to unwind. A screechy voice wouldn't help. "Is that why the place is so empty tonight?"

"Probably." Paulette turned on the shower and stepped back. Cold water burst forth in a tight stream that died to a lethargic drizzle. Wiggling a finger in the drizzle, Paulette waited for the water to warm up then turned the knob off and on again to get a strong steady blast of spray. "Did I mention that Cheryl doesn't believe in workout music?"

Even less good. Music provided the beat for pumping arms and jogging legs. It made the time pass more quickly. And helped me relax. Margie favored the oldies, leaning heavily on Motown. "Has anyone complained?"

Paulette aimed a thumb at her chest. "Me. And dozens of others. Phone calls. E-mails. Letters. We get no response. And nothing happens."

"Sounds to me like she has connections. Or leverage." I twisted a corner of my towel. "Why don't we skip class? We could walk instead."

"No." Paulette inched backward beneath the spray, head stuck out like a turtle's to keep her hair dry. "I think that's what they want us to do."

Chapter 7

"They? Who are *they*?"

"I'm not sure. Anyway, I'm going to class. And you're coming with me. And afterward I'm drawing up a petition." Paulette leveled an exquisitely manicured forefinger at my nose, pale pink polish gleaming in the glow from the fluorescent bulbs above us. "And you're helping me write it and gather signatures and get it to the mayor. Or someone who can do something."

Sheesh.

I was all for the democratic process, but with Dave out of town, my sister's impending visits, and a full week of subbing, there was a lot on my plate. And my plate, by the way, isn't stoneware or China or plastic. It's one of those flimsy paper things. It gets soggy in the middle and folds like a taco, spilling food out of both sides.

"A petition?" I turned on a shower and flipped my hand through what was more mist than spray.

"Or something." Paulette squeezed liquid soap from a container shaped like a penguin, then passed it over to me.

I followed suit and lathered up. The soap in the penguin container smelled like coconut and cherries. "If Cheryl's only filling in, and Margie will be back, why—?"

Paulette's eyes sparked. "Why make a big deal out of it?"

"Um . . ."

"Because rumor has it Margie is planning to retire next month and Cheryl will take her place. And take on other classes, too."

This is the point where someone who didn't know Paulette—or someone foolhardy—might suggest she switch to a different class or even try to ignore Cheryl and concentrate on the workout. But, although I have occasional bouts of foolhardiness, I wasn't inclined to schedule one for this particular moment. Keeping my lips zipped, I rinsed off and followed her to the pool.

(For the record, Paulette hadn't been exaggerating about Cheryl's technique. By the time the hour was up, I felt like I'd been running on a treadmill while someone rubbed a cheese grater across my eardrums.)

"I know you probably thought it was all about me when we went in," Paulette said when we headed to our cars.

"Well, I—"

"I admit that sometimes it is. Sometimes I'm a witchy princess."

"Well, you—"

"But this is about way more than me." She stomped one foot and winced. Stomping works better if you're not wearing ballet slippers and standing on an asphalt parking lot. "This is about saving the rec center pool."

I glanced at the looming building behind us. "Saving it from what?"

"From being shut down and sold to a developer."

52

"Sold? How can they sell it? It's city property. It's been here for 30 years."

"Exactly. It's old. It needs major repairs and upgrades. And the cost of running the pool is huge—insurance, lifeguards, heating and filtering systems."

I leaned against my car, watching the sky above a stand of fir trees turn a velvety purple. "Okay. But what does Cheryl have to do with shutting down the rec center? That wouldn't benefit her. She'd lose her job."

"Right." Paulette lowered her voice as the instructor passed a few yards from us on the way to her car. She'd changed from shorts and a tank top to heels, black leggings, and a sparkly silver sweater cinched with a broad black leather belt. "But I have a feeling she doesn't care. See, she's driving this year's model. And that sweater isn't a knockoff. Even on sale, it's $250 if it's a dime. And those heels run about the same."

I didn't question her assessment. Paulette knew more about designer clothing than I did about brands of cheesy snacks.

"Besides, I think she's part of the plot."

Plot?

I laughed. "Now you're starting to sound like a conspiracy theorist."

"Just because I'm paranoid doesn't mean I'm not right," Paulette said with an impish grin. "I'll send you a draft of the petition later."

And she was gone, hopping in the sporty two-seater she drove when her airline pilot husband was away.

Getting in my beater of a car involved more than hopping. In fact, it was a mini-workout: tugging open the door while reminding myself again to oil or grease the hinges, wrestling with the seatbelt, bracing myself to yank the door closed, and grappling with the steering wheel to get it to a position where it would unlock so I could turn the key and start the engine.

Exhausted, I drove home trying to put together the pieces of Paulette's theory so they made sense. Was Cheryl intentionally irritating people in an attempt to drive them away? If use dropped off, would Reckless River city councilors view the pool as a financial liability? Would they point to newer private facilities and suggest the city get out of the pool business and sell the property?

If that happened, where would I go to get my fix of water aerobics? Sure, I could use the condo pool in the summer. But summer—even with the effects of global warming—was often fleeting in the Pacific Northwest. We were at the mercy of ocean currents, wind, and geography. Summer might linger, and October might deliver a series of dry and clear days, but eventually chilly rains arrived, followed by dank, dark days. And, even if I was made of tougher stuff and willing to plunge into frigid water, condo policy called for the pool to be closed by mid September.

And then there was the larger issue—how much exercise was I liable to do on my own? And how hard would I work without others suffering along?

I was in still pondering when I got home and found Allison at the dining room table with a fork in one hand and a pen in the other. As the fork jabbed pasta salad, the pen alternately jabbed a text and notebook. "This history stuff is so boring," she wailed. "All these guys talking and talking and talking. And wearing weird clothes. What's up with those socks?"

I glanced over her shoulder and spotted a reproduction of a painting of the Constitutional Convention. "That was the style."

"Well, it's pukey. If Josh wore short pants and white stockings and wigs he'd be looking for a new girlfriend."

I didn't mention what women wore in those times. Nor did I say anything about the only word she'd written in the notebook: "BORING!!!!!!" Instead, I pretended I hadn't noticed more than the picture. "Are you taking notes?"

"Yes," she said in a tone implying I had the visual acuity of a mole. "Do you have a problem with that?"

So, it was going to be one of *those* evenings.

I draped my towel and swimsuit over a chair on the deck, filled a tall glass with cool water, and plucked a can of smoked almonds from a cabinet. According to Paulette, a session in the pool should be followed by water and protein. I was in favor of following her nutritional advice, as long as the protein-laden snack came with salt and crunch.

As I drained the glass, the phone rang and Mrs. Ballantine trilled in my ear. "Hello, dear. I can't talk long, but I wanted you to know the little prince and I are having a wonderful time. Everyone adores him. Well, everyone except a cranky old man who makes his home on the second floor and complains about everything under the sun."

That sounded like a male version of Bernina Burke, but I didn't say it. Mrs. B insists I need to be more charitable toward her. Thinking about Bernina led to thinking about the holiday decorating competition. But Mrs. B needed to focus on her dance routine, so I fought the urge to unload. Nor did I bring up the fact that a new name for Krammee's didn't exist yet.

"Cheese Puff barked at a squirrel only two or three times when we arrived, but that codger gave the poor manager an earful. He demanded we use the rear entrance so we don't 'contaminate' the lobby with dog hair. Talk about contamination, he smells like horse liniment. On top of that, he had the audacity to demand I practice without my tap shoes during the hours he sets aside for resting in the afternoon."

Mrs. B hauled in a breath. "Honestly. His room is completely on the other side of the hotel. And he wears a wool hat yanked over his ears all the time."

Trying that be-more-charitable thing, I slipped in a comment. "Maybe he has sensitive ears. Or perhaps he's having problems with a hearing aid."

"And maybe he's a grumpy waste of oxygen who likes to throw his weight around."

Talk about not being charitable. And it was spoken by someone who threw her own weight around—although usually in a generous and helpful manner. "I'm sorry it's not going as well as you hoped."

"Well, life isn't perfect, dear."

Far from it.

"We'll see you on Friday. Saturday at the latest."

I'd no sooner set the phone in its cradle, than it rang again. This time it was Dave. And he wasn't trilling. The signal faded in and out, but his voice was so loud I got every word. "Snakes. Bugs. Ticks. Blackberry vines. Bushes with thorns like sharks' teeth. Plants that make me itch. Hillsides steeper than a cow's face. And did I mention snakes?"

I chuckled. "Except for the cow's face part, you could be describing the condo grounds. If Bernina doesn't stop running off yard services, we'll be hacking our way to our cars with machetes."

"Laugh all you want. I don't know how these search and rescue guys do it. I don't know *why* they do it—especially the ones who volunteer. You should see what I had to fight my way through to get a cellphone signal."

"How's Lola holding up?"

"She's a trooper. Sneezes a lot, but never whimpers. Never whines."

"Unlike her partner."

"Easy for you to say. You're not here."

I stepped onto the deck and slid the door closed behind me. "True. I'm home. Home, where Bernina Burke wants to sign the condo complex up for the holiday decorating competition. Home, where Aston Marsden is planning a write-in campaign for a political office and Paulette suspects there's a plot to close the rec center pool. Home, where your daughter is dissing the wardrobes of the Founding Fathers. Want to trade places?"

Dave's thoughtful silence lasted .027 seconds. "No way. Even with the snakes it's less dangerous here. Don't worry about me. I'll be fine. When I get down from this ridge, I'll eat my rehydrated dinner and crawl in my tent. Then I'll scratch assorted bites and stings until I'm exhausted enough to sleep. See you Friday. Saturday at the latest.

Little did I know I'd see him—and Mrs. Ballantine—a heck of a lot sooner.

Chapter 8

The next day Aston was brimming with ideas and slogans for a write-in campaign. He'd laid half a dozen papers in the center of the table, each with a shot of him in one of his reenactment costumes. He wore an assortment of buckskin, broadcloth, and fur caps. Each page had a slogan scrawled in his atrocious handwriting.

"He hasn't decided which office he'll run for," Doug confided as I waited beside him at the microwave, holding my frozen meal and watching his bowl of chili ride the carousel. "I can't tell whether he's overlooked that step, or figures he'll get to it once he has his message hammered out."

"You know that saying about people who don't know history being doomed to repeat it," Aston said. "Well, I'm the opposite. I know history."

Doug snorted and pulled his chili from the microwave. "He might know history before Teddy Roosevelt's charge up San Juan Hill, but I bet I can name more nations in Africa."

"No bet." I slid my plastic tray of pasta, cheese, and spinach onto the glass carousel and set the oven for three minutes of waves. "I covered his classes when he staged that one-man strike in the spring. Remember?"

"Hard to forget." Doug crumbled crackers on top of his chili. "And you had a front-row seat for the bear grease incident."

I gagged involuntarily, recalling the stench in Aston's classroom when temperatures soared at the same time a mouse gnawed a hole in a plastic jar of bear grease Aston set aside years before. He'd claimed it was part of an experiment in pioneer-style weather forecasting. When the funk reached epic proportions, I tracked the source to a corner cabinet and turned the problem over to Assistant Principal Tremaine Scott.

"You've got a green tint," Doug said. "Let's switch the subject to Aston's campaign so you can swallow your lunch."

"Are you sure that won't make me more queasy?"

Chuckling, Doug took his seat beside Aston and spooned up chili while surveying the campaign poster mock-ups. The microwave dinged, claiming my attention. I hauled in three deep breaths to clear my lungs. Then I ordered myself to forget about rancid bear grease and get something in my stomach to sustain me through afternoon classes.

"A man from the past with vision for the future." Brenda read the slogan beneath a photo of Aston sporting a hat made from a coyote's hide complete with face and tail. "Ha! *Your* vision of the future is a return to the past."

"Nothing wrong with the past." Aston sliced a chunk of smoked salmon and built a sandwich on grainy bread the color of the sacks of soil Mrs. B bought to refresh the rose garden. "Plenty of solid values in the past."

"I suppose there are." Gertrude opened a container of hummus and dipped a cucumber slice. "But I also value things like indoor plumbing, women's rights, air travel, and telephones."

"How far into the past are you reaching for the planks of your platform?" Doug asked.

"Platform? Planks?" Aston frowned and stabbed at the salmon. "Like a stage, where I make speeches?"

Sheesh.

Aston was truly out of touch with the political process. "A platform is a statement of what you stand for," I told him. "It's a summary of your principles and intentions. The planks are your goals, the things you hope to accomplish."

"Will you have a negative platform or a positive one?" Gertrude asked.

Aston glowered and spread screaming yellow mustard on his sandwich with a long knife that would have made any frontiersman envious. "Huh?"

"Are you going to run with the aim of tossing out and tearing down, or do you have specific ideas about improving things?" Gertrude probed. "Would you consolidate departments or create new ones? Emphasize the environment or jobs? Promote tax cuts or call for budget trimming?"

Aston blinked like a shrew thrust into bright sunlight.

"This is a total waste of time," Brenda said, "just like everything that involves Aston. He doesn't know what he's running *for*, so it's pointless to discuss the platform he's running *on*."

"You'll see." Aston whacked his sandwich with the knife, splitting it in half and splattering mustard on the sleeve of Doug's pale blue shirt.

"Cold water," Gertrude advised. "Rinse through the back of the fabric."

Doug leaped to his feet, kicked his chair aside, and headed for the sink.

"Scrape off as much as you can first." Brenda stood and went to work with the edge of a plastic knife while Doug unbuttoned his cuff. "Soak it when you get home. Check the

Internet for advice. See what bleach and water temperature they recommend."

Given the culinary concoctions Brenda came up with, I bet she spent a lot of time searching for the best ways to remove stains.

"Twice a week," Doug grumbled. "Twice a week I'm at this sink trying in vain to salvage a piece of my wardrobe. All thanks to the misguided menu choices of certain people in this room."

"Surely you don't mean me," Brenda objected.

"What do you think?"

Brenda ducked her head and scraped harder at the mustard splatters.

"I'd like to save for a house," Doug railed. "I'd like to save for a vacation. But every few days I have to buy another shirt or another pair of slacks."

"Thrift stores," Aston mumbled around a mouth full of bread and salmon. "That's where I shop."

"Really? I was certain they stocked shirts with frayed collars and mismatched buttons at the mall," Brenda sneered. "You're a walking ad for castoff clothing, Aston. That should be a plank in your platform."

"You could form an anti-consumerism party," Gertrude suggested. "Of course, you'd lose the business vote. And the votes of most of the women I know. I'm all for recycling and repurposing, but I'd be one angry camper if I couldn't lift my spirits now and then by splurging on a new sweater or pair of shoes."

"Wasting money on things you don't need makes you feel better?" Aston squinted at her. "You're kidding."

"She's not." Brenda tossed the plastic knife in the sink and helped Doug work the faucet up his sleeve to blast the stain from inside. "And if you think *anyone* would vote for you on *any* platform, for *any* reason, you've got less sense than whatever it is you're eating."

I expected Aston to launch a defense but, although his narrowed eyes grew flinty with anger, he said nothing. When he finished his sandwich, he dug in the front pocket of his jeans and drew out a fold of bills held together with a paperclip. Peeling off three, he thrust them at Doug, muttering, "Sorry. I never bought a new shirt. Is $30 enough?"

Doug hesitated, but accepted the money. "It's plenty where I shop."

"Good," Aston responded. "Won't happen again."

"I wouldn't bet on that," Brenda told Doug when the door closed behind Aston.

"I wouldn't either," I said. "But it was a nice gesture."

Gertrude shot Brenda a catty smile. "Maybe you should give Doug money to replace the shirt ruined when you dropped the ladle in the vat of strained pea surprise you brought last week."

"Why?" Brenda asked with genuine amazement. "I'm not running for office. I don't need to buy Doug's vote."

Politics and political corruption were on my mind when my sister rang my doorbell shortly after I got home.

I'd never been foolish enough to give Iz a key to my condo, so I lingered behind the locked door, peering through the peephole. Would she leave if I played possum long enough?

"I know you're in there." Iz pressed the doorbell again and followed up with a series of knocks strong enough to register on an earthquake monitor. "I see your car under the canopy."

I gripped the knob, but didn't turn it.

"I hear you breathing."

Really?

Could she?

Or did she simply suspect I was lurking on the other side of the door?

I went with the second choice, backed along the hallway, and yelled in what I hoped was a distracted and mildly frantic voice, "Just a minute!"

Another few seconds and I jogged to the door, flung it wide, and feigned surprise. "Iz!"

Without waiting for an invitation, Iz barged past. "If you'd give me a key, I wouldn't have to knock or ring the bell endlessly. I wouldn't have to pull you away from whatever you're doing."

She spun on one heel and surveyed me through close-set eyes inherited from our paternal grandmother. "School let out less than an hour ago. You can't have been home for long. What *were* you doing?"

Knowing Iz would check—and not in a surreptitious manner—I did the mental equivalent of running in tight circles. "I was, uh, in the kitchen, um, checking the cabinets and refrigerator to see what's running low, what I need to get at the store."

"Hmmph." Iz strode through the dining area and scanned the kitchen counters. "I don't see a list."

Crud.

"I, uh, don't make a list for the usual stuff—bread and milk and eggs and things we stock up on every week. That's automatic. I make a list for the things we don't buy often."

"Like healthy foods." Iz opened the refrigerator. "I don't see a single tub of organic yogurt."

"You're right." I snatched a pencil and notepad from beside the phone. "We're out. I ate the last one for lunch today. With a locally sourced apple and whole-grain crackers."

Iz snorted. "Knowing your disgusting eating habits and lack of foresight, I'm certain you heated up freezer-burned processed food in a cardboard tray."

I opened my mouth to inform her she was wrong—the tray was made of recyclable plastic. Just in time, I spotted the trap. I printed "yogurt" on the notepad while trying for a haughty expression implying I wouldn't be baited.

Iz bent to dig through the crisper drawers, mourning my failure to stock them with broccolini, cabbage, kale, and beets. "What am *I* supposed to have for dinner?"

"Dinner?"

"That meal at the end of the day." She straightened and turned, using her right hand to punctuate her phrases with a chopping motion. "A complete meal consisting of healthy dishes prepared from fresh foods. The meal often shared with family."

For this particular family, the shared meal at the end of the day was, as you've probably already surmised, often pizza or takeout Chinese or Mexican. "I'm all the family there is today. Dave's on a training course. Allison's going for burgers after drama club. And Mrs. B is at a resort with Cheese Puff."

Iz lifted her upper lip in disdain. When it came to pets, she and my ex-husband had the same attitude—they didn't understand why anyone would devote time, attention, and love to an animal. "So you're doing what? Going to that Mexican place to clog your arteries with cheese and sour cream? Ordering baked dough with canned sauce? Stuffing yourself with those puffy orange snacks you don't have the willpower to resist?"

That did it. An insult to cheesy snacks meant it was time to go on the offensive. And the more offensive, the better.

"Speaking of lack of willpower," I said in an offhand voice, "by the look of the cargo inside your cargo pants, you've put on a few pounds."

Iz flushed and sucked in her stomach. Sucking, however, did nothing about her hips.

(For the record, I've rediscovered this sad fact many times, usually while trying to wedge myself in a pair of skinny jeans in front of one of those three-fold dressing room mirrors.)

"I always gain weight when I'm stressed or depressed." I shoved past Iz, got a diet cola from the refrigerator, and fired scattershot questions. "Which one is it for you? Or is it both stressed *and* depressed? What's up with you and Penelope? How's your job search coming? What about that teaching position you wanted the community college to create for you?"

"As if you care." Iz stomped to the sofa and flopped. Cushions wheezed in despair.

The problem with the scattershot approach is that you can't tell which questions strike targets and which fall short or go wide. I popped the cola and went for the soft underbelly of the beast known as my sister. "Apparently you hope I do care. Otherwise you wouldn't have driven over here and attempted to wear out the door to gain admission."

The flush deepened. "I was driving by."

A lie. Getting to Number 90 Columbia Lane involved making a series of turns, the last being on to a dead end.

I let her denial slide, nodded, and sat in Cheese Puff's chair.

When Detective Charles Atwell suspected me of killing history teacher Henry Stoddard last year, he hauled me in for questioning several times. Atwell's questions didn't get to me as much as his silences. He wielded silence like a cudgel. I decided to try the same technique.

Not that it was easy. My sister had weapons of her own.

First, she hit me with a glare that dared me to challenge her statement about driving by.

Fortunately, I had years of experience with her expressions. Clamping my teeth on my tongue, I shook off the creeping implication that I was in the wrong. When I thought I could manage to swallow without choking, I sipped at my cola. From there, I advanced to studying my fingernails. They were sadly in need of scrubbing and filing.

Iz snapped and unsnapped a pocket on her cargo pants.

I examined the state of my jeans. Not bad. Thin at the knees, but soft and comfortable.

Iz cleared her throat. "Penelope says you're a good judge of character and you understand how relationships work. With the exception of Jake."

True. Jake was a recurring asterisk in the narrative of my life. I use my first husband's sudden death as an excuse/explanation for jumping aboard the financial and emotional *Titanic* of my second marriage. But I often wonder if I would have fallen for Jake even if I hadn't been widowed and lonely. His charm camouflaged his faults. And *my* faults—the biggest being low self-esteem—made me a sitting duck.

"She says you're observant and kind and generous."

Iz uttered those words with a tone of surprise and a dash of disbelief, then flipped her hand as if to wave the assessment aside. "Anyway, I thought it would help to talk things through. I'm not asking for advice. Just feedback."

I held my silence, but made with poochy lips to signify I was mulling over her statement.

"I promise not to get mad," Iz said.

Ha!

That was right up there with a female praying mantis telling a potential mate she would never, ever view him as a snack after they shared a mantis moment.

66

I maintained my silence.

"Okay." Iz raised her hands in surrender. "If I get mad, I'll go outside and walk around the complex before I say anything."

I kept my lips zipped.

Iz scuffed the toe of a tire tread sandal on the carpet. "I'll walk around twice."

I pooched my lips once more.

"I'll jog. Fast."

Fast for Iz wouldn't be considered fast for plenty of people, but even after one circuit of the complex, she'd be too tired to snipe, carp, or lecture. "Deal. What's on your mind?"

She scuffed the carpet with her heels. "I love Penelope."

I'd heard her speak that sentence before, but with different names. Within a few months of hearing confessions of love, I'd heard tales of being misunderstood, disrespected, confined, and controlled. Iz's relationships were like trampolines. She bounced on and bounced off again. Sometimes not by choice. And often with a rough landing instead of a smooth dismount.

"Penelope appears to be a wonderful person." I picked my words with the same care you'd use in selecting safe places to put your feet in a minefield. "Of course, we've known her only a few months, but Dave and I and Mrs. B are all fond of her. She's competent, financially secure, focused."

"She is," my sister agreed. "And don't think I don't hear what you're *not* saying."

I didn't move a muscle and went on *not saying* that Iz possessed none of the qualities I mentioned when describing Penelope.

Iz scuffed some more and let out a sigh reminiscent of the sound made by a spouting whale after a deep dive. "Okay. I'll be honest. That's why I'm here." She snapped and unsnapped the pocket three times. "I want to make this relationship work. I want to have a home. I want to stop traveling and putting on presentations about women in history and myth and legend. I want to stop rallying women to causes and leading demonstrations and getting arrested."

She raised her chin and looked me in the eyes. "But it's about more than Penelope. I want to figure out who *I* am. And I want you to help."

Chapter 9

Eeekkk!

Helping Iz—a woman who hates to ask for help—was fraught with peril. Don't get me wrong. Iz *demanded* that people do things for her all the time. Or she simply assumed they would because she was a superior being. But she didn't ask or request or even hint around. Anything short of demanding implied weakness.

I abandoned silence and went with the other handy tool I'd watched Detective Atwell use—complicated questions requiring thought, opinion, and complex answers.

"In what specific ways do you think I'd be able to help you accomplish your search for yourself?"

Iz frowned, opened her mouth, and shut it again. I got the impression she'd expected me to tell her to take a hike, or else agree without setting conditions. I also got the impression she hadn't given much thought to what we might accomplish. Iz was more about passion than process. She made snap decisions, rushed in, and let the current of events carry her. Often that worked. The status quo got a good shaking.

Iz believed in the causes she took on—believed in a way that wasn't influenced by cash. While I was content with love and friendship and a reasonable amount of money, Iz wasn't happy and didn't feel alive unless she had a cause or a mission. If it wasn't for her lack of people skills and her obvious impatience with process and building consensus, she might consider a career in politics. Remembering facts and faces was easy for her. And she'd be terrific at debating—if she kept her cool.

Iz scuffed the carpet again, this time with toes *and* heels. If this kept up, I'd have to rearrange furniture to cover a bare spot. Since Paulette had placed every stick of furniture—all the while sighing and wearing a long-suffering expression implying I had no taste—moving anything even a few inches would require consultation. Consultation would be followed by strong suggestions to truck most of my possessions to the dump and bust the budget for a new sofa, chairs, and "a few decent lamps and tables."

All in all, it seemed less stressful to help Iz with her identity search.

"All right. But you have to keep your promise about how you'll react if you get mad."

Iz stopped scuffing and scowled. "For how long?"

"Until we're finished."

The scowl intensified.

My cringe-reflex kicked in.

I fought it. "And *I* say when we're finished."

Iz did the jaw-flap thing twice. Then she nodded. "What do we do? Where do we start?"

Having sat through dozens of late-night soul-searching discussions in college dorm rooms, I had a few ideas. "First you'll make two lists. Qualities and attributes people have you feel are positive. And those you feel are negative."

Iz slid her feet to heel-scuffing position.

I plunged on. "For example, we agreed that Penelope is focused. Is that a positive quality? Do you admire that?"

Iz scratched her head. "Most of the time. Except when she gets too focused and kind of shuts me out."

"So that quality goes in both columns—with an explanation of when a positive becomes a negative."

I stood, opened the closet under the stairs, and extracted a notebook from the heap Dave bought for Allison before school started. It was the color of those cones highway crews put out to divert traffic, and she'd consigned it to the closet because it wasn't the "right" orange and didn't quite match her top and flip-flops. "Here. You have 70 blank pages. Fill half of them with attributes and your thoughts."

"You're kidding." Iz riffled the ruled pages. "Thirty-five?"

"Not kidding. I can toss out a dozen or more attributes without putting my brain in gear." And, knowing it would light my sister's competitive-nature fuse, I launched a list. "Patience, kindness, intelligence, passion, commitment, caution, generosity, empathy, loyalty, competitive spirit, responsibility, foresightedness, hon—"

"I get it. I didn't donate my brain to science this morning." Iz lurched to her feet, rubbing her butt. "I'm going home. Your sofa is lumpy."

I wanted to tell her the sofa felt the same way about her bottom, but bit my tongue. After all, if she made an effort not to get mad, I could make an effort not to get even.

"I sprained my ankle, burned my hand, ate something that gave me the runs, and was lost for two hours," Dave told me when he called. "What's new with you?"

"My sister wants to change her life. She wants me to help."

"You win," Dave said. "You're in far more danger than I am."

I laughed. "I'm not facing snakes and stinging insects. I might get indigestion from one of the more questionable containers of leftovers in the refrigerator, but I doubt I could get lost around here if I tried."

"After a few days of working with your sister you'll wish you could. Iz wants to change her life the same way I want to give up my favorite T-shirts. The first time you suggest something outside her comfort zone—which is about as wide as a shoelace—she'll turn on you like a rabid dog."

"She promised she'd control her anger."

"And Bush promised no new taxes," Dave pointed out. "You're in deep doo-doo. And you didn't even mention what's going on with my daughter."

"She's up in her room doing homework."

"Can you repeat that? I think we have a bad connection. Or maybe the meeting with Iz scrambled your brain. I thought you said Allison was doing homework."

"Well, I haven't opened the door to check. But, now that you mention it, I hear music and smell nail polish."

"That's my daughter," Dave said. "Hang in there."

"You be careful."

"I will. I've about run out of things that can go wrong. I'll be home before you know it."

"That hateful man," Mrs. B sputtered when she called later. "All he does is complain about noises and smells and, oh, just the least little things, all day long. Not to my face, you understand. But to the desk clerks and the chef and the waitresses. Someone ought to put him out of our misery."

"Sounds like it's not going as well as you hoped," I commiserated.

"Not even half as well. If it wasn't for the stage being the perfect size and the staff being so sweet and the wonderful scenery and incredible food, I'd leave in the morning."

"How's Cheese Puff doing?"

"Well, to tell the truth, I'm worried about him."

I gripped the phone. "Worried that man might hurt him?"

"Oh, no. Not physically. But his feelings have been deeply wounded by that man's comments. And his self-image already suffered so after the duck scarred him for life."

(For the record, all trace of the scars from the small cuts the duck inflicted would be covered by Cheese Puff's hair when it grew out. That fell far short of "scarred for life." At least in my book.)

"He's extremely fragile right now," Mrs. B went on. "Knowing someone doesn't care for him simply because he's a dog is crushing his spirit."

Sheesh.

If she projected this much on my dog, imagine what she'd do for my sister. I considered asking her to take over as a mentor in the school of life changes I'd been recruited to run, but she had enough to handle. "If you decide it's too stressful for Cheese Puff, I'll drive up and get him."

"Oh, no, dear. There's no need. Once that crabby creature realizes I won't allow him to drive me out, I expect he'll tire of his game. You'll see. Everything will be fine tomorrow."

Tomorrow, however, was far from fine.

When I arrived at the teachers' room after a morning of drama involving misplaced pottery projects and misinterpreted artistic advice, I found Aston in a mood more foul than usual.

"Was it you?" He leaped from his chair and leveled a finger at my face. "Was it?"

A year ago I would have recoiled, but I'd learned Aston was mostly bluster. I executed a little jog step and kept going to the refrigerator to liberate my lunch—cheese, apple slices, walnuts, and whole grain crackers.

Doug unfolded the foil from a ham and cheese sandwich on rye. "He thinks one of us told Tremaine Scott about his political plans."

"I don't *think* it. I *know* one of you ratted me out." Aston's flinty gaze swung from me to Brenda and lingered.

"As if I cared enough about you or your career to rat you out." Brenda popped the plastic lid from a glass container of something that resembled frogs' eggs floating in melted lemon sherbet. "Tremaine Scott came to your room this morning because the fire marshal is due soon and he wants to identify issues before we get dinged for them. He checked *all* the rooms on this side of the school."

Aston continued to scowl.

Doug brought me up to speed as I settled in my chair. "Scott dropped in as Aston was explaining what he wanted kids to do for his political poster."

"It wasn't *my* poster. It was for a hypothetical candidate in a hypothetical race." Aston thumped the table with his fork—a fork that appeared to be carved from an antler or tusk. I told myself not to wonder how he acquired it, or speculate about the grayish chunk impaled on the tines, or what else was contained in the fire-blackened tin pot he'd pulled the chunk from.

"It *could* have been hypothetical," Gertrude told him. "If you hadn't informed the kids you were planning to run for something. After you passed on that bit of information, instructing them to design posters can definitely be defined as bringing your campaign to school."

"Using school materials wasn't smart, either," Brenda pointed out. "There are guidelines and—"

"Somebody ought to change them so kids can really learn about politics." Aston thumped the table again. "And what about our rights under the Constitution? Freedom of speech and all that?"

"I guess you'll be able to answer those questions when you finish the report Scott assigned," Gertrude said.

Doug leaned toward me. "'Campaigning and the classroom, what every teacher should know.' Emphasis on 'should.' Three thousand words. Due Friday."

"As if I didn't have enough to do," Aston groused. "Every time I turn around there's a new way of grading and reporting and feedbacking."

"Is that a word?" I asked Gertrude.

"If it isn't, it probably will be soon," she said.

"Stop complaining," Brenda told Aston. "You got off easy. If he came by tomorrow when the project was underway, you might have been suspended. You're not at the top of his favorite-teachers list after the stunts you pulled last year."

"I was standing up for my rights," Aston muttered. "Something none of you did when they changed everything around for no good reason."

Meaning administrators attempted to move Aston to another classroom in order to have all the history teachers in one area and improve collaboration. The plan was scrapped once other teachers complained that collaborating with Aston on curriculum was like collaborating with Godzilla on urban renewal projects.

"There's a right to be dumber than dirt?" Brenda asked. "A right to store revolting substances on school property?"

Aston kicked over his chair, grabbed his tin pot, and stalked from the room, clutching his fork like a spear. We braced for a door slam, Brenda gripping her soup—or whatever it was—with both hands, but Aston closed it with only a click of the latch.

"Well, that was a restful interlude." Doug took a bite of his sandwich.

"And you didn't get splattered," I observed.

"For once," Doug agreed, casting a wary look at Brenda's bowl. "Maybe things are changing."

"Or maybe it was a fluke."

"It was a fluke." Dave waved from his prone position on the sofa, raising a left arm swaddled from wrist to shoulder in a cast. "Could have happened to anyone."

"Anyone and his dog," I noted. Lola, sprawled on the carpet beside the sofa, sported a cast on her right rear leg. "What the heck happened?"

"A bear happened."

"A bear?" I opened the door to the deck, set my school bag on the floor, and set myself in a dining room chair. Whatever happened was over, and they were home. Except for the casts, Dave and Lola looked fine—no gashes, no bite marks. "A bear broke your arm? And Lola's leg?"

Lola sneezed and thumped her tail on the carpet.

"No. See, a bear came in to camp in the middle of the night and the dogs went crazy." He waved both arms, illustrating panic. "Everybody piled out of their tents. Flashlights strafing the dark. Guys grabbing for guns and other guys yelling not to shoot. Dogs barking and howling. It was bedlam."

"Did the bear maul anyone?"

"No. He took off. The only injuries were stubbed toes and a pair of broken glasses." He tapped the cast. "This happened later. Like I said, it was a fluke."

Lola thumped again.

Was she agreeing? Or disagreeing?

"I went to, uh, answer the call of nature and, uh, got turned around and tripped over a log in the dark. I had Lola on her leash. On account of the bear."

"So you both went down."

"And down. And down again. It was one of those rolling falls. Did I mention the terrain was steeper than a cow's face?" He chopped with his right hand, indicating the slope. "We'd probably still be rolling if we hadn't hit a tree."

I let out a long breath. "Good thing you were with a search and rescue team."

"And they had a field day. Broke out all the equipment. Carried Lola on a stretcher."

He rolled to the edge of the sofa, reached down, and patted her flank. "She never whimpered through the whole thing. I think she would have walked on her three good legs if they let her."

Lola raised her head and gave me a look that said he shouldn't be so sure.

"So, will you be reassessing the search and rescue idea?"

"Already did. While I was body-surfing the hill."

"And? What's the plan?"

"The plan is—"

"Ruined!" Mrs. B slid open the screen door to the deck and charged in, Cheese Puff at her heels. "All my plans for a week of rehearsing are ruined. Someone killed that cranky old man."

Chapter 10

With a grunt and a heave, Dave sat up. "What cranky man?"

"The man who lived at the inn." Twisting her silvery hair in tufts, Mrs. B dropped into Cheese Puff's chair and answered in a tone that implied Dave should pay attention and stop asking stupid questions. Cheese Puff, meanwhile, raced to Lola, sniffed her cast, licked her nose, and curled against her belly.

"The man who complained about the noise?" I asked.

"Yes. The one who insisted Cheese Puff be kept out of the common areas and treated like . . . like a dog."

Registering the insult, Cheese Puff yipped and put his paws over his ears.

"I haven't had a chance to tell Dave about him yet," I told her in a soothing voice. "I just got home from school and he was explaining how he broke his arm falling down a mountain last night. With Lola at his side."

"Oh. Oh dear." Mrs. B dropped to her knees to pet Lola. Then she popped to the sofa beside Dave. "Are you in pain?"

"Some," he said. "But I've got killer pills. And the cast comes off in a few weeks. Same for Lola."

While Mrs. B examined his cast, I focused on her outfit—a faded red sweatshirt, baggy checked pants, and a pair of worn black flip-flops patched with electrical tape. Not a pearl in sight. Not even on her fingers or in her ears. "What are you wearing? And why?"

"I'm wearing what the deputies allowed the hotel staff to find for me." She smoothed a wrinkle in the pants. "They took all my shoes and clothing. Even my underwear. And my jewelry. All of it. To check for blood, I suppose. And they towed my car somewhere."

She said all that in an offhand manner, but Dave's eyebrows rose and his lips tightened in a way that made my stomach lurch. "Tell me about the murder," he said.

"I don't know much. Apparently they think I'm a suspect."

She delivered that sentence with mild amusement, not at all the way I delivered a similar assortment of words when I was suspected of Henry Stoddard's murder. "They questioned you?"

"Of course, dear. They questioned everyone at the inn." She made another run at smoothing the wrinkle. "I had the distinct lack of pleasure of speaking with a rotund and balding gentleman reeking of smoke from decades of cheap cigars. He was a heart attack in cheap shoes with knotted laces."

"Harvey Goodspeed. The county's homicide investigator." Dave smiled. "Chuck Atwell refers to him as Hardly Nospeed. But don't repeat that. They have to work together now and then."

Mrs. B and I did the lip-zipping move, me hesitating a second because this was the kind of thing I loved to share with Paulette.

"Who was the victim?" Dave asked. "How was he killed?"

"I have no idea what his name was. The staff referred to him as 215. That was his room number."

"You weren't curious about his identity?" I asked. "If someone was complaining about me, I'd want to know who it was."

"I decided a creature like that didn't deserve a name." She sat up straighter, lifting her chin in a regal manner. "But I *do* know how he died. Well, at least I suspect it had to do with a lamp. I saw the forensic team carry one to their van. And because they're so interested in blood, I assume he wasn't strangled with the cord."

She pointed to the lamp on the end table. "The lamps in my room were taller than that. They had square marble bases. So did the one they carried away."

They sounded like ideal weapons. Long enough to give your swing a good arc. Heavy enough to drive the corner of the square base against a skull or neck. But not so heavy a woman in her senior years couldn't manage. Especially when the woman was in great condition for her age.

"You're not the only suspect, are you?" I asked.

"I expect not. That man was horrible to everyone." Mrs. B shrugged and turned to Dave. "Is being on the receiving end of nasty behavior a motive?"

"You'd be surprised what can motivate people to kill," Dave said. "Goodspeed will probably start by considering the entire staff and all the guests who were there last night."

"There were perhaps forty people for dinner. They put on quite a nice buffet and Tuesday was Southern cooking night. The hushpuppies were delicious. And the pecan pie—" Mrs. B paused and pursed her lips. "But I believe I was the only guest who stayed the night. Except 215."

Not good.

And once Harvey Goodspeed made the connection to Mrs. B's late husband and her past in Las Vegas, the situation might get worse.

"I'm surprised Harvey let you leave so soon," Dave said.

"I'm sure he didn't want to. But I never go anywhere without my attorney's business card. Once I laid it on the table, he assured me I would be driven home as soon as possible."

She stood. "And now that I'm here, I intend to take a long shower and consign these rags to the trash. Then I'll have a large glass of something restorative and order in provisions for an early dinner. You'll join me?"

"Wouldn't miss it." Dave raised his cast. "As long as I can manage with one hand."

Mrs. B smiled and headed for the door, flip-flops alternately dragging and smacking the floor. "How Allison walks in these things is beyond me," she muttered as she slid the screen door closed.

I took her spot on the sofa beside Dave. "Tell me I have a vivid imagination and this isn't as bad as I think it is."

"You have a vivid imagination."

"But . . . ?"

"This looks pretty bad. She was the only other guest in the hotel last night, and I don't doubt she has the strength to swing a lamp."

"So she had means and opportunity. What was her motive?"

"The guy complained about her."

"But she didn't even ask who he was."

"He bad-mouthed Cheese Puff. He wanted him treated like a dog. Mrs. Ballantine has a huge blind spot where your spoiled mutt is concerned."

Cheese Puff sat up, bared his teeth at Dave, and snarled. Lola sneezed and pawed him against her belly again. The snarl ceased.

"I admit she goes overboard sometimes."

"Sometimes?"

"Okay. Frequently. But there's a huge leap from being upset because someone doesn't like dogs, to killing that person."

Dave shrugged. "Maybe he confronted her. Maybe they argued."

"Mrs. B doesn't argue. As you often say, she's a force of nature. If she can't ignore or deflect, she states her views and proposes her concept of a solution. The other person capitulates."

"Maybe this guy didn't." Dave massaged his left shoulder. "Who's her attorney? Must be a big gun if Harvey cut her loose."

"There are big legal guns. And then there's Angus Drummond III."

Dave's eyes widened. "He's a legend. I thought he retired."

"He retired from other clients, but he's still at Mrs. B's beck and call."

Dave didn't say "Good, because she's going to need him," but the way his brow furrowed indicated his thoughts.

"Tell me about Harvey Goodspeed," I said. "It sounds like he's not the sharpest tooth on the county saw."

"Well, he takes his time. He's deliberate. Some people think he's not all that bright. But that may be what he wants them to think." Dave tapped his forehead with his index finger. "On the other hand, he's never had a case that required a lot of gray cells. Every county homicide in the past decade has been a slam-dunk no-brainer. Husbands killing wives, ex-girlfriends killing new girlfriends, fired employees killing bosses."

My fingers and toes grew numb with anxiety. Harvey Goodspeed might not cast his net beyond Mrs. B—no matter how high-powered her attorney.

"You're getting that look in your eyes," Dave said. "The last time I saw it was right before you announced you were going to 'snoop around' the Luke Dylan case. And you know what happened then."

What happened was Bennett Hightower threatened to shoot me and Clarice Hightower tried to run me down in her land-yacht of a car. What also happened was I uncovered the truth, and catnapping charges against Luke were dropped.

"Are you telling me you don't want me to snoop?"

"Nope." Dave raised his hands in surrender. "No way am I telling you I don't want you to do anything."

"Smart man." I patted his knee. "But don't worry about me getting sucked into this. I have to work for the rest of the week, so I don't have time for snooping. Besides, there's no reason. Mrs. B hasn't been accused of anything more than being in close proximity to a crime."

Little did I know how quickly the situation would change.

Chapter 11

Dinner was my idea of delicious—appetizers, salads, and a selection of pasta dishes from a nearby Italian restaurant, plus a huge box of treats from Mrs. B's favorite bakery. As usual, especially when I don't have to pay for or prepare a meal, I ate far more than I should.

Allison pointed that out. "If you go to water aerobics after all the fried zucchini you ate, you'll sink to the bottom."

"Deep water exercise," I informed her in a caustic voice. "We wear flotation belts."

"Better wear two," she advised in a snarky tone.

While my brain searched for a sarcastic comeback, Mrs. B intervened. "Being catty doesn't become you, Allison. And, since you devoured three chocolate mousse cupcakes after a second helping of lasagna, you've put yourself in the position of a pot calling the kettle black."

Allison cast a guilty glance at the bakery box. "What does that mean?"

"It takes one to know one," Dave said. "You'd sink faster than Barbara."

"Would not." Allison ducked her head and picked at one of the many frayed spots on her designer jeans. "And, anyway, pretty soon the pool won't be there so she won't be able to sink *or* float."

I sat up straight—or as straight as I could, considering what I'd packed in my stomach. "What does that mean?"

Allison shrugged. "One of the girls in my English class—her father sells houses and stuff—says he's going to sell the rec center pool next year and get a big check. Then he'll buy her a car. A *new* car."

"The pool is public property. The city council would have to vote to sell. And they'd require reports and hearings first." Mrs. B waved aside Allison's comments. "I think your friend is making up a story."

"She's not my friend. She's a skank who's always trying to hit on Josh," Allison said in a huffy voice. "And she says her father can too sell it—right after the guys in charge of the city vote to close it down. And they're gonna."

I felt a burst of anger mixed with disbelief. Was Paulette's theory about Cheryl accurate?

"Why would they close it?" Mrs. B asked. "The rec center is very popular. They have such a nice gym and workout facility. And I know several people who use the meeting rooms for crafts and clubs."

Allison made a face that implied Mrs. B just fell off the turnip truck. "But hardly anyone uses the pool. Except Barbara and Paulette. And it costs way more to keep it open than what people pay to swim."

I'd never seen the numbers, but I wasn't surprised by Allison's claim. The pool had to be heated and cleaned. It had to be staffed by lifeguards every minute it was open. None of that came cheap. And, since the recent recession, Reckless River leaders were all about the bottom line.

"It's not the only pool in town." Dave tapped my wrist. "If they close it, you can join a club or fitness center until summer.

And when the condo pool opens again, you can do water workouts here."

All true. But I liked the rec center pool better than others. Sure, the facility was old but, for that very reason, the pool was larger and deeper. And the price was in line with my budget. I gripped the edge of the table, my anger rising. This shady scheme had to be stopped.

Mrs. B echoed my thoughts. "This sounds like someone feathering their own nest at the expense of others. If I wasn't so busy—"

"Paulette and I will look into it," I assured her. And everyone in our aerobics classes who couldn't stand Cheryl would line up to help. As Allison had pointed out, there weren't all that many swimmers, but I had no doubt there were enough to raise a public stink.

"If *I* was gonna get a new car," Allison said in a wheedling voice, "I'd learn to drive much faster."

"We don't want you to drive faster," Dave teased. "We want you to drive carefully."

Allison pouted. "You know what I mean. I'd have *incentive*." She emphasized the last word.

"Driving yourself where you want to go isn't incentive enough?" Dave asked.

"Not if I have to drive your car. Or Barbara's."

"Because they're old?"

"Yeeeaaahhh. And, no offense, Dad, but your car is disgusting. It's all full of dog hair and fried pie wrappers. And Barbara's car rattles. And, anymore, it makes weird noises like guys make in the back of class when we have a sub."

"You've heard those noises?" Dave asked me.

"Sadly, yes." As a substitute teacher, I was far too familiar with disgusting noises. Because they almost always occurred when I had my back turned and thus couldn't determine the source, I'd developed the art of ignoring them. Apparently that art now extended to my car. I hadn't noticed a new range of noises emanating from it.

"Barbara can't afford another car and neither can I," Dave said. "But you know where the trash bags are. And the vacuum. You're welcome to clean mine to meet your standards. Although, given the state of your room, I'm a little surprised to find you *have* standards."

Allison made a gag-me motion. "If I cleaned all day and all night, it will still be a smelly old car with dings all over and tape on the driver's seat."

"Hawaiian seat covers are fun," Mrs. B suggested. "And air fresheners come in a variety of scents."

"But I want a *new* car."

"I don't care about new. But I'm definitely ready for *newer*." I took a mental peek at the amount I'd saved toward buying a low-mileage used model outright. Not even close.

"Until you pass the test for your learner's permit, and then pass the driver's test and get a license, there's not much point in winding yourself up," Dave said. "And your car, when you get it, won't be a gift. You'll have to work for it."

That last bit was a message to Mrs. Ballantine.

"You mean I have to pay for it all myself?" Allison wailed.

"Not all," Dave answered. "But at least half the cost of the car and a year's worth of insurance. And you have to earn the privilege in other ways—like doing your chores and getting decent grades."

Allison stuck her lower lip out so far it threatened to unhinge her jaw. She turned a pleading gaze on Mrs. B, the one person in the room who not only could overrule her father, but also write a check for the full price of a new car.

"Your father's right, dear." Mrs. B reinforced Dave's message. "Things you acquire because you work for them mean so much more than those simply handed to you."

Allison's thundercloud expression made it clear she didn't agree, but she didn't argue. In fact, after a moment of hesitation, she cleared the table and helped Mrs. B load the dishwasher and put leftovers away.

I shot Dave a wink. "You can't say your daughter doesn't pick the right person to suck up to. The one with enough loose change to buy an entire car dealership."

Dave smiled for a second, but then his eyes grew dark. "I hope Harvey Goodspeed wraps this case up before she's forced to spend every dime of that change on defense attorneys."

I made it to the pool with 15 minutes to spare and waited beside my car, hoping Paulette would also arrive early and I could share what I'd learned from Allison. When she parked beside me, I swung her driver's door wide and launched in. "You were right about Cheryl. You were right about this being a scheme to shut down the pool and make big bucks for a developer. Allison knows a girl whose father promised her a new car after he collects his commission on the sale of the pool building."

Paulette smiled like a cat full of cream. Or canary. Or maybe both. She unbuckled her seatbelt, grasped the handles of her swim bag, and slid from the car. "It's not much of a secret scheme if word is all around Captain Meriwether."

"Right."

"Meaning the crooks haven't kept their cards close to their vests."

"Right."

"Meaning some of them may be worried their plot will be revealed." Paulette flashed that smile again. "When we're getting our flotation belts on, let's linger behind Cheryl. You repeat what you just told me. I'll express outrage and say we need to find out if the rumor is true. If we can shake her tree, who knows what might fall out."

We shared a high-five and headed for the pool where we unfolded our scheme. Making certain Cheryl heard us was a cinch. Class attendance was off by 50%. That meant the level of last-minute chatting was also off. By the way Cheryl cocked her head and frowned, I was certain she caught every word.

"Lewis and Clark didn't quit when they faced the portage around the Great Falls of the Missouri River." Aston Marsden slammed a dried biscuit on the table, shattering it. He tossed the chunks in a bowl of something that smelled a lot like skunk spray. I dipped my head and inhaled the aroma of my rice pilaf. It did its best, but wasn't powerful enough to override the odor of Aston's lunch. Did people eat skunk? I shuddered, held my nose, and wondered how hungry I'd have to be to try it.

"If *they* didn't quit when their moccasins wore through, *I'm* not quitting because Tremaine Scott is a micromanaging nincompoop." Aston raised his chin and glared across the table at Brenda Waring. "Go ahead. Tell him I said that. I dare you."

Brenda cocked her head and gazed at the ceiling as if considering.

"Relationship's still off," Doug whispered.

Off permanently if she passed along that insult. Tremaine Scott didn't suffer fools gladly. And, while Aston might not be an all-out, all-the-time fool, he had his moments—a whole lot of moments.

"So you're continuing your pursuit of an office," Gertrude mused. "Have you decided which one?"

"Nah." Aston stirred his stew, releasing more of that pungent scent. Doug moved his chair as far away as the cramped seating arrangement allowed. I turned my head to breathe in the fragrance of the lemon cleaning solution I'd used on the sink and refrigerator.

"Haven't had time to research the . . ." Aston raised his spoon from the noxious stew and pointed it at me. "Hey, what's your sister up to? She ever manage a political campaign?"

I gulped air. Iz and Aston? Taking on the political establishment together? I almost felt the blood in my veins and arteries freezing. With my sister at loose ends and searching for a career and/or cause, and with Aston hunting for a partner in political slime, this was a recipe for a mixture more toxic than what Aston had in his bowl.

"Uh, no, Iz never managed a campaign."

"Doesn't mean she couldn't. Give me her number."

"I think that would be a huge mistake. Iz thinks of herself as a visionary. She's not good with details and organization."

In fact, saying "not good" was to give her way too much credit.

"It's only a local campaign. Probably. How much organizing would it take?"

Spoken like a man who had no concept of the number of potential voters in a district. "Iz also has a way of taking over and setting her own agenda."

Aston shrugged. "I don't mind knocking heads with stubborn women."

"Liar," Brenda shrieked.

"As long as they have common sense and know what they're doing," Aston said.

"And how would you know whether they do?" Brenda sniped. "You don't pay attention. You don't care about the movies a woman likes or the perfume she wears."

"And they're off." Doug cupped his hands and did an impression of a racetrack announcer.

"What does perfume have to do with anything?" Aston slapped his spoon on his stew, sending up a geyser of odiferous brown liquid.

Doug dove beneath the table, saving his pale yellow shirt, but subjecting his gray slacks to a rain of ruin.

"Sorry," Aston said.

"Sorry about what?" Doug clambered from his shelter and snatched half a dozen napkins from a stack on the table. "Sorry your batch of toxic sludge wasn't thinner so you could have gotten more distance? Destroyed my shirt? Soaked my hair?"

He jammed his sandwich in his lunch sack, snatched up his can of iced tea, and poured it on Aston's head. "Take that. I'll eat in my classroom. For the rest of the school year."

"You don't have a microwave in your room." Aston wiped tea from his eyes. "Or a refrigerator."

"I have credit cards." Doug tossed the tea can in the recycling tub. "Generally I use them to replace articles of clothing. But that's an expense I won't have after today."

"There goes one vote," Gertrude observed as the door slammed.

"And here goes another." Brenda snapped a lid on a plastic tub filled with something that looked like cottage cheese and kelp and smelled like low tide on a warm day. "Even if you hired an expert, Aston, you don't have a chance because you don't listen, and you won't change. No one's going to support a man who's as shaggy as a buffalo in winter, has no people skills, and isn't aware of events and issues since before women got the vote."

She leveled an angry gaze at me and then at Gertrude. "You two are welcome to join me in my classroom."

After she stalked out, Gertrude and I exchanged glances. Brenda's classroom, where kids learned about nutrition and mastered rudimentary cooking skills, was also where Brenda prepared many of the dishes she shared—or attempted to share—with us. I had no intention of spending time at culinary catastrophe ground zero.

Gertrude apparently didn't either. She opened a container of apple sauce and dug in. I warmed up my rice pilaf and did likewise. Aston, meanwhile, used a wad of napkins to dry his hair and beard and blot his flannel shirt and jeans.

"We're not staying because we're on your side, Aston," Gertrude told him. "And we may not be here tomorrow. There are other teachers' rooms and I'm sure anyone who knows what we've put up with will allow us to squeeze in."

"All I said was—"

Gertrude made a shoving motion with her hand. "I don't want to hear it."

"But all I did—"

"Barbara doesn't want to hear it, either. And if I find out you talked to her sister about your campaign, I'll be tempted to tell Tremaine Scott you called him a lot worse than a nincompoop."

"But Iz—"

"Will make you appear more ridiculous than you would on your own." Gertrude shoved air with both hands. "The last thing you should do, Aston, is put yourself out in public in a role other than those you play when you take part in reenactments. You're far better at acting than at being yourself."

"I could learn," Aston said after a stretch of silence.

"Learn basic table manners? Acquire a wardrobe that isn't pieced together from roadkill? Verse yourself in social skills?" Gertrude scraped the last bit of applesauce from the container. "Not fast enough for *this* election." She tossed the container in the trash. "Plus, you don't have a platform. Not a single cause or issue."

Aston seemed on the verge of arguing, but settled for sitting up straight, placing a napkin on his lap, and eating his stew with stiff and stylized movements.

I finished my rice while thinking about the issue closest to my heart—the scheme to close the rec center pool and sell the property. If the conspiracy was as shady and underhanded as it appeared to be, someone could make a lot of noise. And make political hay in the process. But that someone wasn't Aston. I doubted he'd ever been to the rec center. And, quite honestly, the thought of seeing him in a swimsuit made me queasy.

Oddly, it was that queasy feeling, coupled with Gertrude's use of the word "cause," that made me decide to call my sister and see how she was doing.

C h a p te r 1 2

As it turned out, I didn't have to call. When I got home, Iz anchored one end of the sofa and Dave, his feet on the coffee table, sprawled at the other. A documentary on soap through the ages blared from the television while Iz demolished a bag of store-brand potato chips, a tub of onion dip, and a large bottle of high-calorie cherry soda. The volume of the TV and the chill in the room told me Dave and Iz weren't presently on speaking terms. Cheese Puff and Lola were nowhere in sight, but the sliding glass door was open and I surmised they'd escaped to the deck or Mrs. B's condo.

Iz acknowledged me by lifting her chin half an inch and pointing with a chip. Dave grunted a greeting, but didn't shift his glazed-over gaze from the unopened bottle of beer on the table between his feet.

I bent and kissed his forehead. "Is the beer there because you're going off pain pills?"

"I was planning on it." He slid his gaze toward my sister. "But the pain suddenly got worse and I took another pill."

"Got enough pills for a friend?" I nuzzled his ear. "A really close friend?"

He tapped his shirt pocket, rattling a plastic container. "All depends on how long the pain hangs around."

"I'll see what I can do to alleviate it." I carried the beer to the refrigerator, poured a glass of lemonade, and headed for the deck. "I'm going out for sunlight and *natural* Vitamin D," I called. "The forecast says rain's moving in."

Since I hadn't checked the forecast, I had no idea if my statement about the weather was accurate. But I figured it was pretty safe. In the Pacific Northwest during the fall, winter, and spring, predictions almost always mentioned rain moving in.

Much of the deck furniture had been stored for the winter, leaving one chaise and several hardy molded plastic chairs to battle wind, rain, sleet, snow, and whatever else came our way. I turned a chair toward the sun and toted over a small table to use as a hassock.

As I'd hoped, Iz took the natural Vitamin D bait and trundled out a moment later, her hands filled with provisions. She kneed a chair with wide arms over beside mine, dropped into it with an exasperated sigh, and arrayed her supplies, including the orange notebook. "I don't know what you see in that man."

My sister went for women who were short, blond, and adorable, while I went for men described as tall, dark, and handsome, so there was no point in responding. And, since Iz was all about female empowerment, there was no point in telling her I felt safe with Dave—a feeling I hadn't experienced with my bird-obsessed first husband Albert or female-obsessed second husband Jake.

I decided to practice the technique of silence again.

It had the desired effect. Iz filled the conversational void.

"I asked if there were any openings on the police force for someone like me. He said maybe—if I'd wear a harness and sniff for drugs."

95

I forced myself not to laugh.

Iz studied me through narrowed eyes. "He hasn't suggested that you wear a harness, has he?"

This time I couldn't contain my laughter.

"It's not a source of amusement." Iz glanced toward the open door of the condo and lowered her voice. "I've heard stories about what men get up to in the bedroom."

I didn't mention that women also "got up to" various bedroom activities.

"You'd tell me if there were problems of that nature, wouldn't you?"

I gave her a wide-eyed nod, thinking she'd be the last person I'd go to. First, because I'd have to listen to her say she told me so. Second, because my sister's ideas about solving problems often made things worse. And third, because I was no longer the naïve child she helped bring up. I was able to take care of myself.

Mostly.

Iz blew air between her lips making a motorboat sound that indicated she didn't buy what my body language was selling. "Have it your way. But don't come crying to me later."

No chance of that.

She ate another dozen chips laden with dip, finished the soda, and opened the notebook. "I made the list."

"Good." I tilted my face to the sun and closed my eyes to cut down on reactions indicating disbelief or amazement. "What are your best qualities?"

"I'm *extremely* intelligent. I'm an *incredibly* strong leader. I'm *highly* skilled at mobilizing people behind a cause. I'm *amazingly* well-informed. And I'm *exceptionally* hard-working."

(For the record, I noted every item on her list came with an adverb. Many writers and writing teachers contend adverbs often beef up weak adjectives or verbs. I'll let you decide if that's accurate in this case.)

"What are your worst qualities?"

Iz flipped notebook pages. "There have been occasions when perhaps I should have talked less and listened more. It's possible I sometimes jump the gun and take action too quickly. Every so often I tend to make blanket assumptions. Now and then I don't respect others. And, in a few cases, I may have failed to attempt to reach a compromise when I disagreed with my partners."

Talk about wishy-washy statements.

So far this was going about the way I expected.

"Given all that, what kinds of jobs are you qualified for?"

Iz tossed the notebook to the deck. The pages fluttered as if waving for help. "Obviously I have the experience to run a domestic violence program. But Dave told me I'm not a good fit for the program here because it's 'low profile' and I'm not."

I smothered yet another smile and wondered if he said that before or after his pain pill.

"And, of course, I could run a preschool program for girls. Start raising their sense of worth early, before they're exposed to stereotypes in books and movies, and assaulted by marketing with skin-and-bone models. But Dave said girls that age don't hold still for lectures, and I'd have to integrate the message in play sessions and make learning fun."

The chip bag crinkled as she gripped it. "The rest of their lives depend on how they perceive themselves. How can they take lessons seriously if those lessons are amusing?"

Translation: Iz had no idea how to deliver information except through a lecture.

"This bag is empty. Do you have more potato chips?"

"That's the only bag we had." And—silly me—I'd hoped to have a few to pack with tomorrow's lunch.

"Tortilla chips?"

"Nope."

"Pretzels?"

"Not a one."

"What are you making for dinner?"

What I'd planned was potato soup with carrots, celery and onions, topped off with shredded cheddar cheese and crumbled bacon. But Iz liked that. So, in the interest of getting her gone faster, I went with a menu I knew she'd loathe. "Double hot chili with pork and red beans, and a creamed corn and chopped cabbage casserole."

Iz did a choke-gag thing, and I opened my eyes enough to watch her stuff the empty dip container in the potato chip bag. "I guess I'll go home and see what's in the freezer." She scooped up the notebook. "What do I do next?"

I'd been thinking about this since lunch, thinking about handing Iz the rec center rumor as a challenge and a cause. I'd argued the decision both ways, and finally determined to run it by Paulette first. "Work on a job scenario. Let's say you're hired by an agency or business that does good work but is strapped for cash. Let's say it provides sports and exercise opportunities for kids. How would you promote it? How would you raise awareness in the community? How would you bring it to the attention of the public?"

"How long will this take? I need a job. Soon!"

That's when a light bulb at the back of my mind flashed on.

Actually, it was a whole string of lights.

"I think I have a foolproof way to get Bernina to abandon the holiday decorating scheme," I told Jim a few minutes later. "The condo board agrees to go along with her scheme, but *only* if she hires the assistant the board selects."

"An assistant? How would that make her back off?" Jim tugged at his Father Christmas beard. "An assistant means she'd do less work. And an assistant would cost us more money."

"But for only a few days." I paused. "Or maybe only a few hours."

"A few hours? Are you nuts? The places that win these contests have enough lights to suck all the juice from Bonneville Dam. Not to mention all the other geegaws—animated critters, phony snow, holiday music blasting from speakers. Buying all that and setting it up will take days. Maybe weeks."

"But there won't be any buying or setting up if board members insist Bernina hires my sister."

"Your—?" Jim's jaw sagged then rebounded as he smiled. "Iz and Bernina can't stand the sight of each other."

"Correct."

"They both want to be in charge all the time."

"Exactly."

"Neither of them ever listens to anyone else."

"So true."

"And Iz is militant about commercialism and consumer excess."

"Which the decorating contest is all about."

"There's no way they'd work together."

"Absolutely."

Jim hugged me hard enough to make my ribs creak. "You're a genius."

"Just trying to help," I wheezed.

"How do we get Iz on board?"

"Dangling a few hundred dollars should do it. We can take up a collection from the Committee."

"All right. But how do we persuade board members?" He released me. "Some of them know Iz from the time she and Bernina got in that fight in the parking lot. Or they've seen her on TV. They won't go for it."

Dang.

A flaw in my plan.

I gulped air, my mind churning. "Okay, what if we skip that part? What if someone kind of hints to Bernina that the board is leaning in that direction?"

"Might work." Jim tugged at his beard and then smiled. "Couldn't hurt to try. Maybe I'll ask Sybil if she told Bernina about the plan to hire Iz to help with decorations. Then we'll see what happens."

Sybil served on the condo board not because she had an interest in how 90 Columbia Lane was run or an aptitude for management, but because she dozed off at a membership meeting and was nominated and approved before she woke up. Since her mind probably was more like a pinball game than a filing cabinet, there was a 98% chance she'd assume she'd forgotten about the plan and ask Jim to remind her. He would, and she'd trot to Bernina's office.

"Now who's the genius?" I ruffled his snowy hair and went on my merry way home.

Except my way wasn't all that merry.

And I didn't get home.

At least not in a timely fashion.

As I approached my unit, a county patrol car pulled up in front of Mrs. B's condo, and two uniformed deputies got out.

Chapter 13

Leading with square jaws, the deputies marched to Mrs. B's door.

Uh oh.

I scanned the parking area. No sign of the dark green luxury car she'd rented while investigators worked hers over.

Whipping out my phone, I called Dave.

"A couple of county guys are knocking on Mrs. Ballantine's door. I don't think they're here to shampoo the carpets."

"Don't get in the middle of it," Dave advised in a groggy voice. "If you get hauled in for interfering with an arrest, I won't try to spring you. I'll be in another county, trying to recover from professional embarrassment."

"Fine," I snarled.

"Tillamook County's a possibility. I hear it's nice at the beach today."

"Don't cry to me if you get sunburned."

Fuming, I clicked off. He was right.

And I knew it.

But that didn't stop me from scurrying under the protected-parking canopy, sliding into my car, and phoning Mrs. B.

"Don't come home," I yelped. "Call your lawyer. A couple of county officers are at your door. They have you're-under-arrest expressions."

"Oh my. Why would they arrest me?"

Talk about naïve. This is what happens when you focus on the sunny side of the street. "Because you're a suspect in a murder case?"

"Oh. Of course."

"Where are you?"

"A few blocks away. Cheese Puff and Lola and I were at the pet supply store. I thought a new collar might cheer Lola up."

"Come to the Italian restaurant. I'll meet you in ten minutes."

I told myself I wasn't exactly interfering with an arrest. I was retrieving our dogs and seeing that a friend gave her attorney advance notice. Much as I often resented the fact, money talked. Power also talked. Often in a louder voice. If Mrs. B turned herself in with Angus Drummond III at her side, the treatment she received might be kinder and gentler than if she arrived in a patrol car.

The deputies knocked again and, to my surprise, Dave opened the door of our unit and peered out. He yawned, giving a good impression of someone awakened from a nap and wondering what the commotion was all about.

One of the deputies acknowledged him with a raised hand. Dave nodded, said something I couldn't hear, and pointed to the empty slot where Mrs. B parked her car.

I ducked, counted to twenty, and risked a peek over the dash. Backs to me, the deputies were examining Dave's cast and the cuts and bruises on his face. Easing from the car, I skulked to the rear of the covered parking area, and scuttled off, striving for a brisk but natural pace.

I skirted the trash bins and the hedge Jake mangled last spring, hit the river trail, and sprinted for the restaurant. Mrs. B was waiting, phone to her ear, Cheese Puff and Lola tangling their leashes as they milled around her. Lola wore a green collar and a new ID tag to match.

I took the plastic handles from Mrs. B, unsnarled the leash cords, and listened in to the last of her conversation. It was carried on in a sugary voice. Mrs. B, it seemed, was flirting with Angus Drummond III.

"You're such a dear, Angus. I'll meet you there in fifteen minutes. I'm so glad I have you to see me through this."

She paused then giggled. "I'd love to have dinner with you. As long as I can change to something more presentable than my present shabby attire."

What she had on was a pair of black leather flats, gray slacks, a white silk blouse, and a bright blue fluffy wool sweater that set off her hair and eyes. She was more "presentable" dressed for a trip to the pet supply store than I am gussied up for an evening out. Add two diamond rings and a pearl necklace and earrings, and her outfit was worth more than my entire wardrobe with my car thrown in.

With a final giggle and a promise to say nothing to anyone until they met, she clicked off.

"That promise doesn't include you, dear. Thank you for calling." She kissed my cheek then chewed at her lower lip. "Dave won't be angry, will he?"

"He might go through the motions because he feels obligated. But I know he didn't expect me to stand by and watch you get hauled off."

"Loyalty is one of your finest qualities, dear." Mrs. B gave me another kiss. "For a moment I thought it might be fun—and enlightening—to be taken to jail like a common criminal. I've had so much of the good life for so long. I've almost forgotten what it was like to be at the bottom of the heap."

"But Angus Drummond talked you out of that?"

"He said it was lunacy. And lunacy that might, in the end, cost me significantly more in terms of legal hours billed." She smiled and brushed a strand of Cheese Puff's orange hair from her slacks. "Angus is a dear friend but he is, after all, my attorney. The skill he's honed comes at a price. If I need to make use of it, I have no problem paying."

I wondered if Drummond would bill her for hours devoted to wining and dining, then gave myself a mental kick. It was none of my business. "Well, what good is money if you're locked up and can't spend it? And, like they say, you can't take it with you."

"No, you certainly can't. But you *can* leave it to charity." She plucked a strand of Lola's hair from her sweater. "So let's hope Angus straightens out this misunderstanding quickly."

Spoken as if she was referring to a parking ticket or excessive library fine.

She opened the trunk, removed her purse, and handed me her key ring. "I hope you can spare a few moments to drive me to the sheriff's office."

"I can spare all the time you need." I opened the rear door for the dogs. Cheese Puff leaped in and turned to give Lola an encouraging bark. She got her front feet planted on the seat then paused, whining, until I gave her a boost.

We cruised past the sheriff's office and spotted Angus Drummond sliding out of a black SUV in the center of the next block. He wasn't wearing a kilt and he wasn't playing bagpipes, but he looked like someone who might do both on occasion. Ginger hair frosted with white at the temples and a beard shot through with gray gave him the appearance of an elder statesman.

He opened the door for Mrs. Ballantine and offered his hand to help her out. When her feet were on the sidewalk, she bent and blew me a kiss. "It will be fine, dear. I'll be home in no time."

"Maybe the definition of 'no time' is actually 'never,'" I told Dave as I paced another circuit of the dining room. The kitchen clock, which had read 9:21 the last time I checked, read 9:22.

"Harvey Goodspeed isn't the type who can be rushed. If Drummond tries to speed up the process, Harvey will dig in his heels." Dave thumbed the TV remote, clicking through channels in search of something I doubted he'd watch. Admit it or not, he was as worried about Mrs. B's fate as I was. "In fact, just *seeing* Drummond will make Harvey balk."

That didn't bode well for Mrs. B. I scooped up Cheese Puff and cuddled him. He huffed, but bore with me for a full minute before he wiggled and yipped to be put down. "What about the DA? How does he feel about Drummond?"

"Likes him as a person. They golf together." Dave repositioned his feet on the coffee table and clicked to a baseball game. In a second he clicked past it to what was either mud wrestling or the aftermath of an explosion in a chocolate factory. "But he won't let that influence him. Neither will the fact that the victim may have been a killer himself."

I shivered and grabbed for Cheese Puff again in an attempt to keep my mind from fixating on what Dave had learned from the deputies. My faithless mutt skittered away and slipped under the sofa. Lola opened her eyes and thumped her tail on the carpet. I knelt beside her and stroked her head and ears.

It took Cheese Puff less than a minute to notice attention not directed at him. He darted from his lair, shook off clinging dust bunnies, and threw himself on top of Lola. She sneezed, but took it with her usual long-suffering silence.

"If we harnessed Cheese Puff's jealousy and converted it to electricity, we'd knock our power bill down to nothing." Dave flopped on his side and ran his fingers through my hair.

I sighed and snuck another look at the clock. 9:27.

"Maybe get a treadmill. Get that cat from down the way to hang out at the end of it," Dave mused. "Give the cat one of Cheese Puff's toys and see how fast he runs."

I knew he was trying to distract me, but I couldn't get my mind off the mess Mrs. Ballantine was in. Based on the evidence, would they want to toss her in jail until she went to trial? Would they? If they did, how would she fare? Would she be protected, or victimized and abused?

That thought made my stomach flip. I forced myself to picture her, like my ex-husband, finding ways to make the best of incarceration. She was strong for her age. And determined. She made friends easily. And if she had to buy temporary friendships, she was realistic enough to do so.

"Tell me again about the . . . guy who was killed." I couldn't make my mouth form the word "victim." As Dave told me earlier, the man had been anything but. "Tell me about Big Shiny Scarpelli."

"I don't know more than I did half an hour ago." Dave wound a lock of my hair around his fingers. "I never heard of him until this afternoon. And I only know what's on the Internet—which is mostly unconfirmed rumor. His name came up in connection with several murders and disappearances around Las Vegas years ago, but nothing ever stuck. He dropped off the radar a long time ago."

"Do you think Mrs. B knew him?"

Dave's fingers stopped moving. I suspected he was crafting an answer that wouldn't jack my anxiety level to the heart-attack zone.

"Don't lie. Do you think she knew him in her showgirl days?"

"Possibly," he said after a long moment. "Or he knew who she was. Las Vegas was a smaller place then. And she was a star."

He resumed twining my hair around his fingers. "Now if you're asking whether they were an item, all I can say is, if photographs from back then don't lie, Big Shiny wasn't exactly—"

The doorbell rang.

I leaped to my feet and hustled down the hallway, Dave close behind, dogs at our heels.

Peering through the peephole, I spotted Mrs. Ballantine.

"I'm sorry to bother you," she said as I flung the door wide. "But I gave you my keys."

"No bother." I pulled her inside. "They're on the hook in the hallway."

"Are you okay?" Dave's gaze swept over her. I suspected he noted the smudged mascara beneath her eyes, the lack of lipstick, the quiver of her chin, and the death grip she had on her black leather purse.

"I'm fine." She patted his arm. "Or as fine as I can be considering I'm tired, hungry, and insulted beyond reason." She hissed the final words through clenched teeth.

Uh oh.

"We can fix the hungry part." I drew her toward the dining room. "As long as you're in the mood for spaghetti."

"Did Dave make his famous garlic bread?"

"Two loaves. And Allison ate only six slices." Dave pulled out a chair for her and poured a glass of wine.

"That was during dinner," I corrected Dave's report as I put the microwave and toaster oven through their paces. "She took another three slices up to her room an hour ago."

Mrs. B smiled, but only with her lips. She ignored Cheese Puff's efforts to worm his way onto her lap and folded and unfolded her napkin, her gaze drifting and unfocused. When I set the steaming bowl in front of her, she sprinkled grated cheese on top, then pressed her hands against the sides and leaned forward to inhale the aroma. "If I had to choose between garlic and chocolate, I'd be in a quandary."

The toaster oven dinged and I slid three slices of garlic bread on a plate and brought it to the table.

"Barb would be there with you. But I'd go with garlic every time." Dave snatched one of the slices and bit off a huge chunk.

Mrs. B followed suit, but took a far smaller bite, then speared a mushroom from the tangle of pasta and chased it with a huge swallow of wine. I longed to have a glass of the grape myself, but I'd already downed one. Another day in pottery loomed, and I needed to be sharp—or at least not as dull as a pair of plastic kindergarten scissors.

Dave and I exchanged glances, but neither of us said a word about Big Shiny Scarpelli and the case against her. I wanted to. You bet I wanted to. I was on the edge of my chair with wanting to. But I was afraid Mrs. B would feel crowded, feel her privacy had been violated because Dave had pried the name of the murdered man from the deputies.

She wound a few strands of spaghetti around her fork. "He was smaller and shriveled, but I might have recognized him if I'd seen him without a hat."

Chapter 14

I played dumb. What can I say? I have a gift.

"Recognized . . . the man who was killed?"

"Big Shiny Scarpelli. If I recall, his real name was Sam, but he was called Big Shiny because of his head. Without the hat, I'm certain I would have recognized it."

I continued my act. "His head?"

"Marco had the most luscious hair—thick and wavy. Sam Scarpelli lost most of his in his 20's, and shaved off what few hairs remained. Many men do that and I usually find it far more attractive than combing over a dozen strands." She grimaced and set her fork down. "The thing I didn't like about his head was the shine. Rumor had it he waxed his scalp every morning. Some girls claimed he used car wax. Others said it smelled like furniture paste. One swore he had it buffed at a shoeshine stand."

"What did you think?" Dave asked.

Mrs. B raised her chin and straightened her spine. "*I* never got close enough to develop an opinion."

I felt an involuntary sigh of relief leak between my lips. Mrs. B hadn't been involved with Big Shiny.

"Did you avoid him because he was dangerous?" Dave asked.

"Partly. But mostly because he was disgusting. A horrible man. A squid of a man. That long, shiny head. Arms that hung to his knees. And a big belly." She shuddered. "They said he killed people. And enjoyed it. They said sometimes he did it for no reason."

She shuddered again and hugged herself. "When Marco went on the run, it was because word was going around that Big Shiny wanted to have a talk with him."

The legend of Marco being on the run from organized crime was questionable, so I took the talk-with-Big-Shiny story with a grain of salt. Still, it sounded like something *I'd* run from.

"Did you know he'd moved to Washington?" Dave asked. "That he was living at the River Rise Inn and calling himself Norman Adams?"

Mrs. B grasped her fork and dug another mushroom from the nest of pasta. "I hadn't thought about him for years. I had no idea he was still alive—in fact, I would have bet he'd been rubbed out. If I'd realized he was the one complaining about Cheese Puff, I would have checked out immediately."

"And gone to the police?" I asked.

"Probably not." Mrs. B shot an apologetic glance at Dave. "The police couldn't—or wouldn't—do anything about him years ago. There's no reason to believe they could now. And if I informed on him and he found out . . ."

"You don't want to make a man like that angry," Dave agreed.

Mrs. B nodded, popped the mushroom in her mouth, and wound more spaghetti on her fork. After a glance at the clock— now showing 9:58—I broke down, ate the last slice of garlic bread on the plate, and heated more. We had yet to get to what happened at the sheriff's office, and I needed fuel to compensate for the sleep I'd lose.

Or so I told myself. When it came to excuses for eating, I never ran out.

"I expect you want to know where things stand." Mrs. B pushed her empty bowl aside and patted her lips with her napkin.

"Only if you want to tell us," I said in a tone about as casual as that of someone yelling for help from the roof of a burning building.

"That's Barb's way of saying you better spit out every detail," Dave said.

Mrs. B smiled—the first real smile since she came through the door. "You two are such a comfort to me. And Cheese Puff and Lola as well." She pushed her chair away from the table and patted her lap. Cheese Puff levitated and went to work licking crumbs from her blouse and sweater, his claws doing little to benefit the fabric. Patient Lola laid her head on Mrs. B's knee, waiting for a nibble to be handed to her. I brought a box of dog treats from a kitchen cabinet. Cheese Puff snubbed his, craned his neck, and eyed the garlic bread. Before he made his move, Dave snatched the plate, folded a slice of bread, and stuffed it in his mouth. Cheese Puff yipped in a way that said he was not amused. Dave mouthed something I won't write here.

"Angus fought like a wildcat—but in a lawyer-like way," Mrs. B said. "We were both absolutely exhausted when it was over. Too tired to even consider a meal in a restaurant."

"He must have won the battle," Dave observed. "You're here. Not in jail."

"I'm here." Ignoring Cheese Puff's whines of protest, Mrs. B turned in her chair, raised her right leg, and drew up her slacks to reveal an electronic ankle bracelet. "But I'm still more or less in jail."

Dave opened his mouth, but she patted air to silence him. "I volunteered to wear it. To prove I won't skip town. They seem to think I'm a flight risk because I happen to have a little money."

I almost smiled at the "little money" comment, but this was about murder. "They can't seriously think you killed Big Shiny Scarpelli."

"Apparently they do. And I can't blame them. You see, my fingerprints are on the murder weapon."

I groaned again, loud enough to make Lola whimper.

Dave pressed his lips together and cocked his head the way he did when he was thinking. "He was killed with a lamp," he said after a moment. "Yesterday you said it was the same style as the one in your room."

"Yes. Exactly the same style. There were two in my room. No, four. One on either side of the bed and one on each of the tables beside the sofa."

"And I assume you touched at least one of them."

"Of course. The one on the right side of the bed. And one beside the sofa. I turned them on and off."

Mrs. B glanced at me, a puzzled frown on her face. I patted her hand. By now I saw where Dave was going. I also saw a glimmer of sunlight through the clouds of suspicion.

"Did you touch them other than to turn them on? Did you move one?"

"I don't think I . . . yes, you know, I did. Late on the second afternoon I was there, a woman from housekeeping brought fresh bulbs. The lamps are tall and heavy and she asked me to tip them so she could remove the old bulbs and screw in the new ones."

Mrs. B grasped air, miming what she'd done. "I got hold of the base or the column or whatever you call it and tilted the lamp."

"Leaving your fingerprints on every one of them," I said.

"Oh my." Mrs. B studied the pads of her fingers. "Do you suppose . . . ?"

"That you were set up?" Dave asked. "You bet. Especially if the woman from housekeeping was wearing rubber gloves. And perhaps a wig or a pair of glasses."

"She definitely wore a pair of yellow kitchen gloves. And sunglasses. And something like a shower cap on her head." Mrs. B twisted a pearl earring. "In retrospect, that seems odd. But at the time I was in a hurry to meet the girl who was walking Cheese Puff, and I didn't think anything of it."

Dave retrieved a pen and notepad from the end of the counter and set them in front of Mrs. B. "Describe her—height, weight, skin tone, eye color, moles or tattoos, everything you can remember."

"She was thin. And not too tall. But I'm afraid that's all I remember."

"Exactly," Dave agreed. "You saw someone from housekeeping, someone in a uniform with a name badge and a cart full of supplies."

"Wait. She didn't have a cart. Or a badge." Mrs. B slapped the table, narrowly missing Cheese Puff's paw as he reached for a flake of bread crust. He yelped, leaped down, and darted to the sanctuary of his favorite chair and the crevice between the cushion and the arm.

"I am such a fool," Mrs. B moaned. "I should have known something fishy was going on. I've stayed in more than a thousand hotels in my lifetime and no one *ever* replaced bulbs that were working. In fact, if a bulb blew, it was sometimes like pulling teeth to get a new one."

"Don't beat up on yourself," I said. "With all the emphasis on energy-efficient lighting, I might have assumed she was replacing every bulb in the resort."

Mrs. B shot me a feeble smile. "Thank you, dear, but I should have noticed she had no badge. Instead I just let her waltz in. And then I helped her fabricate evidence."

I turned to Dave. "Do you think that woman worked at the resort and took her badge off and slapped on a cap so she wouldn't be recognized later?"

"Possibly. Or she got in through a side door. Or came in as an early dinner guest."

"Maybe someone at the desk or in the restaurant might remember her," I said in a hopeful voice.

"Or not. We have no idea what she looked like without that disguise," Dave said in a dash-my-hopes-gently tone.

Crud.

I hadn't thought of that.

"She put some planning into this," he went on. "But she still had to depend on luck. She took a chance carrying the lamp from your room and replacing it with another so you wouldn't notice. Someone on the staff might have seen her."

"There isn't much of a staff," Mrs. B said. "The general manager and two young men on the desk. They work in shifts and also sweep the porch and do other chores. Then there's the chef. And the kitchen help, two waitresses, and only one maid. At least only one that I saw."

And someone as low on the staff totem pole as a maid might assume the woman with the light bulbs was legitimate.

"My room was just a few steps from a stairway," Mrs. B added. "And I was out a lot working on my routine. If she had a key, she could have slipped in almost any time and taken a lamp."

"A key?" Dave asked. "Not a key card?"

"An old-fashioned heavy brass key attached to a polished slab of wood with the room number on it in gold paint."

Dave groaned. "A burglar's dream. Barbara could have unlocked your door with a nail file. But that's good news for your defense."

"I never thought the word 'defense' would sound so dreadful." Mrs. B shivered. "What I don't understand is why. I don't mean why anyone would kill Big Shiny, but why anyone would frame me."

"Perhaps it's someone from your past," I suggested. "Someone from Las Vegas."

She thought for a moment, and then shook her head. "I can't imagine who. Or why that person would wait so long. Big Shiny was an old man. And I'm not exactly a spring chicken."

She stood and stretched. "Lord knows how this will affect the show. I'd better call Dario." She headed for the hallway and her keys.

"Wait," I called. "Didn't you tell me the resort owner was an old friend of Dario's?"

"Yes. Not a close friend. An acquaintance."

"From Las Vegas?"

She twirled the key ring on her finger. "Yes. Farley Dole managed a men's clothing store. He worked in Baltimore or maybe Philadelphia until a year or so after Marco and I left Las Vegas. I never met him until this week. He hit a jackpot on the slots. That's how he bought the inn."

"If this acquaintance knew a mobster was living in his resort, would he mention it to Dario?"

Mrs. B's sapphire eyes flashed. "If Dario knew, he would never have allowed me to go there."

"If Dario knew," Dave muttered, "he might have done more than that."

"And if Farley Dole knew, and didn't say a word." Mrs. B steadied herself against the wall. "Then he might have been working for that horrible man."

"Or not working for him, but too afraid to open his mouth and reveal his identity," I speculated.

"That's another trail for Angus Drummond to follow," Dave said. "It leads to more potential suspects, like Farley Dole."

"Maybe he got tired of playing host to a killer who could turn on him any time," I said. "Or maybe he wasn't playing host by choice. Maybe he was footing the bill for Big Shiny's retirement hideout."

"And maybe he decided to stop the financial bleeding," Dave offered. "It sounds like the hotel wasn't doing a booming business."

"I'll call Angus first thing in the morning and tell him about our conversation. Right now I need to rest." Mrs. B cast a rueful glance at her ankle. "If rest is even a possibility with this contraption."

Chapter 15

When I returned from school the next day, I went straight to Mrs. B's condo for what she'd called "a council of war." Allison and Josh beat me there, adding to the crush in the living room, a crush that included Dario, Paulette, members of the CPCCC, Lana Dylan, and my sister. Looking like a sugar bowl between two dainty salt shakers, Iz hunkered on the sofa with Verna and Sybil. Lana perched on a hassock, Josh and Allison sprawled on cushions beside the coffee table where they had easy access to snacks, and Jim gave an antique rocker a workout. Paulette, notepad on her lap, sat with perfect posture in a wooden dining room chair with broad arms, and Dario paced. Or rather he attempted to pace. Every other circuit of the dining room found him on a collision course with someone bound for the kitchen to refill a glass, pour nuts or chips in a bowl, retrieve a fresh container of dip, or arrange more cheese and crackers on a tray.

"Pull over a chair, dear." Mrs. B pointed to one by the dining room table. "There's room beside Paulette if she squeezes closer to Jim."

Dario nudged me aside and hoisted the chair. His purple shirt was damp under the arms, his gray and pink tie hung

117

askew, and a grease spot shone on one knee of his black slacks. With a grunt, he slammed my seat in place and stepped aside, glaring at Mrs. Ballantine who sat in her favorite wing chair, a legal pad on her lap.

Dario is a large unit and well versed in using body language to convey displeasure. Since he became part of the crowd several months ago, I'd seen a variety of scowls and frowns, but I never expected to see a glare aimed at the woman he worshipped.

"For the last time, Dario," Mrs. B said in raw voice, "please contain yourself. You're making Cheese Puff tense."

As if to punctuate that statement, Cheese Puff interrupted his nap and bared his tiny teeth.

"This situation is making *me* tense," Dario said.

"Then pace if you must. But please don't drive up to that resort."

Dario growled again.

"If you interfere, you might make things worse." Mrs. B aimed a finger at his chest and softened her voice. "*I* know you're a cream puff, but there are others who find you intimidating."

For example: me.

Dario tugged at his tie. "I want answers, Muriel."

"And if one of those answers is that Farley knew who was living in his hotel, what will you do?"

"What I have to." Dario pounded a fist on the dining room table.

Cheese Puff bared his teeth again. Sybil and Verna gasped. Paulette pressed against the back of her chair and fanned herself with an interior design magazine. I seized the handle of a pitcher half full of frothy pink liquid and filled a tall glass.

"What *you* have to do?" Mrs. B asked.

Dario nodded.

118

"Not what would be best for me and for my defense?" Her voice tightened. "You do see the difference, don't you?"

Dario's hands curled into fists. He scraped the sole of his right shoe—a black leather loafer that appeared to be at least a size 14—against the carpet. He reminded me of a bull about to charge.

Acting on the belief that the more relaxed I was, the more likely I'd be to survive whatever Dario wrought, I gulped my drink.

"I want answers just as much as you do," Mrs. B went on, her voice softening. "And if we don't get them, then we may have to pursue other avenues to reach the truth. But I don't think that time has come."

Dario drew in a breath that made me fear for the buttons on his shirt, and then took up a position behind her chair, his hands on her shoulders. Verna and Sybil relaxed against the sofa cushions, careful to lean away from my sister. Cheese Puff swatted a catnip-stuffed mouse from the end table, circled in Mrs. B's lap, and returned to his snooze. She stroked my entitled dog with her right hand and touched Dario's fingers with her left, tipping her head to smile at him. "I've got the best attorney in the Northwest."

"You saying you don't need me?"

"You know I do. But you have a job and responsibilities in Las Vegas."

"And if you don't get back, that pushy-pushy Jackie will take over your office," Allison added.

Dario blew air between his lips, but then nodded. "We're behind schedule, so I'll head back this evening. But call me if—"

"I will. You know I will." Mrs. B blew him a kiss, and then her gaze clicked across the faces of the others in the room and she was all business. "If things go wrong, I may end up in a jail cell before long. And even if things go well, I presume I'll have to spend a great deal of time with my attorney. So we need to settle the issues hanging fire. First, where do we stand on a name for the restaurant?"

Jim, Verna, Sybil, and Josh exchanged sidelong glances. Paulette tapped manicured nails on the arm of her chair. Lana studied the carpet at her feet. Allison huffed a sigh that clearly said, "Nowhere."

"Have you at least narrowed the possibilities to two or three?"

More sidelong glances indicated they hadn't.

"When we were hatching this plan," Jim said, "we should have done a little more homework."

"And checked on menus outside of Reckless River," Josh added. "There are hundreds of places that do way more than slap cheese on bread and grill it."

"I haven't had a grilled cheese sandwich since I was a little girl," Verna said. "I had no idea there were so many variations."

"And so many ingredients and kinds of cheese," Sybil elaborated. "I guess that's why there are so many different kinds of cows."

I smothered a giggle. So did Paulette. Iz and Dario groaned. Allison and Verna rolled their eyes. Jim closed his and rubbed his temples. Mrs. B shot Sybil an indulgent smile. "So I assume many of the names you came up with are already taken."

Paulette nodded. "We spent hours on the Internet ruling out ideas and concepts because they'd been trademarked or done to death."

Verna leaned forward in order to see around Iz and directed her gaze at Sybil. "A lot of the names *some people* came up with were stupid or silly. Toasty Cheesy Pleasy. Really? And that was the best of the lot."

"And the names *other people* came up with were as dull as dishwater," Sybil shot back, wagging a finger at Verna. "Much More Than Cheese. That was all you had."

Iz raised her elbows to keep them apart. "Penelope thinks unless you come up with something brilliant you should keep the name clear and simple. Don't go with anything too cute."

"No one even listened to any of my suggestions," Allison wailed. "Just because I'm not really on the committee. They were good ideas, too. Like having the witch from that old movie standing on a sandwich and screaming she was melting."

Jim spread his hands in an appeal for Mrs. B to recognize what he was up against as chair of the Krammee's Reconstruction Committee.

Mrs. B tented her fingers, the diamonds in her two large rings flashing. "All right. I think Penelope makes a good point. Thank you, Iz, for conveying it to us. We'll go with clear and simple. The Reckless River Sandwich Shop."

"That's pathetic." Allison groaned. "It doesn't say anything about the grill. Or the kinds of cheese."

"That's true, dear," Mrs. B said in a patient but firm tone. "Cheese is the core of the menu. But, as Josh and Paulette have told us, the best cheese names are already taken."

Lana cleared her throat, but kept her chin tucked and spoke in a voice not far from a whisper. "Perhaps we could use cheese in the logo."

"Like a picture of a grilled cheese sandwich?" Josh asked.

"I like it." Paulette scribbled on her notepad. "Maybe toasty brown bread and melting orange cheese on a thick white plate? With the name of the restaurant written around the rim?"

"Works for me," Jim said almost before she finished. Obviously, he was ready to be finished with this process, get the restaurant open, and pass on as much responsibility to Lana as possible.

"I'm on board," Josh chimed in. "If we all approve, I'll get with Corcoran McGuckin."

Corcoran, a Captain Meriwether student, was noted for his caricatures of teachers and administrators. He was also an accomplished artist and—pardon the pun—fast on the draw. I bet he'd have preliminary sketches before sundown.

"Be sure you check existing logos," Jim advised. "There's only so much you can do with a drawing of a grilled cheese sandwich. We've got to make sure ours doesn't duplicate anyone else's."

"The sandwich logo goes nicely with the color scheme," Paulette said. "Soft yellows and whites on the walls, and the brown picnic-style tables." She shifted her gaze from Verna to Sybil and back again. "And, as you know, we're right at the deadline for submitting artwork for the signs."

After a long moment and several glances at each other behind Iz's back, Sybil and Verna nodded.

Allison pouted and puffed out enough air to send a small kite spinning into the sky. Josh put his arm around her, kissed her cheek, and slipped a chocolate-covered almond between her lips.

"Then it's decided." Mrs. B clapped her hands. "On to the second issue—*Still Got That Strut*. Even if the cloud of suspicion lifts in time for me to travel to Las Vegas, how will I be able to perfect my performance if I'm under house arrest? The little studio upstairs is fine for practicing individual moves, but I need more space to rehearse the whole routine."

She raised the hem of her beige slacks to display the electronic monitor. "And even if I have space, how can I dance with this? It throws me off balance."

She tipped her head to peer at Dario. "In fact, this whole mess has thrown me off balance. What I'd really like to do is postpone my appearance."

"I think," Iz said, "you should cancel it."

Dario opened his mouth, but Allison beat him to the conversational punch. "She can't cancel! If she doesn't compete, then Glorree Morning might win the big prize."

Iz snorted. "Who cares who wins? Shows like this make all women who compete into losers."

"Now, Iz," Mrs. B said in a steely voice, "I believe we had this discussion earlier. And I believe I made my position clear."

"Muriel intends to compete," Dario said. "And she intends to win. Got it?"

Iz nodded to indicate she got it, but her body language and a couple of muffled rude noises demonstrated her dislike. When she simmered to silence, Dario went on. "Whether she competes in the slot we have scheduled, or another one later in the season, she's going to take the stage. It's up to us to help her get ready. Who has ideas?"

Again there was an exchange of sidelong glances, and then Josh raised his hand. He did it the way students do when they're not sure of the answer, but figure they'll see if they can score points with the teacher. "If we took everything off the deck, would that be enough space?"

Mrs. B turned to gaze through the sliding glass door to the double deck area formed when she removed the privacy panels after arranging for me to buy the unit next door. "I'd have to measure to be sure, but it certainly appears large enough."

"What will you do if it rains?" Jim asked.

"You mean *when* it rains," Verna corrected.

And it would. So far we'd had only a few fall showers and a single day of drooling drizzle, but the winds were shifting and the nozzle of the weather pattern hose would soon point right at Reckless River. "I suppose it would be against condo regulations to put up a giant canopy," I offered.

"Probably," Jim said. "It would obscure the view for other residents."

And Bernina Burke would demand it come down.

"The canopy wouldn't be up forever," Verna said. "What if we got the residents who would be affected to sign off on it for a set period of time? Would the board approve?"

My money said the board might, but not if Bernina could help it. Ever since she'd lost the pet-limit battle, Bernina had it in for me and Mrs. B. The incident involving a monster mutt that destroyed the interior of her car hadn't improved relations.

"She'll fight it tooth and nail," Jim said, "rule and regulation. She'll drag things out until it's too late to do any good."

Glum nods greeted his remark. Dario patted Mrs. B's shoulders.

Desperate times called for desperate measures. I had to sacrifice my scheme to use Iz to stop Bernina. "What if we had a bargaining chip?"

Heads turned my way. Eyebrows arched. "What kind of a chip?" Jim asked.

"The holiday decorating contest," I said in a small voice. "If we all agreed to get on board, Bernina might agree to the canopy."

"But tomorrow I was going to . . ." Jim groaned and shot a glance at my sister. "Going along with Bernina will cost us a fortune in mechanical reindeer, dancing elves, and twinkly lights. Not to mention the power bill."

"The cost is on me," Mrs. B said.

"It may be steep," Jim warned.

I snickered. Because Mrs. Ballantine was so down-to-earth and so much a part of the group, there was a tendency to forget she was loaded. In fact, I often thought that she forgot. Although she loved jewelry and travel and fine food, Mrs. B placed more value on friendship and comfort and community than on the status of an address or membership in an elite group.

"If it's more than I can afford," she responded with a smile, "I'll put it on my credit card and pass on buying another pearl necklace."

"That's the spirit," Dario said. "That's my girl. I'd love you if you didn't have a single pearl to your name."

"Pearls." Allison shot to her feet. "That's how you'll do it."

C h a p t e r   1 6

Mrs. B fingered her three-strand necklace of shimmering pink pearls while Cheese Puff looked on with interest. "How I'll do what, dear?"

"Balance the electronic thing so you can practice. Get the guy at the jewelry store to make you a pearl ankle cuff that weighs the same." Allison pointed at the ankle monitor. "No, you need two ankle cuffs."

"Good idea, kid," Dario said. "But we could make up the weight and bulk a lot cheaper by using a big watch."

Allison shook her head. "But if those things stay on too long, it will feel weird when they're gone. And they might not be gone until right before the show. So you need two pearl cuffs so you'll feel even."

Josh scratched his head, my sister shook hers, Dario grunted, Paulette chewed her thumbnail, Sybil and Verna exchanged puzzled looks. But Lana nodded in agreement. Mrs. B's fingernails clicked on her pearls as she considered the plan. Then she beamed a smile at Allison. "I'll call my jeweler and costume designer right away. Pearl ankle cuffs will be a stunning addition to my costume."

Dave looked more stunned than stunning when I found him sprawled on the sofa, staring at the ceiling. "How was the council of war?"

"Not bad. Mrs. B pre-empted the committee and named the restaurant, and Josh and Allison came up with a plan for her to practice her routine." I set Cheese Puff in his favorite chair and decided I wouldn't mention my contribution and how it doomed us to holiday lighting displays bright enough to scorch our retinas. "How's your arm?"

Dave raised and lowered it. "Not hurting too much." He patted the sofa beside him. "Is it my imagination, or are these cushions getting lumpier? Anyway, sit down. There's something we need to discuss."

Uh oh.

My brain speed-wrote a list of possible discussion topics— he was breaking up with me, he was asking me to marry him, he was quitting his job, he was pursuing work in another city, another state, or another country.

"I guarantee it's not any of the things you're thinking."

"How do you know what I'm thinking?"

"I'm a trained observer."

"Right. How come you never notice fingerprints and smears on the refrigerator?"

"Because my mission isn't to observe the refrigerator. Since entering this relationship, my mission has been to observe you and the fascinating ways in which your convoluted brain blows things out of proportion." Dave laughed and patted the sofa again. "Come on. This has nothing to do with you and me. At least not directly."

I still didn't like the sound of that, but I slunk to the sofa and sat next to him, avoiding eye contact and leaning away to make it clear there would be no touching. Until I knew the topic of discussion wouldn't turn my future on its ear, I'd keep physical and emotional distance.

Dave studied my posture, raised his eyebrows, and made a show of shoving his hands in the pockets of his jeans. "Okay, here's the situation. Harvey Goodspeed had a heart attack this morning."

My heart and lungs seemed to halt their work, but my brain hit warp speed. How would this affect the investigation? Would it drag on longer? Would evidence be compromised? Would there be pressure for Mrs. B to go to jail until her trial?

"He was in his office. The building is crawling with guys who know what to do. They got him to the hospital in time."

I gave myself a mental kick for not asking about him before I started worrying about Mrs. B. "How is he?"

"Okay, considering they had to crack his chest and do so much bypass work his heart looks like an aerial view of a Los Angeles freeway interchange."

Chest cracking sounded painful, dangerous, and like something that would take significant time to recover from. My brain resumed worrying about Mrs. B's fate.

"The sheriff's office is understaffed and the guy who worked with Harvey took a job in Idaho a few weeks ago. They're bringing in an outside investigator. He's experienced and has knowledge of the case."

Experience and knowledge were good things. My frantic brain slowed.

"He also knows Mrs. Ballantine."

Was that a good thing? I adored Mrs. B, but there were some who . . .

Yikes.

I swiveled to face Dave and gripped his arm. "Tell me it's not Detective Atwell."

"If I did, I'd be lying."

"But he's always been suspicious of Mrs. Ballantine."

Dave pried my fingers loose. "Chuck's suspicious of everyone. That's his nature. It's a good quality if you're a homicide investigator."

On the surface that appeared logical. "But he's not open-minded. He doesn't listen to ideas. In fact, he hates it when people have ideas."

"People in general? Or you in particular?"

"Maybe not me in particular, but me especially. He only pays attention to my ideas if *you* pitch them." I took a deep breath and played the card my sister was so fond of slapping on the table. "And I don't think it's because you're a cop. Or because you're his friend. I think it's because—"

"You're a woman?"

I nodded.

"Not because he's a careful and deliberate thinker and you have a way of tossing theories like confetti? Not because you occasionally rush off to act on them and wind up in trouble?"

Okay, so those were possibilities. But no way would I admit it.

"I know you're worried about Mrs. Ballantine, but she might be better off with Chuck in charge." Dave pulled me against him and kissed the top of my head. "The investigation will be thorough. It will be better organized. And it will move at a faster pace."

"When someone's being railroaded, it's usually at a fast pace."

Dave tipped my chin and kissed me long and hard. But even with every nerve ending tingling, a small part of my brain realized he hadn't said that his buddy Detective Atwell would never railroad anyone. I had a sinking feeling that if Atwell concluded Mrs. B was guilty, all the pearls in the world wouldn't persuade him otherwise.

The sounds of swearing and metal clanging on metal woke me early Saturday morning. A glance out the window revealed six men stretching a pink-and-white-striped canopy across the deck and assembling poles to hold it aloft. That meant Bernina had accepted the bribe. She was probably gearing up for an assault on a home improvement store for extension cords, gutter clips, and other supplies. Making a mental note to buy a sleep mask, I crawled in bed beside Dave and willed myself to return to dreamland.

As you've probably figured out by now, willpower isn't my thing. Besides, even with a pillow folded around my head, I couldn't muffle the sounds from the deck. Those sounds were my fault, a consequence of sacrificing the concept of using Iz as a deterrent.

Iz was like a nuclear weapon. You didn't have to drop it on a city in order to scare people. They simply had to think you would. Maybe Iz should capitalize on that and take on assignments that matched her talent. Granted, they'd likely be quick and dirty gigs, but a few might pay well.

I abandoned attempts to sleep, pulled on a pair of sweat pants and a fleece, and went downstairs to make coffee. Enjoying it on the deck was out of the question, so I settled for the sofa, shifting twice before I found a spot with fewer lumps than in Allison's last attempt at mashed potatoes. What were cushions stuffed with? Did the stuffing break down and clump up as time passed? Could cushions be restuffed?

I was clueless. But Paulette would know. All I had to do was remember to ask her.

Sipping coffee, I watched workmen tying ropes to the railing and to eye bolts screwed into the deck, and hanging white canvas screens that would roll down on all sides and insure privacy. I wondered if Bernina had been aware of these additions to the canopy plan, then decided I wouldn't be the one to bring ropes and screens to her attention. The canopy blocked the sun and view, but it would also keep out the rain—a feature Cheese Puff and Lola would appreciate. Apricot, being a cat and wanting to avoid moisture, would also welcome the protection. And, hopefully, the canopy wouldn't be up for long.

I crossed my fingers on that thought and returned to considering my sister's employment future. Odds were she'd drop by at least once this weekend. I'd given her a job scenario to work on, and I had little doubt her efforts to construct it would be interesting. But as she pointed out, what she needed was a job. And she needed it now.

I'd balked at linking her up with Aston Marsden. Entertaining as it would be to watch him charge in to the political arena like a wounded grizzly, his campaign would reflect badly on other teachers. I'd feared my sister's contributions would make things more embarrassing. But now I saw that if anyone had the power to stop him in his misguided tracks, it was Iz. She'd go ballistic at the idea of working for Aston, but if I insisted she do anything but, she might take the bait. She and Aston would tear each other apart and demolish his political aspirations in the process.

Did I feel guilt about hatching this plan? Remorse? A tiny bit of regret?

Nope.

After all, Aston had asked me to connect him with my sister. What happened next would be *his* fault.

"No." Iz tossed the slip of paper with Aston's phone number to the floor, prompting Cheese Puff to jump from his favorite chair and investigate. When he discovered it wasn't edible—or at least not tasty—he raised his upper lip, returned to his chair, and burrowed between the cushion and the arm, his rump to my sister. If she noticed the snub, Iz wasn't concerned. She leaned back on the sofa and rested her feet on the coffee table beside the plate that had held the two sandwiches she'd demolished. Dave had forgotten to take them along when he headed off for an afternoon of paperwork at the cop shop. When she'd turned up shortly after he left, Iz displayed scenting skills Lola would envy and sniffed them out through foil wrapping and a brown paper bag. Now, after emitting a soft belch, she folded her arms across her chest, obscuring the male-bashing slogan on her XL T-shirt.

(For the record, I assumed it was a male-bashing slogan since her wardrobe runs to T-shirts with messages defaming men. This one, however, was in Greek. And that, to borrow from Shakespeare, is Greek to me.)

"Why would you even suggest I run a campaign for a bumpkin in buckskin?"

I held in a snigger. She'd hit on a campaign slogan. "Because you need a job."

"So I should work for the man who asked you to dress as a camp following hooker for one of his Civil War reenactments?"

"Yes."

"The man who brought fried rattlesnake to a potluck lunch?"

"He claimed it tastes like chicken."

"The man who smells like the hind end of a buffalo?"

"Only in the summer. And only on humid days. Otherwise he smells like the front end of a buffalo."

Iz glowered. "You shouldn't attempt humor, Barbara. You have no sense of timing. And you have no sense of what is amusing."

I felt like holding a mirror up and asking if she was actually describing herself, but I let it slide.

"I should get out and campaign against him." Iz shifted her haunches. "What are these sofa cushions stuffed with? Corn cobs? Kitchen utensils?" She shifted again. "What I should do is sabotage his campaign, shoot it down before it even gets off the ground."

Exactly what I had in mind. But I'd long ago learned if I wanted my sister to go south, I insisted north was the only way. "You're right. I don't know what I was thinking."

"As usual, you weren't."

Ouch.

I'd expected that, but it still hurt. "Delete this conversation. Let's review your strong suits and I'll see what else I can come up with in the way of a job."

"Probably something even more ludicrous." Iz drummed her fingers on the arm of the sofa. "And while you're wasting my time, someone will take the job and run the campaign. That shining example of idiocy might win."

"Yeah," I agreed with a can't-be-helped sigh. "Anyway, if you took the job and managed his campaign to oblivion, it would be too obvious."

Iz glowered. "Are you saying I'm not subtle?"

I thought of three snarky responses, but left the question unanswered. I pointed to the deck and the slight young woman with a tape measure and clipboard surveying the covered area. Her hair was black, shiny, and spiky, her eyebrows thin, her chin pointed, and her long nails painted metallic purple. She looked like an elf, but a sneaky elf bent on a series of misdeeds—poking holes in mushroom umbrellas, making off with acorn plates and cups, or whatever elves got up to in the way of crime. "Who's that with Mrs. Ballantine?"

"I have no idea." Iz leaned forward to scratch her ankle, retrieved the slip of paper with Aston's phone number, and tucked it in a pocket of her cargo pants. "And I have no intention of sticking around and watching you snoop in your neighbor's business."

Never mind that I preferred to think of snooping as research. And never mind that Iz did plenty of it herself.

I pasted on a contrite expression.

"Don't bother to stress your brain any further." She heaved herself from the sofa and, leaving her dirty plate and glass on the coffee table, headed for the door. "I can manage to find employment worthy of my talents without your help."

She delivered the word "help" with a heap of sarcasm that made it almost impossible for me to contain a triumphant smile.

I was giving myself ten points for winning our conversational skirmish when she turned at the door and called out, "Isn't it about time you visited Mom and Dad?"

Crap!

Direct hit.

Shot down with a big guilt gun she hadn't brought out in years.

Chapter 17

The door slammed behind her and I felt myself drowning in the should-have sea of regret. Never mind that my parents had abandoned me—and Iz—in an emotional way after my brother died, it had been weeks since I called or wrote, and almost two years since I made the journey to Missouri to visit. I should check airline prices right now. I should—

Hold on a second!

When was the last time Iz visited our parents?

I'd bet the last dark chocolate malted milk ball hidden in the empty instant coffee container in the far left kitchen cabinet that my sister hadn't set foot in their senior-living gated community in years. And I'd bet the cheesy snacks stashed in the largest mixing bowl that she had no intention of doing so in the near future.

I couldn't blame her.

Iz had not only suffered emotional abandonment, she'd also taken on the role of responsible adult, and raised me. Granted, it wasn't what you'd call high-quality raising. But she made sure I didn't play in traffic too often, took baths now and then, wore mostly clean clothing, ate a reasonable assortment of semi-nutritious foods, and made it to school generally on time.

Besides, my parents, with their card games and dancing and rounds of golf, were okay. Removed from reality, but okay. And, in my defense, they didn't reach out to me.

Still, it *had* been nearly two years. Perhaps I'd get a good deal if I traveled before the Thanksgiving rush. Or before the Christmas rush. Or after the turn of the year.

Mulling that, I called to Cheese Puff and strolled to the deck.

"This is Jackie DeWill," Mrs. B told me as she picked up Cheese Puff for a cuddle. "She's a production assistant on *Still Got That Strut*."

"Barbara Reed." I shook hands. Although she'd appeared elf-like, her grip was powerful. I almost heard my bones rub together. "Neighbor, friend, and owner of the world's most entitled mutt."

Without a glance at Cheese Puff, Jackie flashed teeth as pointed as her chin. "Nice to meet you." Her brittle words were spaced like ornaments on a shelf.

"Jackie's measuring the deck," Mrs. B volunteered. "She'll outline the stage dimensions and note the columns and staircase. I'll chalk my marks as I practice."

"As I pointed out," Jackie said, "it would be far more efficient if I watched your routine and chalked the marks as you went along."

Mrs. B's sapphire eyes darkened. "I'm not opposed to efficiency, Jackie, but I intend to keep the nuances of my performance under wraps as long as possible."

Jackie frowned, thin eyebrows almost meeting above her nub of a nose. "You do realize it's my job to see things run smoothly, don't you? To do that, I have to know what contestants have planned."

"Of course. But Dario assured me that if I gave him a diagram of my movements, I would be allowed to hold back specific details until I got to Las Vegas and began to rehearse on the actual stage." She patted my arm. "Not even Barbara knows what I'm up to."

The frown locked on her face, Jackie pointed at the door to my condo. "She *will* once you start practicing out here. She'll have a front row seat."

"With a terrific view of a fabric screen," I noted in a tone that leaned 40 degrees toward snarky. "And I'll pull the drapes for good measure. I'm all in favor of keeping secrets."

(For the record, that isn't exactly true. I'm all in favor of keeping *my* secrets. But I admit to being fascinated by what others try to shield from public knowledge, and the lengths they go to. When I can pass it off as investigating, I enjoy trying to uncover secrets. But I make an exception for Mrs. B. In general, because she's a good friend. And, today, because there was something about Jackie that irked me.)

"What if the set designers want to make changes?" Jackie persisted. "If I'm familiar with your routine, I can negotiate with them."

"I appreciate your concerns and dedication." Mrs. B rubbed noses with Cheese Puff. "But the little prince is the only one allowed to watch."

"Suit yourself." Jackie's curt tone implied she'd exact revenge by informing others on the production staff that Muriel Ballantine was an uncooperative contestant who wouldn't accept advice and might cast blame on others.

"I almost always do suit myself," Mrs. B said with a twinkling smile. "Let me know when you're finished, or if there's anything I can do to help."

"Fine," Jackie said in a tone that made it clear the status of the situation was anything but. "Then we'll discuss your costumes."

Mrs. B's twinkles turned to sparks. "Discuss? What is there to discuss?"

"What you'll need our wardrobe people to develop."

"I have my own designer and seamstress."

"All right. But what if—?"

"Something rips? I'll have duplicates of everything. And the seamstress will be there when the show is recorded." Mrs. B raised her chin in the defiant way that always made me back off at warp speed. "I already communicated that to the head of your wardrobe department as well as to several others."

Jackie waved that aside. "Communication's always an issue on shows like this. So many details, you know. Someone always drops the ball."

I wanted to jump in and tell Tacky Jackie that the ball-dropping someone wouldn't be Mrs. Ballantine. When it comes to details, she has an iron grip.

"I'm certain some people fumble now and then," she said in a bland voice. "And I'm certain that when it comes to pointing out communication failures, you have significant skills."

Jackie's eyes narrowed. I imagined steam rising from her brain as she tried to decide whether she'd been complimented or insulted. Turning aside so I wouldn't make eye contact with Mrs. B and rupture myself trying to hold in a laugh, I pretended to check a bolt in the deck.

Jackie cleared her throat with the kind of kak-kaw cough you might employ if you swallowed a fish bone. "Let's talk about your hair and makeup needs."

"Taken care of. I've hired a team of experts."

"Of course," Jackie muttered.

"Knock on the door if you need anything."

Tapping my arm, Mrs. B pointed toward my unit. I lingered for a second, snapping a picture of Jackie so Allison could see what the woman who was "all pushy-pushy" looked like. When we were inside, Mrs. B slid the door closed, and set the latch.

"Trying to keep me in?" I joked. "Or keep someone else out?"

Mrs. B carried Cheese Puff to his favorite chair and sat, not seeming to care about the orange hair that would adorn her black leggings when she stood later. "You may think I'm paranoid, dear, but the core of *Still Got That Strut* is competition. I don't intend to go down there with empty sleeves."

"As in not having any tricks left up them?"

"Exactly."

"And you think Jackie would spill your beans? To Glorree Morning?"

"Not intentionally." Mrs. B settled Cheese Puff on her lap, ensuring a coating of hair on the front of her black tights as well as the rear. "But you know what they used to say about loose lips sinking ships. She might mention something to a set designer or lighting expert, and someone might overhear."

I nodded, and for a few moments we watched Jackie measuring and marking.

"I could have done that myself," Mrs. B muttered. "I think Dario sent her up here to get her out of his hair. He didn't want an assistant."

"Then why did he get one?"

"It wasn't his decision. Apparently, when he came up last month to help fight off those men who threatened Cheese Puff, a few little thing on his list didn't get done quite on time."

Mrs. B made it sound as if the problem was on a par with leaving a pan of cookies in the oven for a minute too long.

Having worked as a radio producer, however, I knew how "some little thing" could be the toppling domino that caused a hundred others to clack against each other and go down. Dario had never explained exactly what he did, and he spent a significant number of days in Reckless River each month, so I always assumed he held a figurehead position based on his Vegas connections. Color me rethinking my assumption. "So, someone up the food chain decided he needed help."

"Yes. And that person did the hiring." Mrs. B scratched Cheese Puff's ears. "It's not that Jackie isn't competent. Dario says she's thorough and never misses a deadline. And she's full of ideas."

"And full of herself?"

"Well, I haven't known her for more than an hour, but it's clear she has definite opinions and doesn't hold back from expressing them." Mrs. B rewarded me with a smile. "But many of us do, so I can't fault her for that. And she's a little unclear about boundaries, but she *does* have experience. She worked for two casinos and held production positions on several TV programs."

"Maybe they'll get used to each other."

"I doubt it, dear. Dario's my age, you know. As we get older, we tend to get a tiny bit set in our ways."

In my experience with both of them, "a tiny bit" meant "a whole heck of a lot." But I kept the thought bottled up.

"And in a few months Jackie will be someone else's problem." Mrs. B leaned toward me and lowered her voice. "Dario's retiring after the final show of the season. We're planning some lovely trips. Tahiti, Madagascar, Belize."

I made a T with my hands. "Not so fast. He's not going anywhere until Allison passes her driver's test."

Mrs. B smiled.

I gripped her wrist. "That's not a joke. He's the only one with nerves strong enough to see this through. Although there are times when I hope it doesn't get seen through. The thought of Allison behind the wheel—"

Jackie rapped on the glass door. "All done," she called.

Mrs. B stood and laid Cheese Puff across her shoulder. "You don't mind if I borrow the little prince while I rehearse, do you?"

"Borrow away. I have to pick up Allison at the library."

"Excuse me." Mrs. B's exquisitely plucked brows arched. "Did you say the library?"

"Yes, but fear not, there's no studying involved. The theater club didn't like the play their advisor chose. They're looking for one with juicier roles."

Mrs. B chuckled as she headed for the door. "And I bet I know which budding actress was behind the juicy-role rebellion."

I was spending quality time scrubbing grunge from the far corners of the shower stall when Dave called. "Meet me in the parking lot," he said in what definitely wasn't the tone of someone about to reveal he'd bought me a new car. In fact, the tone was more like that of someone about to reveal that all four tires on my sorry excuse for a vehicle were flat.

Knowing it was pointless to ask what was up, I set aside the sponge, stripped off a pair of always-so-attractive yellow kitchen gloves, and strolled outside.

Dave waved from the far end of the covered parking area. Behind him loomed the huge trash bins that served the condo complex. Those bins figured prominently in our how-we-met story. Dave had been lurking in their vicinity last December, staking out the unit occupied by my ex-husband and a murderous redhead who had built a business selling steroids.

Because of his lurking, he was in position to paddle to the rescue when Jake's girlfriend shoved me and Cheese Puff into the Columbia River.

I counted months and came up short of the 12 that would make this an anniversary assignation. Dave's hands were empty—no flowers or candy or even a card. Lola, who sat by his side, had nothing tied to her spiffy new collar. So much for the idea that Dave hadn't remembered exactly when he pulled me from the chilly current.

Curious—and more than a shade anxious—I joined him. He delivered a full-body hug and a kiss that made my toes tingle. "Let's go to the trail," he whispered. "I have something to tell you."

The trail offered a view of the river and the spot where I'd hurtled into it. Was Dave thinking of popping a question besides "What's for dinner?" or "Have you seen my favorite T-shirt?"

I shook that off. If I wasn't ready for an aisle walk—and, after financial and emotional turmoil with Jake, I definitely wasn't—Dave was even more not ready. "You can't tell me here?"

His gaze swept the area, taking in the asphalt parking lot, trash bins, mangled hedge, and gravel border. "Uh, I'd feel safer on the trail."

Chapter 18

He hooked an arm around my neck and steered me past the end of the complex. "Some of those chunks of gravel are big enough to damage my head."

"Damage?" I slid out from under his arm and faced him. "What are you talking about? Do you expect gravel to jump up and impact your skull?"

"Not on its own."

I folded my arms and shot him the substitute-teacher glare. "What does that mean?"

"Um . . . it means sometimes you get, uh, worked up. Sometimes you, um, throw things."

(For the record, those things were dirty socks left on the bathroom floor, a sopping sponge abandoned in the center of the dining room table, and the cardboard tube from a roll of used-up toilet paper he hadn't replaced. Let the record further show that I tossed those items at the clothes hamper, the sink, and a trash can, in that order. That he was standing nearby at the time was hardly coincidental. Sometimes mere words aren't enough. Sometimes action is required to make a point.)

"And you think I'd lob a load of gravel at you?"

Dave ducked his head and scuffed at the trail.

That was all the answer I needed. What he had to say would undoubtedly push at least one of the red reaction buttons labeled—in ascending order—ARE YOU KIDDING ME?, SERIOUSLY?, WHAT WERE YOU THINKING?, ARE YOU OUT OF YOUR MIND?, and MAD? NO, I'M NOT MAD. I'M FURIOUS.

I marched to the opposite side of the trail. "Tell me. Don't try to whitewash it. Just spit it out."

Dave squeaked like a cornered hamster. Without meeting my gaze he said, "Chuck wants me to help him work the case. The chief is on board."

Every one of those red reaction buttons flashed on.

I hauled in a breath.

And held it.

Dave raised his hands in surrender. "I didn't say I would. I told them I had to think about it."

His eager-puppy tone signaled he deserved praise for not making a snap decision.

"But I want to do it. I know you're thinking of the negative side, but this is a good thing."

I let out the breath I'd been holding and hauled in another. "Yeah, a good thing for your career when you play the widow-of-reputed-mobster card and railroad Mrs. Ballantine."

Dave recoiled. Lola whined, sneezed, and eased in front of him.

"Sorry," I mumbled. "I know you'd never do that."

He lowered his hands. "But you're not so sure about Chuck, right?"

I nodded. When I was a suspect in the murder of Henry Stoddard, Detective Charles Atwell grilled me like a burger at a summer barbecue. Grilled me until I was long past well done. Grilled me until I believed his mind was as open as a time-locked bank vault after hours. Which is why, when I got a chance to check out a piece of evidence for myself, I went for it. Mrs. B had helped me concoct a story to screen the extent of my distrust and amateur sleuthing.

So, yeah, even though he was Dave's buddy and often dropped by, I couldn't shake my first impression of Atwell. I wasn't about to knit him a pair of warm socks for Christmas—or any other occasion. Not that I know how to knit, but you catch my drift.

Dave stepped past Lola, crossed the trail, and put his arms around me, locking his gaze on mine. "This really is a good thing, and a heck of an opportunity. I tagged along lots of times, but this gives me official, on-the-record experience working homicide."

"But isn't it a conflict of interest? Because Mrs. Ballantine is the prime suspect? And you live next door?"

"It's a conflict for Chuck, too. He's been over here for parties and dinners. But he's the only one able to jump in right away. Everything we consider, everything we do or discover, will be run past our lieutenant and Harvey Goodspeed."

"But he had a heart attack!" I clutched my chest. "He's in the hospital!"

"Not for long. You'd be surprised how fast they kick them loose, even after surgery like that. And all he has to do is read our reports and make suggestions. If it looks like we're slanting things, he'll call us out."

I grasped at a straw. "And if it appears you're not doing enough to clear Mrs. B's name, will Angus Drummond do the same?"

"You bet."

I considered for a moment, snuggling against him, heedless of passing joggers and dog walkers. It seemed like a workable way to get the investigation rolling. "Mrs. B trusts you." I kissed his chin. "She'll probably be relieved to know you're involved."

"Yeah, well, she might not." Dave cupped my face in his hands. "She might react like you did. So it would be better if you didn't tell—"

"What?" I pulled away. "If I don't tell her, and she finds out, she'll be mad at you *and* me. Mad enough to . . . well, I don't know what. But really mad!"

Dave rolled his eyes. "How about I finish before you fly off the handle?"

"Make it fast," I snarled. "My grip on the handle is slipping."

"Noted. It would be better if that information came from her attorney. Chuck and the lieutenant are meeting with him now. If he has major objections, we'll scrap the idea."

"Oh."

"Feeling silly, are we?"

"No," I said in my sulkiest tone.

He kissed my forehead. "Feeling like munching on happy hour snacks?"

"Maybe."

"Feeling like sharing a table with me?"

"Possibly. If you don't expect me to share the snacks, too."

Dave chuckled. "I may not be the greatest at communication. And I know I suck at cleaning up the kitchen. But I'm smart enough not to get between you and an order of crispy shrimp or sweet potato fries."

"Or one of those baby pizzas?"

"I not only wouldn't get between you and one of those, I'd sit across the table and keep my hands behind my back while you ate it."

I stood on tiptoe and delivered a smacking kiss to his lips. "Then what are we waiting for?"

Sunday morning, after whipping up a batch of his famous cheddar cheese, corn flake, and green onion waffles with sour cream, Dave announced he was headed for the River Rise Inn with Detective Atwell. "I read the reports and looked at the photos and drawings, but there's nothing like seeing the lay of the land—corridors, stairways, balconies a killer could rappel from to avoid being seen, stuff like that. Plus we'll conduct follow-up interviews with everyone Goodspeed talked to, and track down anyone he didn't question."

"Sounds like you're saying I shouldn't wait up."

"I'm also asking if Lola can stay with you." Dave bent and scratched her ears. "Chuck's compact isn't what you'd call dog-friendly."

"Neither is Chuck."

Dave didn't laugh. "He likes Lola okay."

Cheese Puff got the subtext and raised his upper lip in a snarl.

I scooped him up and rubbed his stomach. "You have enough fans without Detective Atwell."

"More than enough," Dave added as he headed for the door. "Oh, by the way, Farley Dole, the River Rise owner, claims he had no idea who his long-term guest was."

"Well of course he says that! You don't believe him, do you?"

"Harvey Goodspeed did."

I snorted. "As if that's an endorsement."

"True. But a sergeant who was up there with Goodspeed said Dole was scared spitless when they told him. Claimed Big Shiny and his ilk were the main reason he left Vegas for the woods. Offered to take a lie detector test."

"That could prove nothing."

"Also true." Dave stepped close and glanced left and right as if checking for eavesdroppers. "So I ran it by Dario."

I didn't ask if he'd run that by Chuck or his lieutenant first, because his body language told me he hadn't. "And?"

"Dario says it squares with what he's learned, but he'll check around some more."

I let out a breath. If Farley Dole didn't know the identity of his guest, a Las Vegas connection and premeditation probably hadn't been part of the frame constructed around Mrs. Ballantine. So—at least in my mind—the frame might have been more a spur-of-the-moment, opportunistic thing.

"Gotta run." Dave kissed my forehead and headed for the door once more.

"Not so fast. What about your daughter? What are her plans for the day? What sort of aberrant behavior should I watch for?"

Dave winced and glanced up the stairs toward Allison's bedroom door—a door that remained closed despite the aroma of waffles permeating the condo. "Would you think I'm the worst father in the world if I said I didn't know?"

"Hardly. I'd be surprised if she told you, surprised you remembered, and more surprised if she actually did what she said she intended to."

Dave gave one of those quick head tilts that indicate a high degree of befuddlement.

"You're cute when you're confused." I kissed his chin. "I'll watch Lola and ride herd on Allison."

"And, um, clean up my mess in the kitchen."

I sighed.

"I'll make it up to you. I'll unload the dishwasher for a month."

That meant I'd spend a month hunting for measuring cups, serving spoons, spatulas, and assorted bowls. They seldom got to their "rightful places" unless I put them there. "Forget the dishwasher. You go look for clues that Mrs. Ballantine didn't bash Big Shiny."

With a relieved grin, Dave snapped a salute and escaped.

A few minutes later I was deep in the Sunday newspaper ads when Mrs. B came in wearing tap shoes, black leggings, and a lilac shirt I assumed once belonged to Marco. The electronic bracelet on one ankle balanced a twist of pearls on the other. "I need Cheese Puff with me while I practice."

"Need him for what? An audience?"

"Well, yes. I've always fought stage fright by pretending to be performing for just one special person." She wrested Cheese Puff from the crevice in his favorite chair and laid him across her shoulder. "And I know you won't believe this, dear, but he's an excellent judge of what works and what doesn't."

"Hmmm." To contain an explosion of laughter, I pretended deep interest in an ad for a fiber supplement.

"He's an inspiration." Mrs. B rubbed her nose against Cheese Puff's neck and made kissy noises. "An orange spark of creativity."

"Hmmm." I turned to an ad for cream to fade age spots. Seemed the paper was courting an older demographic.

Mrs. B made a tutting sound and turned on one heel. "I'll pull the drapery as I leave, dear. I expect I'll be practicing much of the day, and then I'll take the little prince out to dinner as a reward."

I glanced up to see Cheese Puff smirk and—no, it wasn't my imagination—stick out his tongue as they left.

"I don't know what you see in him," I told Lola.

She sneezed and thumped her tail, but didn't bother to open her eyes.

"I guess when you find a man who amuses you and understands that you want a career and agrees you need time to yourself and doesn't make too much of a mess, then you go with it. Right?"

"Go with what?" Allison jumped from the third step, making the silverware on the table rattle. "And what about a mess?"

"Don't make one in the kitchen."

"No problem. There's hardly any place left to make a mess."

True. When Dave made waffles there was always batter spatter—and not just on the counter. Add in a crusty bowl, cutting board, cheese grater, waffle iron, dirty plates, and coffee mugs, and every square inch of formerly clean space was compromised.

Allison got a clean plate, plopped a waffle on it, and stuck it in the microwave.

"After you clean up the kitchen," I ventured, "what are your plans for the rest of the day?"

Allison turned, eyes wide, mouth gaping. "Me? Why do I have to do all the work around here?"

As if.

By now I'd heard this question—in varying forms and delivered at varying volumes—hundreds of times. I went on perusing an ad for hearing aids.

The microwave dinged and Allison stopped carping long enough to slather butter and sour cream on her waffle and carry her plate to the living room. Feet on the coffee table, TV remote in her left hand, fork in her right, she channel surfed and stuffed her face. "Josh is coming over. We're going to check out the leaves on Mount Hood for photography class, okay?

"Sure. As soon as the kitchen is clean, you can hit the road."

Never missing a bite, she managed to pout, scowl, and twitch her shoulders in annoyance. When the waffle was gone she asked, "How clean?"

"Clean." I studied a coupon for a lift chair. It looked pretty comfy.

"I mean, really, really clean? Or like it was when Dad started cooking?"

I didn't take the negotiating bait. When Dave got out the bowl for waffle batter, he'd shoved a phalanx of dirty glasses and popcorn bowls to the rear of the counter instead of loading them in the dishwasher. "Clean enough so Mrs. Ballantine wouldn't make that little noise of disapproval."

"The one that's kind of like a chicken amping up to squawk?"

"That's the noise."

Allison emitted a lung-emptying sigh. "But cleaning up will take all day."

"And all night if you don't get started soon."

Another sigh, followed by a replay of body language designed to demonstrate how difficult her life was, and how nobody cared.

I gathered the sections of the paper and folded them together on the coffee table, then headed upstairs to change the bedding and line up outfits for the week ahead. At the moment my schedule was clear. But every substitute teacher knows that a clear schedule is temporary.

Chapter 19

Sure enough, at 9:03 PM the phone rang and a mechanical voice asked if I'd be interested in a job. Since jobs mean money, I punched the button for "Yes." The voice moved on to the specifics. Captain Meriwether High School. History. Aston Marsden.

My index finger hovered over the button as I recalled the last time I subbed for Aston—the hastily scrawled lesson plan, the video I never found, the stench of rancid bear grease. Not to mention Aston's anger when he returned and discovered I'd called in Assistant Principal Tremaine Scott to identify and dispose of the grease.

The bookkeeping portion of my brain pointed out my old car wouldn't last forever and the price of almost everything was rising. A sympathetic chunk of gray matter opined that if Aston was ill, he'd appreciate having someone familiar in his classroom.

My hand shook.

My finger stabbed the button.

A few minutes later the phone rang again.

Aston skipped over a greeting. "The movie's on my desk."

Proving I wasn't born yesterday and had subbed for Aston before, I asked a few key questions. "Which desk? The one in your classroom? Or the one in the teachers' room? And where on your desk? Under something? In a drawer?"

"The desk in the classroom, you ninny. Right on top. In the middle. Even *you* couldn't miss it."

Biting my tongue, I held back a barrage of caustic comments. Then, because he sounded perfectly healthy and I suspected was taking the day off to work on campaign strategy with my sister, I went on the attack. "Are there worksheets to go with the movie?"

"Worksheets?"

I took that to mean there weren't. Aston apparently hadn't attended the last few staff meetings. Or he hadn't paid attention to directives about guided video viewing. "So, uh, if Tremaine Scott drops by and asks why kids are watching a movie without worksheets, what should I tell him?"

"Tell him to pound salt."

Like I'd be dumb enough to do that. Although, if I made it clear I was quoting Aston, the result could be interesting.

"Maybe you could put questions on the board as you go along," he suggested.

Maybe. If I was subbing for a teacher who hadn't called me a ninny.

Aston seemed to read my thoughts. "Okay," he grumped. "I'll make a worksheet and e-mail it to Big Chill and tell her to make copies."

And wouldn't she love being told—not asked—to do that in between rounding up room keys, information packets, and timesheets for subs, as well as arranging coverage for positions not filled. I hoped she didn't decide to take her supreme displeasure out on me. And I really hoped she didn't cancel our previous bargains—especially the one keeping me out of PE and the band room most of the time.

"What should I say when someone asks if you're sick or taking a personal day?"

"Tell them to mind their own business. And you mind yours."

Sounded like confirmation of my political-brainstorming theory. Not that Aston—as my sister would soon discover—had much of a brain to storm.

It was after midnight when I woke to the sounds of Dave undressing—the swish of fabric as he yanked off his T-shirt, the thud-thud of shoes kicked in the direction of the closet, the clink of coins as he dropped his jeans. I pulled the pillow over my head, but couldn't muffle the hum of the electric toothbrush, a flush, a stumble, and a curse as he tripped over his shoes.

When he hit the bed—and I mean literally because Dave has a way of levitating, assuming a horizontal position in the air, and executing a body slam on the mattress—I abandoned ideas of slumber. "Make any progress?"

"We might have." He flailed at the sheet and light blanket. "If it wasn't for Dick McBain."

"Dick McBain? As in, your nemesis?"

"Is there another Dick McBain? Because if there is, I'll volunteer to start a settlement on Mars."

Vitriolic sarcasm, but I knew it was aimed at the man who'd had it in for Dave for years. "How did McBain get in the way?"

"In a classic case of locking the barn door after the horse is gone, Farley Dole hired a security company—the one Dick went to work for last month. Dick horned in on every interview we attempted with the staff. And he's holding up the video from the camera in the lobby."

"Wait." I sat up and turned on the lamp. "It's been days since the murder. Why didn't Harvey Goodspeed have the video already?"

Dave rolled bleary eyes. "Take a wild guess."

"He didn't realize there was a camera? He didn't request the video?"

"Ding. Ding. You win!" Dave pounded his pillow with his cast. "And because Chuck and I didn't see a mention of a camera in the reports, we assumed there wasn't one." He lofted the pillow and booted it with both feet. "Assumed! We're idiots! We deserve the crap Dick shoveled on us."

"But that doesn't give him the right to impede a homicide investigation."

"You'd think. But the Dickster said, 'Crossing the Ts of the letter of the law is not impeding an investigation.' I had to hold Chuck down or there would have been a second homicide."

"You'll get the video eventually, right?"

"Yeah." Dave executed a kind of jackknife move, retrieved the pillow, and flopped beside me again. "Tomorrow. But I doubt it will give us much—if anything. The person who killed Big Shiny was no dummy."

"Neither is McBain," I said. "Not when it comes to being vindictive."

Dave held the pillow aloft and hit it with an uppercut. "I spent half my day wondering what the heck I did at the academy to make him hate me."

"And you came up with?"

"Nothing that would play anywhere outside of kindergarten." He dropped the pillow, rolled over, and wrapped his good arm around my legs. "Sorry I woke you."

I ruffled his hair. "It's okay."

"It's not. I bet you have to work tomorrow."

"I do. For Aston Marsden."

"Ugh. Now I'm really sorry." He slid the hand without a cast beneath my nightgown and walked his fingers up my thigh. "I'll make it up to you."

The disciplined cells in my brain said I needed my rest. The go-for-it cells said I'd sleep better afterward.

While the cells were arguing it out, I heard a gasp and realized I was the source.

I switched off the lamp.

Monday dawned through scudding clouds, gusting wind, and blasts of horizontal rain. Inside Big Chill's office another storm raged.

"That man!" Big Chill pounded her fist on a stack of worksheets labeled "The Missoula Floods." "That man should be hauled into this century and taught some lessons about . . . about everything!"

She raised her fist to slam the worksheets again, but I snatched them away and stuffed them in my briefcase, glancing at the first question as I did. "What was the ice dam made of?"

Really?

"I bet you reminded him he needed worksheets," Big Chill said.

I didn't respond.

"I knew it. And I bet he's as sick as I am." She rubbed the edge of her hand and checked the status of cherry-red nail polish that matched her lipstick, the dots on her scarf, her belt, and her high heels. Big Chill was nothing if not coordinated. "I don't know why you'd want to save his sorry backside. Or any other part of his anatomy."

I shrugged. I'd met Aston Marsden my first day at Captain Meriwether. He had, in his blustery way, been kind. He'd advised me to ignore Henry Stoddard, the school bully who later was murdered by Susan Mitchell, another member of the lunch bunch.

"By the way," Big Chill said as I signed my timesheet. "I assigned someone to that desk in the teachers' room where you hang out."

"Susan's desk?" I squeaked.

"Is there another empty desk in that room?"

I thought about Doug and Brenda abandoning ship last week, but kept my lips zipped and shook my head.

"I know some think bumping off Henry was justifiable homicide." Big Chill wagged a finger at me. "But most judges won't agree. And even if a temporary-insanity defense flies, Susan's not coming back to Captain Meriwether." She shot a glance toward the office next door, the office of Principal Jerome Morrow, a man spotted so infrequently there were rumors he'd died or taken a job elsewhere. "I've got orders to make better use of limited resources."

I refrained from howling with laughter. Everyone knew Big Chill was the power behind Jerome Morrow's throne. Orders or not, she mostly did what she pleased. Apparently, what pleased her was reassigning Susan's desk. And, with the desk, went a seat at the lunch table—the seat we'd discouraged anyone from appropriating since the day Susan confessed.

"Who is it? Someone new? Or a teacher from another room?"

"You'll find out." She made a shooing gesture with her fingers. "Now move along. You're not the only sub checking in this morning."

I turned to see two middle-aged women sipping from giant mugs of coffee. Beyond them was an eager young man who didn't appear old enough to have a teaching certificate or need a razor. "Sorry."

157

"Take your time," the first woman said. "I've got PE and I'm in no hurry to hit the locker room."

"Because the odor in the locker room hits back?" the second woman asked.

"It won't be bad on Monday," the eager beaver said.

I sniggered. Captain Meriwether High School had been around for more than half a century. It hailed from the days when air circulation involved opening a window. At night and during weekends, school windows were closed and locked. During those hours the odors of sweaty bodies, smelly shoes, and all manner of deodorants, perfumes, and colognes, mingled to create a menacing miasma. Like London fog of old, it sent tendrils along the floor and up the walls. It swirled into the coaches' offices and through the gym.

"Maybe you'd like to swap," I suggested to the eager beaver.

The sub assigned to PE got the hopeful expression of a drowning woman who spots a life raft.

Then the eager beaver said, "Sure. I've got band."

Tough choice. An assault on your nasal passages or an assault on your eardrums. Rock, meet hard spot.

I'd usually go with band, but only because I possessed a pair of state-of-the-art, high-quality, battlefield-tested earplugs. I'd spent a small fortune on them last year and no way would I offer to loan them out. Rent, maybe. But I didn't have time to negotiate a price.

I eased past the sub assigned to PE while she chewed her lower lip. The other woman shook her head.

"I haven't got all day," Big Chill said in a voice caustic enough to remove nail polish—along with the nails it was painted on. "Decide something."

"I'll stick with PE," the first sub said with a mammoth sigh.

I made my escape to the attendance office to pick up roll sheets and check Aston's mail cubby. To my total lack of surprise, it was stuffed solid with notices and memos dating to the start of the school year. And I mean stuffed. This was no neat heap with the oldest on the bottom, this was a collection of folded and wadded and compressed papers, much like what you'd find in the bottom of a trash compactor.

I stood on tiptoe and reached out to grasp a handful, but Gertrude Suttle gripped my shoulder with a plump hand. "Don't even think of cleaning that out for him."

"Thanks for the reality check." I lowered my arm. "Did you hear that the Chillster assigned someone to Susan's desk?"

"No, but Friday I heard Tremaine Scott telling the custodians to box up everything in the drawers and on the bookshelf." Gertrude shifted her armload of folders and scowled. "Of course, no one asked us what we thought."

We headed along the corridor toward the staircase. "Maybe new blood will be a good thing," I ventured, "especially if Doug and Brenda don't return."

Gertrude delivered a glare that said new blood would be as welcome as dysentery at a debutante ball.

"Maybe after a few days of Aston this person will move to another room."

We tackled the first tier of steps.

"Or maybe the new person will decide to eat in a classroom. Or . . . or somewhere else."

"Or I will," Gertrude huffed.

I held my next thought until we were within a yard of the top and she was taking in air like a dolphin that had stayed underwater too long. "Isn't it possible we might like this person?"

Gertrude staggered up the final two steps. "When I'm shut out of the decision-making process, my policy is not to like the outcome, no matter what."

Whoa.

Up until this moment I'd thought of Gertrude as flexible and pragmatic. But each of us has at least one line in the sand, and the tone of her voice told me this was hers. So I didn't argue or pose hypothetical questions as we trucked along the upper corridor to the teachers' room.

"You got a key handy?" Gertrude asked.

I jingled the set clipped to my lanyard and bent to unlock the door. As I was wiggling the key from the sticky lock, Gertrude pushed past.

"Mornin'," a voice said.

A familiar voice.

Chapter 20

I last heard that voice when I subbed behind bars.

"Ardie?"

"One and the same, sugar."

I yanked the key free and, doing my best to ignore Gertrude's frown, wove my way around chairs to hug Ardette Johnson.

As she had at the juvenile jail, Ardie appeared to be a charcoal sketch of a rangy woman—meaning that everything except the whites of her eyes, the palms of her hands, and the trim on her sneakers, was a shade of black. It was her signature style, and I couldn't imagine her in anything else.

She drew me tight against her black denim jacket, and I inhaled the far-off scent of gardenias and warm earth. "Why did you leave the juvie jail? How did you get transferred to Captain Meriwether?"

"I told Big Chill how much I missed you and she waved her magic wand."

More like she called in favors. Or twisted arms. "Really?"

"Of course not." Ardie chuckled and patted my head. "Not that I didn't miss you, but I wouldn't have presumed to ask a favor. Not after you fixed it so the Chill and I were even."

"So, she called you."

"More like called someone who called someone who sent me an e-mail from the central office with an offer involving more pay. The Chill moves in mysterious ways."

"And we're pawns in her game."

I turned to Gertrude, who was observing Ardie with the wary intensity of someone spotting a new species of venomous snake. "Gertrude, this is Ardette Johnson. Ardie, meet Gertrude Suttle, lead counselor."

Gertrude didn't extend a hand to meet Ardie's. "What's your job description?" she asked in a tone only slightly warmer than the outside of an igloo on the night of the winter solstice.

Ardie withdrew her hand and answered without a hint of defensiveness. "Right now it's what you might call 'loose' or 'indeterminate.' I'm a classroom assistant, a floater. I'm assigned to teachers with big classes. And freshmen."

"Isn't that just the way?" Gertrude opened the refrigerator with such force the door banged off the counter and rebounded against her arm. "Some people get help when they don't ask for it. The rest of us are expected to do more on our own."

She slammed the refrigerator door so hard jars rattled and something thudded inside. Then she tore it open again. A squeeze bottle of mustard tumbled out and rolled under the table. Gertrude retrieved her lunch. "I'll eat in my office today." With a withering glower in my direction, she stalked out.

"That had nothing to do with you," I assured Ardie.

She hugged herself. "Felt like it had a lot to do with me."

"Well, okay, it has a little to do with you. But it's not prejudice—at least not of the usual variety." I glanced at the clock. "It's a long story and I don't have time to tell it now. See you at lunch?"

"Wouldn't miss it. Should I bring a pad and pen? To take notes?"

I started to laugh, but caught myself. "Probably not. Unless your memory isn't what it was a few weeks ago. Like I said, though, it's a long story."

A few hours later, between bites of a sandwich made with cream cheese, celery, grapes, and walnuts, I filled Ardie in on the dynamics of the teachers' room. I started with the murder of Henry Stoddard and ended with last week's Lunch-ageddon that sent Doug and Brenda fleeing for the safety of their classrooms.

"And I thought the juvenile jail was rife with potential dangers," Ardie marveled. "I might need body armor. Hope it comes in black." She nibbled at a potato chip. "Think Gertrude will come around? Or should I see if the Chill can find another spot for me?"

"I don't know. Gertrude's always seemed like the practical and level-headed one in here, but she's been under a lot of stress since they assigned her the Family Support Room. Even more since someone started stealing from it."

I filled Ardie in on the way the room was run, how food, clothing, and supplies were donated, delivered, and doled out. I added the names of those who had keys, and Gertrude's conviction that the thefts occurred early in the week.

"Stealing from the charity closet," Ardie mused. "You gotta be a nasty piece of work to do that—or a needy one. And if you're in need, and if the food and clothing and whatnot are free . . .?"

She left her thought hanging, folded the top of her chip bag, and secured it with a paperclip. "I see why Gertrude is carrying a load."

"Load or not, she had no right to treat you like dirt."

"I've been treated worse, sugar. And you know what? I find when people are honest about their feelings and motives it's easier to move on."

"You think you and Gertrude might be friends?"

"Maybe not friends. But cordial co-workers." Ardie stowed the chips in the desk that had once been Susan's.

"Does that mean you won't ask Big Chill to find another space for you?"

"Not just yet." She plucked a gold tube of lipstick from the top drawer of the desk and applied a lustrous coating of purple-black gloss. "Now I gotta help with a reading group in the media center. You have a good afternoon—if that's possible in a classroom you described as a hoarder's starter home. Don't give this little bump in our road another thought."

That, of course, was easier said than done, even with the distraction Allison provided. She'd ridden home with Josh and, when I arrived, was dancing around the living room, waving a note printed on bright green paper.

"Bernina Burke wants me to help her with the holiday decorations! She's going to pay me and everything!"

"Minimum wage." Josh shifted on the sofa, pounded the cushion, and shifted again. "And the job won't last long."

"Will so." Allison fanned him with the note. "It says we're putting up miles of lights so we can win the competition. That will take, like, forever."

"If it takes forever, you won't be finished in time for the judges to check it out."

"Oh." Allison took two steps back, nearly tripping over Lola. "Right."

"And you know what? You better ask your dad before you take the job. And you better have his permission before you go up on the roof." Josh shifted again, winced, and stood. "If you get hurt, he'll explode. And that note doesn't say anything about insurance or safety precautions."

He shifted his gaze toward me in a way that implied Allison wouldn't follow those precautions if they existed. I turned a thumb up in thanks. Allison, however, stuck out her tongue.

"I'm off." Josh scooped his backpack from the coffee table. "Lana needs me to help organize the freezer over at Krammee's. I mean, at the Reckless River Sandwich Shop."

Allison leaped into his arms for a hug and a 20-second liplock, and then resumed her manic dance. "I got a job. A fun job. Not like making sandwiches."

Josh opened his mouth, but apparently decided not to take the bait and defend his position as assistant manager. Although I dreaded the pain a breakup would cause Allison, I wondered how much longer he'd stick with this relationship if she didn't start moving toward maturity.

"I gotta see Bernina." Allison toed on a pair of hot pink flip-flops that matched her scoop neck T-shirt. "I have a ton of ideas."

Piled on top of the grandiose plans Bernina already had, they'd achieve critical mass in no time. Mrs. B would be writing checks until the muscles in her hand seized up.

"Hold it," I said, using the substitute teacher's you'd-better-quiet-down-and-pay-attention-or-I-guarantee-there-will-be-a-test-tomorrow voice. "You can talk to Bernina. Talk. That's all. What you can't do is agree to take the job until you run it by your father."

Allison presented me with a pout so extreme I feared she'd need physical therapy to put her lower lip back in place. Wondering if Dave's insurance would cover that, I toted my briefcase to the closet under the stairs and hung it on the designated hook—after moving Dave's ball cap to its own clearly labeled spot.

"When will Dad be back?"

"I have no idea. Did he leave a note?"

Allison circled the dining room table and then checked the kitchen counters and the refrigerator door. "I don't see one."

I checked my cellphone, but found no message. I wasn't surprised. Or worried. When Dave worked a case, he worked it hard; everything thing else went by the wayside. Right now the case he was working affected Mrs. Ballantine's future—and the future of all of us who loved her. If he failed to call or leave a note, I wouldn't complain.

But Allison would.

"He's not answering." She shook her phone at me.

"Leave a message. He'll call when he can."

"What if he doesn't call until really late?" she wailed. "What if Bernina decides to give the job to someone else?"

Like people would be standing in line to work with Bernina.

Still, peace and quiet depended on me coming up with something to soothe the savage teen.

"Tell her you'll have to check with him to be sure. Tell her there's a good chance your father will let you take the job, *but only* to help with safe decorations at ground level. That means no heavy lifting, and no standing on anything taller than a kitchen step stool. It means don't go near high voltage or frayed cords or overloaded sockets."

"You mean no doing stuff like Jake did when he was the handyman? Like when he blew up the pressure washer?"

"Right. If it sounds like something Jake would do, then don't do it."

Jake had been a crap husband, but no one could claim he wasn't a terrific bad example.

"So I can take the job?"

"That wasn't what I said. And you know it."

Allison ducked her head and shuffled her feet. "Yeah. I guess."

"Come again."

"Yes. I know. I can't take the job until I talk to Dad. But I bet every other kid in the universe doesn't have—"

"Been there. Heard that. I'm done with this conversation."

Allison delivered a scowl that implied I was worse than any wicked stepmother in a fairy tale and she hoped I never married her father.

I delivered a fake smile that said I didn't much care what she thought.

Our game was all tied up.

"Fine," Allison said.

"Fine," I agreed.

"Fine," she said once more.

Recognizing her need to have the last word, I only nodded. Then she was off, racing along the hall and out the door to the parking lot.

"Another day, another drama," I told Lola.

She responded with a sneeze and a thump of her tail.

"I'll take you out for a walk in a few minutes."

Another thump assured me there was no hurry.

I opened the sliding glass door, heard no sounds of tapping, but called through the curtain anyway. "Can I come out?"

"Come ahead, dear. I'm taking a little break."

I parted two canvas curtains and eased onto the deck. A series of Xs and Os and check marks crisscrossed the rectangle representing the Las Vegas stage. Mrs. B, dressed in a pair of red leggings and a long black T-shirt, sat in a chair at one corner. A jeweled and feathered headdress lay on a small table beside her. Cheese Puff sprawled on her lap while she tapped an electronic tablet.

167

"You'd be amazed at what you can order on the Internet and what they'll deliver right to your door," she informed me. "Why, this morning I bought three new cat toys for little Apricot to play with when she comes to visit. All the others have disappeared. Who would steal stuffed mice and feathered balls with bells?"

"Not me. Lola has no interest in toys, and Cheese Puff already has a huge collection of squeaky creatures thanks to the Committee." Although, apparently feeling superior to most dogs, he never played with any of them. The lone exception was a plush penguin he'd appropriated during a visit to a pet supply store. And all he did with that was cart it around and leave it in Dave's shoes, Lola's food dish, Allison's backpack, or any cabinet he found open.

"Perhaps they rolled beneath the sofa, or accidentally got sucked up by the vacuum."

Or perhaps members of the professional cleaning squad that descended on Mrs. B's condo once a week sucked the toys up accidentally on purpose.

"Well, anyway," Mrs. B said, "after the cat toys, I bought enough groceries for the rest of the week, an adorable jacket for the little prince, and a new set of bath towels. And I started shopping for a small RV for Larry to use as a waiting room at the auto repair shop, but then I thought it would be more practical to expand the office area. What do you think?"

"Excuse me?" I'd heard nothing after "jacket for the little prince" because I'd been staring at the black satin vest and tiny top hat Cheese Puff wore. "What was the question?"

She speared me with her sapphire gaze. "If you don't intend to pay attention, dear, please say so. Then I won't attempt a conversation."

That comment was over the line into Uncalled For Territory, but I chalked her testiness up to the oppression of being under house arrest. "Sorry. I got distracted by Cheese Puff's outfit."

Mrs. B smiled, apparently forgiving me. "Isn't it darling? I'm trying to decide if I want a male dancer as part of my second presentation. Cheese Puff has been filling in so I get a feel for having someone else on the stage. And he's helping me decide whether I want that person to have an active role or simply be eye candy."

Cheese Puff raised his chin in what I took for a show of pride.

The top hat tipped.

"Wardrobe malfunction," I said.

Mrs. B set the tablet aside and straightened the hat. "My seamstress will be by later to take a tuck in the strap."

Of course. We couldn't have a dog with a tilting hat.

"Does Cheese Puff's formalwear mean your showboy will wear a tux instead of something skimpy?"

"You're as nosy as Jackie," Mrs. B said with a tinkling laugh.

Put in my place, I sat on the deck beside her chair and dropped my little bombshell. "Bernina Burke wants to hire Allison to help with the decorations."

Mrs. B's fingers fluttered to her pearl choker. "Oh, my."

"Exactly. Did you set a limit on how much you'd pour in to the project?"

She clutched the choker. "Oh, my."

"Yeah, as in 'oh, my bank account is empty.' Allison has no clue about budgeting. And since Bernina's spending your money, she'll see no reason to hold the line."

Mrs. B surveyed the tent, and then shifted her gaze to the electronic bracelet on her ankle. "I suppose there's no chance they'll decide less is more."

"About the same chance that Iz will decide men are human."

Mrs. B sighed. "Well, it can't be helped. And it's only money." She raised her right leg to display the ankle monitor. "And if I go to trial, I'm sure more will go for attorney's fees than twinkly lights."

"Speaking of the case, what happens if they don't catch the killer soon? What happens if you aren't allowed to go to Las Vegas?"

Chapter 21

"Angus is working on a series of proposals, including armed guards to travel with me." She laughed in the brittle way people do when they'd rather cry but refuse to give in. Then she rocked forward and blotted her eyes on the hem of her T-shirt.

I thought of a dozen platitudes, but decided Mrs. B knew them all. Scooching closer, I laid my head against her knee. I tried not to think about my life without her next door, or about her life behind bars. But I couldn't stop my brain from conjuring images of an empty condo, and Mrs. B shivering in a cell. "If . . . if they don't find out who killed Big Shiny, and if it looks like you'll be convicted, I'll cut off your monitor and help you get away."

"Get away to where, dear?"

"I don't know. A country where they can't bring you back." I tipped my head to face her. "Stash money in an offshore account. Fly out on a private jet. Use a fake—"

"No." Mrs. B stroked my hair. "Thank you for being so loyal, but I have to believe this will be settled soon. I have to imagine I'll get on a plane without a guard or an electronic monitor."

"And you have to believe you'll win."

Her hand came to rest on the back of my head. "It's strange, but that doesn't matter now."

I noted a faraway look in her eyes. "But I thought the whole point was to kick Glorree Morning's nipped and tucked bottom. And donate the prize money to women's programs."

"Oh, I still intend to make major donations. But while I was at the River Rise Inn without all of my friends around, and without as many distractions as a day normally offers, I had time to think. And what I thought about was Glorree and why she felt she had to outdo me at everything."

"And what did you decide?"

"That we're two sides of the same coin." Mrs. B finger-combed sections of my hair and braided them. "She came from a family as poor as mine. That explains her discipline and drive. And I'm sure we have the same painful memories and the same fears about waking up and finding we're cold and hungry and losing hope."

I tried to imagine Mrs. B that way.

I couldn't.

"So, what made you different?"

"I suppose I never let myself go too far down the It's Not Fair Highway. Of course, when I was young I envied those who had more than I did, but I made up my mind not to show it. And I never wanted to take what someone else had partly because I wanted to see them lose it."

"And Glorree did?"

"I don't know. But she was certainly envious. And she never seemed content."

"And you were?" Again, I turned to peer at her.

"Oh yes." She beamed a smile. "In just a few years I had so much more than I ever hoped for. And when I fell in love with Marco and knew he loved me, well, then I had everything."

Her voice trailed off and I thought about love and how it affected my view of the world. When I knew Dave cared about me, the sun seemed brighter, clouds scattered more quickly, and little things I'd stressed about became sources of amusement. "Glorree must have had admirers, didn't she?"

"Dozens. A few stinkers. Some fine men. But all she saw was what other girls had, and especially what I had. I don't know if it makes sense, but I think she was driven more by pain and emptiness than greed."

I considered that, wondering if Mrs. B had felt so generous then. "What happened after you and Marco left? Did she fixate on another showgirl who had more than she did? Did she ever marry?"

"I don't know." She tugged the braid loose and fluffed my hair. "I hadn't thought about her in years, not until I agreed to do the show and Dario told me Glorree would compete against me."

You might think Mrs. B was blowing smoke, but I knew better. If she said she hadn't thought about Glorree, she meant it. *I'm* not that highly evolved. I can't seal off the past. My mental file cabinets are stuffed with clear memory snapshots of incidents involving female competitors, especially in the romantic arena, all the way back to first grade. I sort through them far too often.

"Well, it's time for me to get dancing before my legs stiffen up and I trip over my own feet." Mrs. B patted my head. "Don't you worry about Allison and Bernina. Their wild ideas may cancel each other out. We might end up with something almost tasteful."

"Almost?" I gripped the arm of her chair and unfolded, stamping my left foot to get feeling back. "But not quite?"

Mrs. B smiled and stood, cradling Cheese Puff in her arms. "Where some people are concerned, I've long ago given up expecting anything more than the low end of almost. Now with others, like your Dave, I anticipate miracles."

Was she referring to Dave's role in the investigation?

I played dumb. "What do you mean?"

"You can stop pretending." Mrs. B shifted Cheese Puff to her shoulder, took my arm, and walked me to my door. "Angus told me Dave is working the case with Detective Atwell."

"And you're not angry?"

"Oh, no. It's made me feel so much better about what's ahead. Not because I think Dave would ever slant things, but because I know he'll turn over every rock and shake every tree and dig out every nugget of information."

She chuckled as I parted the curtain. "Listen to me. Is there a cliché I didn't toss in?"

I kissed her cheek and tickled Cheese Puff's chin. "I think you left out going the extra mile and keeping his nose to the grindstone."

Laptop propped on her knees, yellow pad and pen at the ready, Allison sat on the sofa. Sat, that is, if you abandoned all preconceptions of posture and defined a pretzel-like configuration of arms, legs, and spine as sitting. She turned the laptop my way. "Come see this."

Light blazed from the screen. I squinted and made out a herd of mechanical deer and an army of inflatable angels and elves. They marched toward a collection of cartoon characters from every movie made in the past few decades.

"We should definitely do this." Allison made a note on her pad. "Or maybe this."

She brought up another image, this time of a house strung with enough icicle lights to start an avalanche, ornaments the size of compact cars, and a sleigh and eight inflatable polar bears on the roof. "No way could we lose!"

I headed to the kitchen, visions of dinner dancing in my head. "What would something like that cost?"

"Bernina said money is no object."

Of course. It wasn't her money.

"How long would it take to set it up?"

"Not too long. Not if we can get a crane to lift the stuff to the roof and if I get Josh and some kids from school to help with all the strings of lights."

Memo to self: 1) Get Jim and other members of the Committee to lean on the board to review condo liability insurance coverage. 2) Talk with Josh and advise him to avoid being pressured to do stupid stuff and advise his friends to do the same. 3) Send an e-mail to Dave so I'd be on the record with my concerns.

I opened the refrigerator and used the door as a shield against blowback. "Remember to get your father's permission before you officially accept this job."

"I knooooooow."

The way she groaned the word implied I was nagging, harping, and generally failing to recognize that she was on top of things.

A year of subbing in classrooms packed with teenagers taught me the correct response to her statement was no response. First, because even saying something like "okay" or "good" often set off a volley of pent-up complaints about adults running and/or ruining her life. And second, because not responding was more annoying than any form of response, and therefore allowed me to chalk up a point.

I got busy cooking chicken breasts and chopping red onion and an assortment of veggies. As long as she was in a snit, Allison would snub anything I offered, but she'd have no qualms about scarfing up a wrap or two after I left for the pool. And Dave, when he returned, would probably be hungry for something offering more nutritional value than coffee, doughnuts, and chips. I made several shredded-chicken wraps, secured them with toothpicks, and popped them in a large container with a snap lid.

Allison, meanwhile, pouted and poked at her laptop keys. "Bernina's ideas are stupid," she muttered as I carried my wrap to the dining room table.

"Hmmm." Cleverly, I said nothing about the ideas Allison had presented.

"She's all about giant wreathes and bells and electric candles and setting up a forest of trees and dumping truckloads of fake snow and building a sleigh and hitching real reindeer to it and having Jim drive them up and down and give out candy and play like he's Santa Claus. Only not Santa. Another guy."

"Father Christmas?"

"Yeah."

Poor Jim. He looked the part, but no way would he want to act it. As long as the canopy stood, however, he'd feel he had to go along with the scheme.

"He wouldn't even wear a red suit," Allison griped. "Bernina showed me a picture and I swear the guy had on a brown bathrobe." She thumped the sofa cushion, then slid to another spot. "Can we get a new sofa sometime before I die?"

"Probably."

"When?"

"When we have money to spare."

"That usually means 'never.'" Allison gave the center cushion a one-two punch. "If Bernina gets real reindeer to pull the sleigh, do you think she'll let me drive?"

The obvious answer was Bernina might, but Dave wouldn't. Where did you find a team of reindeer, anyway? And how hard was it to hitch reindeer up and control them?

I had a vision of reindeer grazing on condo hedges and plucking winter greenery from decorative pots along the walks. The vision expanded to include renegade reindeer loose in Reckless River, pooping on downtown sidewalks, snarling traffic, trampling pedestrians.

"The only good part about Bernina's plan is my wood nymph costume."

I swallowed a bite of chicken wrap and, suspecting I wouldn't be crazy about the answer, asked, "What does a wood nymph costume look like?"

"Like a leotard and tights and ballet shoes." Allison made swishy motions with her hands. "And a floaty skirt you can kind of see through."

Certainly my idea of the perfect outfit for early winter weather. An outfit that would offer no protection against rain, wind, and temperatures hovering around 40 degrees.

"And I'd have kind of a crown." Allison mimed placing a circlet on her head and adjusting it. "But probably not with jewels. Probably ivy."

As long as it wasn't poison ivy. Or a flowering plant or trailing vine that was toxic to dogs.

Dave would have his hands full when he got home. I glanced at the clock. And if I was going to get that cover-my-butt e-mail written before I headed for the pool, I better hustle.

"I haven't had time to do any digging into rumors about the sale of the pool building," I told Paulette when we met up. "I don't know the name of the real estate guy. I don't know which of the city council—"

"That's okay. I've been thinking we should take an easier approach." Paulette took my arm and led me toward the building. "I know you enjoy research, but we need speed. And heat. And pressure."

I recoiled. That sounded like Paulette intended to call in my sister. And, although I'd considered the idea, I'd decided our mission called for a surgical strike, not carpet bombing.

Before I could protest, Paulette asked, "What's the name of the reporter you tipped to the Bigfoot tracks a few months ago?"

"Stan Stewart. Why?"

"If you dangled another tip, would he come running?"

"He might. He got a lot of mileage out of those tracks. His stories were picked up by papers all over the country."

"Well, let's see how fast he runs for a city government scandal. Get out your cell and give him a call."

Chapter 22

I dug the phone from my swim bag. "In your vision of how this goes down, I tell him . . .?"

"To meet you here in an hour to question a woman about her role in shutting down a city service for financial benefit."

"You mean Cheryl?" I snorted a laugh. "She'll tell him to buzz off—in an annoying voice."

Paulette shot me another satisfied smile. "Maybe. But don't forget we planted worry seeds in her brain about the scheme becoming common knowledge. With a little nudge, she might spill her guts to save her butt."

I liked the anatomical imagery and rhyme scheme. But how eager would Cheryl be to fink on a golden-egg-laying political goose? I decided that depended on whether she believed the goose was about to be cooked. "You're going to exaggerate the extent of our knowledge when you nudge her, aren't you?"

"*Moi?*" Paulette cocked a hip and placed her forefinger on her chin.

"Don't go all Miss Piggy on me. You'll lie through your teeth."

"My fresh-from-the-dental-hygienist-just-this-morning teeth," she corrected as we entered the pool building. "And you bet I will. When she scurries out the door after class, she'll believe she has two choices—rat out her pals or go down with their ship."

"And she'll scurry right into Stan Stewart's clutches?"

"Mere moments after you prime him." Paulette dug in her bag for her pool pass. "Of course, you'll have to leave class early, but if the other choice is listening to Cheryl for a full hour, you won't consider that a hardship."

And I didn't.

When Paulette gave me the nod, I hauled myself over the lip of the pool, hooked my flotation belt in the rack on the wall, ignored the sign that said NO RUNNING, and raced for the locker room. Figuring I'd have a genuine shower in the morning, I went with a quick rinse, yanked on my clothes, and trotted to the parking lot.

Stan Stewart, appearing no less scruffy than he had when last we met, slouched against a car two years overdue for a wrecking yard. His scowl and crossed arms said, "This better be good. My time is valuable."

The subtext didn't faze me. After all, if he was as wonderful as he thought, why was he still working for the *Reckless River Roundup*? Plus, even though the message I left on his phone had been vague, he'd hustled right over.

I tossed my swim gear in my trunk. "This might not go national like the Bigfoot story, but I can almost guarantee statewide interest. And it has legs."

Meaning, this wasn't a one-shot deal but, with some digging, might be milked for days and accompanied by sidebars and background pieces.

"That remains to be seen." Stewart maintained the scowl, but uncrossed his arms and dug a pen and reporter's notebook from the sagging, ink-stained pocket of a corduroy jacket. Except for deeper creases on the sleeves and more fraying around the buttonholes, the jacket looked much as it had early in the summer. Maybe *Roundup* reporters didn't make enough to afford food, lodging, *and* clothing. Or perhaps Stewart thought of the jacket as a uniform. Perhaps he considered creases and stains to be badges of honor.

Shoving wardrobe musings aside, I made certain we were talking off the record before I plunged in. Stewart stopped slouching and made notes, his pen leaving blotches of ink. When I wound down, he squinted and tapped the pen against his teeth—a dumb move given the smear of ink left on his incisors. "What's your interest in this?"

"I use this facility. I like it. I don't like the possibility of a group of people shutting it down to line their pockets. And I *really* don't like government corruption."

"Me, neither. But it sells papers." Stewart tapped his pen against his lip, leaving another smudge. I made a mental note to buy him a dozen pens. "How much of this can you prove?"

"Proving is your job," I told him. "I've been out of the research business since Rick Rivers decided he could do without a producer for his radio show."

"Guy's an idiot," Stewart muttered.

He didn't say whether he made that assessment because Rivers laid me off or because Rivers was, well, an idiot. Deciding the two were closely connected, I moved on. And fast. A glance over my shoulder revealed Cheryl heading our way, gnawing her lipstick, and still wearing the tank top and shorts she'd sported on the pool deck. "I wouldn't want to tell you how to do your job, but I'd start by interviewing that woman."

I turned and pointed at Cheryl.

She shot me a glare frosty enough to chill vodka to perfect martini temperature. Hesitating, she peered behind her. Paulette, still in her black bathing suit, spread her arms and raised the corners of a black-and-gold-striped towel. With her jeweled headband and glitter-trimmed flip-flops, she looked like a tiny avenging angel.

"I'm thinking you'll have to promise not to use her name."

Stewart groaned.

"On the positive side," I went on, "if the snakes you poke demand you reveal it and haul you to court, a few days in jail might boost your career."

Stewart gazed into the distance as if imagining life in a bigger city, on a bigger paper, with a bigger salary. Then he hustled to intercept Cheryl.

I got home just in time to cut off Allison as she headed for Bernina Burke's office with a sheaf of photos scavenged from the Internet. We had the usual conversation about homework, chores, and returning before 9:00. In other words, I brought those issues up and she tap danced around them.

Sigh.

Inside, I picked up a call from the electronic service that matched subs with jobs. Aston Marsden needed me again. Once more I mentally added the number of days I'd worked in this pay period and computed my take-home pay. I thought of Ardie. I thought of the cost of a visit to my parents. Then I tapped the number and accepted the job.

Aston called a few minutes later. "How much of the movie is left?"

"Not much. Maybe ten minutes."

"Hmmm."

I suspected Aston was wondering whether he dared suggest I launch a 40-minute discussion following the final frame. Projecting an icy silence I hoped said "No way," I waited him out.

"Okay. Answer any questions they have. Then tell them to start reading the next chapter."

"Which is?"

"I don't know. Do you think I carry the darn book home every night? Use your head. Figure it out."

Spoken like a man who didn't want me to sub for him again. Ever. I lowered the temperature on my silence.

"That kid in first period will know," he mumbled. The one who sits up front in the center. Always wears a white shirt. Has a pocket protector."

I knew the boy he was talking about. He was one of a group of self-proclaimed geeks who spent their lunch hours in the library playing chess. Crew cuts and pocket protectors were their emblems. He'd probably already read the chapter. Heck, he'd probably already read the entire book.

"Tell them to answer some of the questions at the end."

"Some? How many is that?"

"Five. Six. Are you dense?"

Apparently. Why else would I have agreed to sub for him?

"And what were you thinking when you told me to hire your sister? She did nothing but undermine ideas and sabotage plans and wear me out arguing. I finally fired her. Then she had the gall to demand half the amount we agreed to for a week. Threatened to haul me to court. The woman is a harpy."

He'd get no argument from me.

"The next time you have a hare-brained scheme that involves her, keep it to yourself. From now on I'm running this race alone, doing things my way."

Aston hung up without a farewell. Fine by me. The less I had to listen to him the better. But now that Iz was, once again, jobless, it appeared I'd spend more time listening to her.

Muttering, I made my way to the office, fired up my computer, and checked airfares to Missouri.

The numbers made my hands shake.

I went to the kitchen for a restorative drink and found only a few drops in the adult-beverage bottle. Recalling there was far better stuff next door, I headed that way. Halfway, I halted and told myself not to mooch. Pacing, I gave that deeper thought and decided I wouldn't be an *obvious* mooch if I had a legitimate reason for dropping in, like, for example, collecting Cheese Puff for his evening walk.

I found Mrs. B seated in her favorite chair, Cheese Puff on her lap. In addition to his hat and vest, he wore what appeared to be a tiny pair of spats. Packages of frozen vegetables chilled her knees and ankles and another rested against the back of her neck. She held a martini with two huge olives.

"Overdo it this afternoon?" I asked.

"I hope not. But if I did, this usually nips the swelling in the bud." She patted a veggie pack. "Getting old isn't for the faint of heart."

"Good thing you're the poster girl for kicking Father Time's butt."

She smiled and preened, fluffing her hair with her fingers, an act that drew the attention of Apricot, the half-grown cat from next door. Apricot was a climber, and liked to hang out on top of bookcases, cabinets, and refrigerators. When she spotted something of interest, she'd sail from the heights, legs outspread like a flying squirrel.

And that's what she did, landing on the back of Mrs. B's chair, and mock attacking her fingers. Mrs. B made cute-kitty sounds. Cheese Puff growled. Lola, on the floor beside the sofa, sneezed. Apricot leaped from the chair, raced in circles, and shot out the door to the deck. Cheese Puff barked a farewell.

"You do know that store brands of frozen vegetables chill as well as the high-end organic types, right?" I asked.

"You do know that I'm on house arrest and have to make do with what's in the freezer, don't you?"

184

Direct hit.

I winced and didn't mention that she was also "making do" with little goodies ordered through the Internet.

Mrs. B marked her score in the air and smiled. "Mix up a little something and sit with me for a bit."

Exactly the invitation I'd hoped for. Trying to move more slowly than a genuine mooch, I eased to the kitchen, poured coconut rum and ginger ale in a tall glass, and added crushed ice and a couple of cherries. Taking further advantage, I liberated a can of giant cashews from a cabinet.

"Bring that new box of dog biscuits," Mrs. B called. "Lola looks hungry."

"She probably is. I forgot to feed her before I took off for the pool."

"And I know why." Mrs. B patted Cheese Puff. "The little prince wasn't there to remind you."

Meaning he wasn't there to shove his dish around the kitchen and yip at me to do my job.

She took the box and fed Lola half a dozen small biscuits. "I hope these meet with your approval. They're apple and pumpkin and peanut butter. All organic and not a bit of grain." She stroked Lola's silky ears. "It's entirely my fault you went unfed. I was so intent on practicing, I quite forgot about Cheese Puff's obligations."

Since she was looking right at me when she spoke that last bit, I refrained from any physical reaction suggesting my entitled mutt never felt obligated to do anything except accept adoration from his fans. I took a seat on the sofa, the can of cashews at my side, and set about fortifying myself.

Mrs. B fed Lola two more biscuits, and broke another in small pieces for Cheese Puff. "I don't want to pry, dear, but you have the look of someone either in a quandary or about to fall off a cliff and land in one. We've discussed Dave and Allison,

185

and we've covered whether I should attempt to escape to another country, so would this be about your sister?"

"Close. My parents."

"Ah." Mrs. B adjusted the sack of petite peas on her left knee, shifted Cheese Puff a few millimeters, and fed Lola another biscuit. "I'm ready to listen when you're ready to talk."

I'm never "ready" to talk about my parents. My feelings are so varied and conflicted—love, anger, guilt, loss, sadness, frustration. I swallowed half of my drink to prime the conversational pump. "I feel like I should visit them. I call almost every week, but mostly they're not home because they have so many activities. And I hate to admit it, but I'm kind of relieved when I get the answering machine. It's difficult to talk to them. The last time I felt like they hardly remembered me."

I choked on tears and groped in the pockets of my jeans for a tissue.

"There's a box of tissues with lotion on that lower shelf of the little bookcase beside the rocker," Mrs. B said in a soft voice.

I plucked out a trio and snorked. "Did you stay in touch with your parents after you left home?"

"At first. I wrote. And sent what money I could spare."

"Did they write back?"

"No. Perhaps their pride wouldn't allow it. Or perhaps they wanted no more contact. So, after a time . . ."

I handed her a pair of tissues and we sniffled together for a few moments.

"I'm sure your parents care, dear," she said. "But their scars are deep. They would hardly know where or how to begin to connect with you again. And, of course, whether they admit it or not, they're afraid if they do, and then somehow lose you, the pain would be too great to bear."

I'd never considered that. "So what can I do?"

"Take care of yourself. Treasure your memories. Live the happiest and most fulfilling life you can."

I wadded my tissues and sipped my drink. "That's it?"

"Write to them. Send birthday and holiday cards and pictures. Tell them if they need you, you'll do whatever you can."

"But . . . but don't call? Don't visit?"

"I didn't say that, dear. By all means, go to Missouri if that's what you feel you must do. But think about what you hope to achieve. You can't change the past. You can't fit the pieces of your family together the way they were."

That last sentence created a vivid image in my mind—my parents, Iz, and me as pieces of a jigsaw puzzle. The pieces were bent and torn. They had knobby protrusions that would never lock into the correct indentations of another piece. That piece, the piece known as Bryce, was gone.

Before Bryce died, we'd been a family. We fit together. And yeah, maybe the picture we formed wasn't perfect, but it was still recognizable. Now we were only a collection of pieces. And not even a complete collection.

I didn't say a word, but Mrs. B nodded.

Her piece and mine fit together. And they fit with Dave and Allison and Dario and the members of the Committee and even, sometimes, with my sister.

I raised my glass in a toast.

She raised hers.

We drank to family.

C h a p te r 2 3

Thinking about family and Mrs. B's future sent me to the computer to search out Glorree Morning. Despite the fact I was once a radio news producer and pretty good at digging, I discovered not much. The news release from *Still Got That Strut* listed her as one of the competitors and named a few of the venues where she'd performed. A ten-year-old "Where-Are-They-Now?" story carried a picture of her wearing an enormous sunhat and shorts while showing off a flower garden in the yard of a Nevada home I wouldn't describe as "palatial." The article made no mention of her actual name, and no reference to a husband or children. Close examination of the picture revealed no evidence in the form of backyard play equipment, a basketball hoop, or multiple cars in the driveway.

I was about to log off when I hit on a blogger fascinated by sequins, sparkle, and showgirls. Peabody Fontaine—his photo showed a large white-haired man in a pink shirt, paisley ascot, and fuzzy green jacket—gushed hundreds of words each day, the majority adjectives and adverbs. He dished dirt, resurrected rumors, suggested scandals, tattled, and titillated.

Peabody Fontaine billed himself as a huge fan of *Still Got That Strut*, but his reviews of performances were more scathing than those delivered by the judges. He reveled in pointing out missteps and wardrobe disasters. He also revealed details of tummy-tucking surgeries, facelifts, and failed diets.

If anyone had anything on Glorree Morning, it would be Peabody Fontaine.

Rubbing my hands in glee, I was about to search his blog when the door slammed and Allison's feet pounded past the office door. "I'm only eight minutes late," she yelled.

I bookmarked the site. Duty called. "That's still late," I called.

"You're not gonna tell Dad, are you?"

I heard the refrigerator door open and then a pop and hiss.

"No carbonated drinks before bed."

"I'm having orange juice," Allison said in a voice oozing phony innocence.

"And I'm walking on the moon." I turned off the computer.

"It's *not* a cola."

"That's *not* the point. You won't sleep well." I snapped off the desk lamp.

"Well, what should I do? Dump it down the sink?"

"I'll put a note on it. Your father might drink it when he gets home."

"When will that be?"

"Later." I headed along the hallway to the kitchen, Lola and Cheese Puff shuffling in my wake.

"When later? He's gotta say okay for the decorating job. And I need money for lunch and stuff."

"What kind of stuff?" I reached the kitchen and spotted Allison rooting through cabinets.

"Snacks. And don't say I can bring them from home, because we're out of potato chips." Her wailing tone was the type you'd expect from people announcing a tornado was about to strike.

"Take something else."

"I don't want something else." She turned to face me, hands on hips. "Why aren't there chips?"

Gazing at the ceiling, I placed a forefinger against my cheek and pretended to think. I was playing a game of Chicken with Dave—a game he wasn't aware of. Sunday had been his day to shop. I hadn't expected him to, because he'd been investigating Big Shiny's murder. But I *had* expected him to remember it was his turn—after all, it was clearly marked on the calendar stuck to the side of the refrigerator—and arrange to swap. When that didn't happen, I decided I'd prove I was every bit as forgetful and distracted.

Since the truth behind the lack of chips didn't paint me as a highly evolved person, I hit Allison with a blatant lie. "There aren't more chips because the condo elves living under the deck said they'd take care of it. But they couldn't get to the store because of the canopy."

Allison stomped toward the door. "Fine. I'll go borrow some from Mrs. Ballantine. She *always* remembers *everything*."

A comment she obviously thought would make me realize how far short I fell. Little did Allison know I'd abandoned hope of even carrying the water bucket in Mrs. B's league.

I scavenged items for lunch—a chicken wrap and a container of pudding two days shy of its sell-by date. As a bonus, I discovered a pack of dry-roasted almonds behind a pyramid of soup cans. Adding a can of generic cola, I tucked my finds inside an insulated lunch sack and stashed it behind a bottle of sparkling cider on the top shelf of the refrigerator. The unopened bottle, a housewarming gift, had been in the same spot for months, evidence that no one had the least interest in sampling what promised to be a tangy treat for the taste buds. I'd considered moving it to a cabinet, but it provided cover for items I claimed as my own, so I left it alone.

190

Allison returned with three family-size bags of chips—regular, crinkly, and barbecue. "See, I told you Mrs. B would have lots of chips."

I didn't recall saying she wouldn't, but my experience with teenagers in general, and Allison in particular, told me not to mention that. There were times when Allison showed glimpses of adult behavior, but not when she was feeling put-upon and/or not cared about.

"I'm gonna take a whole bag." She stuffed the crinklies in her backpack. "So I can share with Josh."

"If you have chips, do you still need money?"

"Duh." She treated me to an eye roll of such speed, magnitude, and duration I feared her eyeballs would launch from their sockets. "Chips make me thirsty."

And that many chips would require a lot of liquid. That, to the delight of her teachers, would be followed by requests for the restroom pass.

"See what's in the tea canister." I pointed at the smallest of a quartet of copper canisters ranged along the counter near the stove. Dave and I seldom drank tea that wasn't premade and chilled, so the container had become a catchall for rubber bands, twist ties, chip clips, and coins—many of which bounced to the floor when Allison pulled off the lid and dumped the contents.

Barking, Cheese Puff pursued a quarter down the hall. Lola sniffed a nickel, snorted, and headed for the bedroom. I was right behind.

Dave was beside me in the morning, but he burrowed under the covers when I spoke to him. I took that for a sign things hadn't gone well yesterday, and zipped through my morning routine as quietly as possible.

When I opened the door of the teachers' room, a clean lemony scent tipped me that change was in the air. The change extended to the table. A bright yellow tablecloth—actual cloth, not plastic—had replaced Susan's. It wouldn't stand up five minutes to a Lunch-ageddon assault, but it was cheery. In the center of the table, blue glass salt and pepper shakers flanked a silver napkin holder stuffed with striped napkins. The countertop gleamed. So did the sink.

Balancing on a chair, the sleeves of her black shirt pushed past her elbows, Adie scrubbed at the upper shelf of the cabinet above the microwave. "Mornin'," she called.

"Back at you." I slipped my lunch in the refrigerator, noting the shelves were far cleaner than when I finished scrubbing them last week. "Trying to clean your way into Gertrude's heart? Or just making this place less of a death trap?"

Ardie chuckled. "Not door number one because she's set in her ways. But so am I." She jumped down and rinsed the sponge. "I'm cleaning to show she can't run me off. Not only that, the longer she stays away, the more I make my mark on this room."

I saluted her attitude with a raised thumb. If I'd been treated like Ardie had yesterday, I would have slunk to my car and eaten alone—if I wasn't too upset to eat. Ardie, however, had guts. And she was far more self-contained. I bet she hadn't mentioned Gertrude's attitude to Big Chill—or anyone.

"Can I give you a hand?"

"Nope. Almost done. Saving the cabinet under the sink for tomorrow."

"Bring a gas mask," I advised.

"I live for a challenge," Ardie said.

"This might be the challenge you die for," I muttered under my breath as I headed for Aston's room.

Assistant Principal Tremaine Scott stood beside the door, muscular legs set wide, muscular arms folded tight across his muscular chest. A former college football star, Scott put in a dozen hours a day at Captain Meriwether, so I had no idea how he found time to stay in shape. But then, I'd never been in shape, so I had no idea what it took to hold the line.

Being a sub, I didn't have to worry about him checking my lesson plans, evaluating my teaching ability, or appointing me to serve on one school committee or another. Subs were pretty much immune to all that. But we weren't bulletproof. Scott might recommend the district pass on hiring me for a full-time position. He could also strike me from the Captain Meriwether subbing roster and consign me to—gasp!—middle school. Consequently, while I didn't suck up, I often walked on eggs when he was nearby.

Scott's voice rumbled like distant thunder. "Aston gave you lesson plans, right?"

I nodded.

"I heard you showed a film yesterday."

"With a worksheet," I squeaked. "With questions." Never mind how lame they were.

"And today?"

"The rest of the film. And they'll read from the textbook. And answer more questions."

I crossed my fingers, hoping to ward off the curse of Scott asking which chapter and how many questions. If I told the truth, Aston would assume I volunteered the information with the aim of making trouble.

Realizing Scott might ask whether I knew what kind of illness Aston had, I crossed my legs for further luck.

Apparently my ballet-school-dropout position did the trick. He gave me only about a tenth of the scowl he once used on opposing linemen. "All right. Let me know if you have problems."

"Definitely."

"And thanks for covering for Aston. After the bear grease incident, no one would fault you for turning him down." He uncrossed his arms and hooked a thumb toward the teachers' room. "I hear you have a new cohort."

"Ardette Johnson." I grinned. "I worked with her at the juvie jail last month. She's terrific."

"I'm glad you think so. I hear not everyone agrees."

How did he know? Had Gertrude complained?

"Some people have more trouble with change than others," I said, keeping it vague. "Give it time."

Allison rode home with me, whining about restrictions Dave had set—in an e-mail—on her job with Bernina. To my mind, they made a lot of sense. In addition to cautions about climbing on the roof or a high ladder, warnings about electricity and overloading sockets, and concerns about her curfew, Dave also made it clear the job wasn't to interfere with homework or chores. That last part was at the core of Allison's complaints.

"If I'm working and making money, I shouldn't have to do dishes and stuff."

I resisted the temptation to point out that A) she wouldn't make all that much, B) the job would end in a few weeks, C) Dave and I worked and didn't get a pass on chores, and D) with "lots of money" she could hire someone to do her chores. And that someone might do a far better job.

In fact, I resisted the temptation to say anything to prolong my agony. When we approached the condo and I spotted Bernina with a tape measure and a clipboard, I braked hard. "Better see if your boss needs help."

"Huh?"

194

"Bernina." I pointed. "She looks like she's about to do some measuring."

"So?"

"So she's probably figuring how many feet of power cord she needs."

"So?"

"So you need power for the lights. And decorations. The ones you'll be setting up for the con—"

"I *know*."

Could have fooled me.

Allison wrestled the door open and slid out. "Take my backpack inside."

I smiled and reached for the door she hadn't closed, thinking I'd tote her pack inside a few minutes after never.

That, coincidentally, was the same time frame I heard Mrs. B referring to when I opened the door to my condo.

Chapter 24

"My position hasn't changed," Mrs. B said. "And it never will!"

Her voice, usually so measured and well-modulated, rose steadily. Even though she was on the deck and the sliding door to my place was open only a few inches, I'd have to be wearing my special earplugs not to hear every syllable. For a moment I was tempted to dig the plugs from my briefcase and stick them in place. But if Mrs. B wanted a private conversation, she would have carried her phone inside her unit. Or lowered her voice. Satisfied that I wasn't snooping, I made my way to the living room.

"I provided you with a diagram and noted the marks I'll hit during my performance," Mrs. B said. "I've talked with Dario and the lighting experts and they're fine with it. There is no reason I should let you watch me rehearse or send you a video of my routine or provide photographs of my wardrobe just yet."

I hung my briefcase in the closet, got a glass, and filled it at the tap, making no attempt to be quiet. Carrying the water, I strolled to the sofa and took a seat.

I moved to my left. And to my right. The cushions were getting lumpier every day. I eased farther to the left and watched Mrs. B's sun-cast shadow on the canvas curtain. Her free hand clenched and unclenched, then punched air. Cheese Puff's shadow circled hers, and then circled a hump of shadow I guessed was Lola.

When Mrs. B spoke again, her voice was low and her tone was menacing—although in a formal and polite way. "I understand that you believe you're doing your job—as you define it. If you're convinced I'm obstructive, and you're certain you must make a case for me to be disqualified, then by all means, go over Dario's head."

Mrs. B's shadow raised its left hand as if to throw the phone, then lowered it. "Did you hear all that, dear?" she called.

"Only from the part where you said your position hasn't changed. I assume that was Jackie."

She pushed the curtain aside, slid the door open, and went to the sink. Her face was the color of borscht after you've mixed in a dollop of sour cream. Not that I'd ever waste sour cream on a bowl of beet soup, but you get the picture.

"I can't understand why that woman is badgering me." Heedless of her silky blue blouse and the phone in the pocket, Mrs. B splashed water on her face and neck. A few drops fell on Cheese Puff and he yipped and scampered for the safety of his favorite chair. Sneezing, Lola limped behind the sofa.

"Everyone else seems satisfied with my arrangements," Mrs. B raged. "Everyone else understands I want my routine kept secret as long as possible."

She cupped her hand and drank from the faucet, something I'd never seen her do, and never imagined she would. Mrs. B always used a glass. And she always used the correct glass for the occasion or particular drink—a tumbler, snifter, goblet, cocktail glass, or stemmed flute. She served lemonade from a green pitcher that matched a set of thick, tall glasses. Further, cream never appeared on her table in a carton,

197

but in one of several glass or silver pitchers. Butter was always in a special dish. With a silver butter knife.

And yet, in her childhood, pitchers and silver and stemware must have been scarce. For all I knew, she'd had nothing to put in a glass except water. So the civilizing touches of her life were learned later. And now they'd been cast aside along with her even temper and tendency to give the benefit of the doubt.

Mrs. B splashed more water on her face, wiped her hands on her blouse, and turned off the tap. "And now she plans to go to the executive producer and tell him I'm uncooperative and obstructive *and* a no-talent diva *and* I'm bringing down the quality of the product. Can you believe it?"

Actually, I could. Having worked in the media, I'd run across several people like Jackie, people who got a little power and wanted more, people who marked their territory and made reams of rules. Many were young and on the way up. Others were older and on the way out.

Mrs. B slumped to the sofa beside me.

Yes, slumped.

Another indication the veneer of civilization had been stripped away. "It's like a vendetta. And it appears to be more about me than rules and requirements for the show."

She slumped even more and chewed at her thumbnail.

That did it.

I didn't like this uncivilized Mrs. B. I loved and depended on the controlled and civilized version. This one was . . . well, this one was too much like me.

"Maybe you're the first person who offered any resistance. Maybe she didn't know how to handle that and, um, escalated."

Mrs. B snorted. "Don't tell me that Glorree Morning isn't giving her 'resistance.' Glorree wrote the book on my-way-or-the-highway behavior. She was the queen of ultimatums. I bet she hasn't changed one little bit."

"Maybe Glorree already gave Jackie so much crapola she's had it up to here." I raised my hand to eye level. "Maybe you're getting backlash."

"Hmmm." Mrs. B brushed at the water spots on her blouse, then drew the phone from her pocket, and punched a few numbers. She held it to her ear, but tipped so I heard Dario's booming voice when he answered. "Kitten!"

"Sweetie Bear," Mrs. B purred. She made kissy sounds, and then got down to business, telling him about Jackie's demands and her threat to go to the executive producer.

Dario laughed. "Stick to your guns. Keep your routine under wraps."

"But she said—"

"She's gone over my head so many times I'm thinking of tying a ladder to my back to make it easier on both of us."

"You're not worried?"

"Waste of time. Don't need the money. They cut me loose, I spend more time with you."

Mrs. B blushed and made more kissy sounds.

"Ask him about Glorree Morning," I prompted.

Mrs. B nodded and straightened from her slump. "Barbara and I were wondering whether Jackie and Glorree are at odds with each other as well."

"Not that I know of. But hang on. I'll check around."

Dario put us on hold and Mrs. B tapped the phone against her chin while we listened to something that sounded like a disco version of "Bohemian Rhapsody." As I finished sending a mental apology to Freddie Mercury out into the universe, Dario came back on the line. "If they argue, they do it in private. Word is they get along."

So much for that theory.

"Don't worry about it, Kitten. Gotta go."

Dario made smoochy sounds and disconnected.

"Well, either Glorree has changed, or it's me," Mrs. B mused.

I patted her shoulder. "Maybe it's a personality conflict. Perhaps you remind Jackie of a teacher who flunked her. Like Dario said, you shouldn't worry about it. Focus on your routine."

"You're right. And that's what I'll do."

She got to her feet, rubbing her hip. "There isn't a soft spot anywhere on that sofa. I wonder if I can order a new one on the Internet."

I wouldn't put it past her. And I was certain the sofa would be expensive, attractive, and durable. But she paid for too many things as it was.

"I'm sure you can." I took her arm and steered her toward the door. "But you need to practice, not shop. Besides, you exceeded your on-line limit for the week."

"There's a limit? I didn't know there was a limit." Her eyes narrowed. "Are you joking?"

"Only about the limit. Not about practice."

"I see." She pushed the curtain aside and called to Cheese Puff. "Rehearsal time."

I closed the door behind them and, since Dave was missing in action, went about jotting down a grocery list.

The process of shopping and schlepping, stashing and storing, snacking and sampling used up most of the evening. Badgering Allison about homework ate up the rest. At 9:00, while compiling a mental list of ways Dave could make it up to me, I checked the sub line. No jobs listed for tomorrow to offset the check I wrote at the supermarket.

Another downside to tomorrow's blank date wasn't financial. It was the early-morning waiting game. If I wasn't committed to a job, but hoping to snag one, I rose at 5:30, showered, dressed, and got ready to fill in. If the phone hadn't rung by the time I finished breakfast, I bided my time.

Time biding involved doing things like reading the paper, rearranging drawers and cabinets, or swishing the dust mop up and down the hall in pursuit of dog hair. Time-biding projects couldn't be too strenuous or messy because, if I got a call, I wouldn't have time to do more than apply fresh deodorant or change a stained T-shirt. Ideally, tasks should also be of short duration so there was less chance of having to dash off and leave one unfinished.

The time-biding process began at 6:40 when I would normally hop in my car and head for Captain Meriwether. The end time, however, wasn't as exact. Middle school started later than high school. And teachers might decide after one or two periods that they couldn't make it through the day. I'd been called as late as 11:00. That made for serious time-biding.

Reminding myself I'd subbed all last week and put in two days for Aston already this week, I vowed to bide until 8:30, and then make myself unavailable for the rest of the day. I'd take a long walk, hit a morning water aerobics class, or wander through a bookstore. I'd definitely write to my parents.

Immediate future decided, I nagged Allison about homework and bedtime, took the dogs out for a last squat or leg lift, then hit the sack.

Dave, snoring softly, didn't move when my alarm buzzed the next morning. He was still in the same position when I emerged from the shower, and hadn't shifted an inch when I came upstairs after grabbing breakfast, swilling the single cup of coffee I'd made, taking the dogs out, and telling Allison six times to get to the bus stop because I wasn't driving her. In stealth mode, I went to work on the bottom drawer of my dresser where I tossed T-shirts I wasn't ready to part with yet and single socks waiting for mates to turn up.

I've never understood the sock thing. I know I'm wearing two at the end of the day when I peel them off and toss them in the hamper. But somewhere on the journey to the washer, or back upstairs from the dryer, one sock goes AWOL. I've checked behind the washer, under the sofa, and inside the vacuum bag. I've searched Dave's dresser drawers, and once sent Paulette to Allison's room on sock patrol—all to no avail. When mates do return, they materialize in places I swear they weren't the day before.

Since I've adopted the policy of tossing single socks in the lower drawer and pretending I don't care if they reunite with their mates, more of them have matched. I guess it's one of those watched-pot-never-boils things. Or reverse psychology. The less I care about whether they pair up, the more socks yearn to be a couple.

So I wasn't surprised when I dumped the drawer—quietly— at the foot of the bed and found three sets of pairs waiting to be rolled together and elevated to the top tier of drawers.

Slam dunking them among other pairs may possibly be what woke Dave.

He groaned the way stone doors do when they open by inches in fantasy or horror movies.

"Sorry," I whispered, hoping his mood would be better than that of the dragon, vampire, ax-murderer, or whatever hung out behind cinematic doors. With bags under his bloodshot eyes and lines around his mouth, he looked like a creature I wouldn't want to encounter in a cave—or anywhere else.

"It's okay. Gotta get up anyway." He rubbed his eyes. "Gotta go over everything again. And again."

"Coffee." I headed for the stairs. "Coming up."

While I brewed a full pot, I stuck an English muffin in the toaster oven, then dialed in and made myself unavailable. It sounded as if the investigation had stalled. And that meant Dave might be inclined to share details and bounce ideas. Sharing and bouncing sometimes led to breakthroughs.

Whether Detective Charles Atwell admitted it or not, I had a knack for fitting snippets of information into a cohesive narrative. I attribute the knack to my background as a radio producer, a genetic tendency toward snooping, my enjoyment of gossip, and the tingling thrill I get from showing up a certain professional detective.

Coffee and OJ poured, muffin covered with toasted cheese and ham, dogs at my heels, I raced upstairs. Well, actually, I raced until I was two steps from the top, then I slowed to a saunter. Appearing too eager might make Dave less likely to spill. The trick was to pretend the status of the investigation was at the bottom of my pyramid of interests, far below searching out new recipes for kale or reading up on the latest movie star divorces.

Arraying my offerings on the nightstand, I returned to straightening the bottom drawer and listened to Dave slurp juice and coffee.

"Are you home because all the teachers in town are on the job today?" he asked.

"Possibly," I answered, skipping around the truth while feeling guilty about taking myself out of the sub pool, and guiltier about making exactly no money today. "Aston didn't request me so I guess he returned from his political sabbatical. I can't remember, did I tell you he hired my sister as a campaign consultant?"

"No. How's that working out?"

"About like you'd expect. He fired her after one day." I abandoned the drawer and sat at the foot of the bed. "Yesterday he claimed he intended to work on his own. He didn't mention what office he's running for."

"And you don't want to ask?"

I nodded and went on to tell him about Ardie's arrival and Gertrude's chilly reception. I admitted to considering whether I should meddle in the situation, try to talk sense to Gertrude, or get Doug to return to the teachers' room so Ardie would have company.

"She'll have Aston," Dave said. "After driving two others out, he's committed to staying, no matter who Big Chill transfers in there."

"True." And I'd already filled Ardie in on his many faults and foibles. I had no doubt she'd find him more amusing than irritating. Maybe she'd cajole or threaten him into improving his behavior.

"What about the pool situation?" Dave sat up and attacked his muffin sandwich. The dogs took up positions on either side in case a bit of ham, shred of cheese, or crumb of muffin should drop.

"Taken care of. Paulette leaned on the water aerobics instructor and sent her into the arms of Stan Stewart. Remember him? The Bigfoot beat reporter?"

"The one who slouches and appears as delighted to be in Reckless River as I'd be if Dick McBain was police chief?"

Bingo!

Dave had opened a door. I waltzed through. "That's him. Hey, speaking of McBain, what happened with the video?"

"We got it. For all the good it did."

Chapter 25

Every snoop cell in my body went to high alert, but I played it cool. Working a burr from the hair on Lola's tail, I waited for Dave to chew and swallow. "The only video we got is from the lobby. Camera at the rear entrance hasn't worked since last winter. One in the elevator was shut down during maintenance and never powered up again."

"There's nothing helpful on the lobby video?"

"Nothing we found so far." He stuffed the last chunk of muffin in his mouth and talked around it. "But aside from the woman with the fresh light bulbs—and there's no sign of her— we don't have any idea who we're looking for. And we don't know why Big Shiny was killed."

"That fact that he was mobbed up isn't enough?"

Dave swallowed and wiped his mouth on the back of his hand. "The guy's been disconnected for years. Unless it was a personal thing, I can't see what there was to gain by killing him. And from the condition of his heart and lungs and liver, he didn't have long to live. Why risk a murder charge?"

There were a dozen questions I wanted to ask and things I wanted to suggest, but Dave had probably thought of most of them. If he got the impression I was telling him how to do his job, he'd clam up. So I didn't ask how he knew for sure Big Shiny wasn't still connected. I mean, it wasn't like he posted his status on social media as "retired mobster." It wasn't like he'd unfriended wiseguys he used to hang with, or been unfriended by them. But I imagined there were experts who kept up on underworld players and would know if someone wanted Big Shiny dead.

And I didn't ask whether Dave thought a member of the hotel staff might have been fed up with the cranky old guy's demands and snapped. Or, been fed up, but paused before snapping and figured out how to frame Mrs. B.

"The guy was obnoxious. Treated the staff like serfs. But he tipped like the last of the big spenders." Dave finished his coffee and set the mug aside. "Anyway, the feeling was he complained to show he still had control. He handed out so much cash the tradeoff was worth it."

"So Mrs. Ballantine is still a suspect?"

Dave's eyes shifted left, then right.

I felt something cold and nasty uncoiling in the pit of my stomach. "She didn't do it. You know she didn't."

Dave's eyes shifted again.

"But why? Why would she kill him? And if she did, why would she leave her fingerprints on the lamp?"

"Misdirection," he muttered. "Make it look like someone framed her."

"That's such a reach." I stood and paced a tight circle between the bed and the dresser, my voice rising. "That's not a theory. It's a pathetic excuse for a theory. I bet your buddy Detective Atwell came up with it."

Dave didn't deny my charge.

"He never liked her, right from the start. He resents her wealth. He'd love to see her behind bars."

Dave stood and put himself in my path. "You're overreacting."

"I am not." I sidestepped. "But even if I am, you're under-reacting. This is Mrs. Ballantine we're talking about. Our *neighbor*. Our *friend*. The woman who brought us together!"

My voice rose to a screech. Cheese Puff yipped and burrowed beneath the pillows. Lola belly-crawled to the closet and clambered behind the shoe racks.

Dave gripped my shoulders. "I'm not out to get her. I'm not her enemy."

"Well you're not acting like her friend."

"If I did, I'd be off the case."

Oh.

Yeah.

Right.

I slumped to the edge of the bed and avoided his gaze by picking at a loose thread on the outside seam of my jeans. In a moment, Dave sat beside me and put his arm around my shoulders. I leaned against him, remembering how I'd leaned against Mrs. Ballantine and how, later, I'd thought of us as pieces of a puzzle that fit together to form a family. She loved me. And she loved Dave and Allison, and Lola and Cheese Puff.

I felt that cold thing uncoiling again. Big Shiny had complained about Cheese Puff and insisted he be banned from certain areas of the hotel. What if he'd taken it further? What if he'd threatened to harm the little dog Mrs. B treasured? Would she—?

No!

I shook off the idea. If Big Shiny had threatened Cheese Puff, Mrs. B would have packed up and left the hotel to keep him safe.

But suppose he didn't threaten. Suppose he snatched Cheese Puff, took him to his room, and—

Sheesh.

The man was ancient. In poor health. Plus, Mrs. B said he smelled like horse liniment. No way would Cheese Puff go near him.

But suppose a member of the staff, angling for an enormous tip, chased Cheese Puff down and brought him to Big Shiny's room? Mrs. B wouldn't have hesitated to do whatever it took to rescue him.

I snuggled against Dave's bare chest. His skin smelled like sweat and sleep, pepperoni and garlic. Amateur sleuth that I am, I surmised he had pizza for at least two meals yesterday. "Was there any evidence Cheese Puff had been in Big Shiny's room?"

"I don't know. Why?"

Stupid me. If Dave hadn't checked for Cheese Puff's hair in Big Shiny's room, it meant he hadn't developed the dog-in-jeopardy theory. Now I'd practically handed it to him.

"Just wondering if, uh, maybe he'd gotten in there when they first arrived and if that was the reason Big Shiny took such a dislike to him."

"Hmmm. Are you sure you weren't thinking Big Shiny dognapped Cheese Puff, and Mrs. B scattered his corpuscles in retaliation?"

"Um, possibly."

Dave chuckled. "I know how she dotes on that dog, and I'm sure she would have kicked in the door while wearing high heels if Big Shiny snatched him. And if one hair on his little orange head was harmed . . ."

Dave didn't elaborate.

"But all that would make noise and attract attention."

"Right. And I think if Mrs. Ballantine took out Big Shiny to save Cheese Puff, she would have called Angus Drummond and turned herself in right then."

"And thrown herself on the mercy of the court," I agreed. "Does this logic progression mean you believe she's innocent?"

He didn't answer.

I counted to 20. Then on to 30. And 40.

"I'd like to believe she is, but a couple of questions keep nagging at me. Why would the killer frame her? Why not someone else? Why not a member of the staff? Or someone who came by now and then—the woman who delivered his special vitamins and mineral water, the plumber, or the termite inspector?" Dave scratched his chin. "Framing someone as wealthy and connected as Mrs. Ballantine guaranteed an all-out defense, turning every stone to find the killer, or find enough doubt to weaken the case and get her off."

"It sounds like you're saying the murder was secondary and the main objective was to frame Mrs. B."

"Officially I'm not saying that. Officially I'm not even having a fleeting thought resembling anything remotely like what you said." Dave tipped my chin and held my gaze. "It's speculation. A wild-hair theory. It doesn't leave this room."

"Right." My busy brain churned up a list of people who had their differences with Mrs. B. There was my sister, who disagreed with her philosophy. And there were others who envied her financial situation. And then there were those who had bigger issues—jealousy and personality conflicts. That was a short list. It was mostly Glorree Morning and Jackie DeWill and Bernina Burke.

Since she now had a pot of money for her holiday decorating competition, Bernina wasn't actually on the list. She was more like standing nearby in position to get back on at a future date. Plus Bernina was lazy. And not all that smart. Hatching this frame-up—if that's what it was—took brains. It also took energy.

As far as Jackie DeWill was concerned, her conflict with Mrs. B hadn't erupted until later, until Mrs. B was forced to practice on the deck.

So that left Glorree Morning. If Mrs. B wasn't cleared soon, she'd either win their competition by default, or be matched with another former showgirl. But Glorree Morning was Mrs. B's age. Could she slip in and out of hotel rooms, swing a lamp with enough force to kill, and escape by jumping from a balcony if that's what it took? And, really, was she so obsessed with winning that she'd kill to send her rival to prison?

That cold slithery thing uncoiled in my gut again. Mrs. B in prison would be like an orchid in a freezer. "If Mrs. B goes to prison, she'll die."

"She's tougher than you think." Dave kissed my forehead. "But I wonder who would profit if she died. Has she ever talked about her will?"

"No." And I'd never brought it up. Partly because it was crass, but mostly because it would involve admitting she wouldn't go on forever.

He did a kind of grunt/groan/sigh thing. "I better ask her. Do you think she's up?"

I glanced at the bedside clock—almost 8:00. "Probably. I hope you plan to shower before you interrogate her."

"It's tough to shower with a cast." Dave did that thing guys do where they raise their arms and sniff their pits. "She doesn't go for gamy?"

"No way."

He leered, then rubbed his stubbly chin against my cheek and breathed in my ear. "How about you?"

"Ditto."

He nuzzled my neck. "You sure?"

I held in a gasp of pleasure. For the next five seconds, I had a choice about what happened next. Then my hormones would overpower my brain. Much as I'd enjoy the activities that followed, what I wanted more was to help Mrs. B.

I pulled away and pointed to the bathroom. "Shower. Interrogate. Get Mrs. B off. Then I'll reward you in many strange and wonderful ways."

He pulled me close for a kiss. "Exactly how many ways? And how strange?"

"How about we negotiate as we go?"

"Works for me." He nibbled my lower lip. "There's nothing I like more than give-and-take negotiating with somebody who's willing to be, um, flexible."

Once again, my hormones threatened to take over. I promised they'd be in complete control later, struggled from Dave's grip, and headed for the stairs. "Want another muffin?"

"Or two. But I'd better go with fruit and oatmeal or something better for me than what I've been eating." He tossed aside the sheet, revealing a pair of black boxer shorts covered with green and yellow snakes. They gave me the creeps, which is why I'd tossed them in the trash at least twice since Dave moved in last spring. Did he have more than one pair? I vowed to search through his drawers (no pun intended) after he left.

"Anything's better for you than the pizza from Ronzo's Royal Rounds."

He turned in the doorway. "How do you know I had pizza? And how do you know it was Ronzo's?"

"You reek of garlic. Ronzo's uses more than other pizza places. It's close to the cop shop. It's a buck a pie less than most." I ticked off additional points on my fingers. "They open early. They stay open late. They deliver. And when you're focused on a case, you don't care what you eat."

"Impressive."

"Elementary."

I trotted downstairs and found Mrs. B coming through the door from the deck—hair combed, makeup flawless, blouse fresh and crisp, tap shoes polished. Despite that, she seemed weary, exhausted, as if she hurt all over.

"If you're looking for Cheese Puff," I said, "he's upstairs under my pillow."

Mrs. B gripped the back of a dining room chair. "Is he sick?"

"No. He's, uh, keeping a low profile. He might come down if you call. If not, I'll pry him out."

"I'll call in a moment." She sat with an audible sigh and laid her cellphone on the table. "Might I have a cup of coffee?"

As if she needed to ask. Heck, the beans I ground this morning probably came from a sack she dropped by last week. "My coffee is your coffee."

I filled a mug with a picture of Thor, bare-chested and ready to throw his hammer. No fancy cups and saucers in this condo. Besides, given a choice between drinking coffee with Thor or from a cup decorated with gold swirls or little flowers, I'd take the guy with the hammer.

"What a fine-looking man." Mrs. B turned the mug to get a better look. "Of course, Dave is also quite handsome and muscular."

I handed her a napkin. "But he's no Thor."

"Few are," she agreed.

That settled, we sipped coffee and, being in practice, I bided my time. Biding activities included rounding up a pan, measuring oatmeal, slicing a banana, digging a sack of strawberries from the freezer, and dumping a few in a bowl to thaw in the microwave.

"No job today?"

"Nothing came up." At least not before I took myself out of the running for the day. "I'm all yours if you need errands run.

212

And if Jackie calls I'll tell her to buzz off so you can save your voice."

"That's kind of you, dear." She set her mug down and folded her hands at the edge of the table. "I've never been a quitter, you know that, but this is taking more out of me than I ever dreamed. I'm starting to think it's not worth the effort."

C h a p t e r 2 6

I felt a pang of selfish loss that had little to do with the possibility of missing out on a trip to Las Vegas. "Would you feel that way if you weren't wearing an electronic ankle bracelet? If you weren't at the center of a murder investigation? If you didn't have to practice on the deck?"

"Maybe not. But everything you mentioned defines my situation." She traced the outline of Thor's hammer with her forefinger. "I haven't felt this helpless since I was a child marking the days until I could break away."

I gave the oatmeal a final stir and turned off the heat. "If you gave up the show, no one would be mad. Except maybe Allison. And she'd get over it. After a year or so."

Mrs. B flashed me a wintry smile and glanced at her cellphone. "I suppose Dario could find someone to compete against Glorree."

I thought of my Glorree-as-killer theory. "I guess she'll be relieved if she doesn't have to go up against you. She'll have a better shot at the big prize."

Mrs. B shrugged. "Probably. I wouldn't be surprised if she needed money. Glorree always lived for the day."

Up until now, I'd been thinking of this mostly as a grudge match. I hadn't considered how important the money might be to Glorree. "But if you withdrew, she wouldn't actually beat you, would she? And I bet she'd always wonder if she could have."

"Could have what?" Ten feet thudded on the stairs. Dave joined us with Cheese Puff and Lola close behind. "What are you talking about?"

"Whether Glorree Morning would wonder if she could have won—if Mrs. B drops out of *Still Got That Strut*."

"No dropping out!" Dave aimed a finger at her. "You're going to Vegas and you're going to trounce that woman."

He sounded 500 times more confident than he had half an hour ago.

Mrs. B glanced at her ankle bracelet.

"Chuck and I are working on that." Dave scooped oatmeal into a bowl and tossed strawberries on top. "We're making progress."

He sold the lie well.

"As a matter of fact, I was about to come talk to you." He poured coffee in a mug with a cartoon woodpecker wearing a crash helmet and neck brace, and brought it to the table along with his oatmeal.

"About what?" Mrs. B seemed to shrink into herself. She raised her hands as if to ward off a blow. "Should I call Angus?"

"Might be a waste of money. This is unofficial."

"All right. Perhaps I'll see where our conversation goes."

"I won't be offended if you call a halt and bring him in." Dave hooked a chair with his foot, sat, and mashed berries and oatmeal with a soup spoon. "This is awkward, so I'll get right to it. We haven't been able to come up with a solid motive for killing Big Shiny, so I'm exploring the possibility his murder was about you."

"Me?" Mrs. B's hands flew to her four-strand pearl choker.

215

"And your money," he added. "If you die—let's say sooner rather than later because of the stress of this situation—who benefits?"

She turned her sapphire gaze on me. "Why, Barbara does."

My lower jaw dropped with an audible click. Dave's loaded spoon halted halfway to his mouth. I groped my way to a chair and sat.

"Did I not tell you?"

I swallowed. Shook my head.

"Apparently you didn't," Dave said. "She's stunned into silence."

"I'm sorry." Mrs. B squeezed my hand. "I absolutely meant to right after I signed the document. But you were so stressed when you were subbing at the juvenile jail. And then Jake put up the blog and endangered the little prince." She pushed her chair away from the table and patted her lap. Cheese Puff leaped aboard and licked her chin before sniffing the table for crumbs. Lola, ever patient, waited for whatever came her way. "And we were caught up with decisions about the restaurant. I guess it just slipped my mind."

Dave stuffed his mouth and gave me a head nod and eyeball shift. Uncomfortable and emotionally off balance, I swallowed again, and made an attempt to get down to specifics. "Um . . ."

"Of course, a lot of what I've acquired will go to charities. Then there are bequests to members of the Committee and Iz and Penelope and Lana—$50,000 each. I'm forgiving my loan to Larry for the auto repair shop. And I set up college funds for Josh and Luke and Allison."

Despite the gravity of the situation, I smothered a laugh. With the grades Allison was getting, we'd have to *buy* a college for her to attend.

"I'm leaving my condo to Dario because he so loves sitting on the deck in the summer and spending time with you. And I thought he'd like my car."

I visualized Dario, wearing a gaudy Hawaiian shirt, tooling around in Mrs. B's red luxury model, a beer in the cup holder, Jim riding shotgun.

"Now some of the rest is set in stone, like the fund for your wedding and honeymoon. But your little nest egg will fluctuate depending on the markets." Mrs. B stretched out a hand. I locked fingers with her. She totted up numbers in the air with her free hand and announced a sum that nearly stopped my heart.

Dave choked and drooled oatmeal. "If that's a nest egg, it was laid by a bird the size of Vermont."

"Marco was a very good money manager. I simply followed his lead."

"I don't care how much it is." I stroked Mrs. B's fingers. "You know I'd rather have you than all the money in the world."

"That's why I'm delighted to leave it to you. But you'll have a job to do before you can relax and enjoy life." She released my hand and tapped her necklace. "You'll be in charge of liquidating my jewelry. I'd like a few pieces to go to Verna and Sybil and Paulette. And there are simple earrings that might suit Penelope and a few watches your sister may like. And you should keep anything that takes your fancy. But the rest you'll sell to establish the Cheese Puff Care and Comfort Fund."

At the sound of his name, Cheese Puff came to attention and raised his right paw in an approximation of a salute.

"Such a good boy. He learned a new trick." Mrs. B rewarded him with a kiss that left a smudge of pink lipstick on his ear. "The fund isn't for the little prince. It's for less fortunate dogs."

"Compared to him," Dave observed, "almost every dog is less fortunate."

"What about cats?" I asked.

Cheese Puff abandoned the salute and raised his upper lip in a snarl.

"We have to be fair," Mrs. B told him. "Of course the money will help cats. And rabbits and birds. My thought was you'd establish a fund that paid interest. Each year you'd distribute the interest to education programs, shelters, and spay and neuter clinics. I don't know what the laws and tax regulations are, but my accountant will help you. If you need a board of directors, I imagine members of the Committee will be happy to serve."

I nodded, still half-stunned by the amount I'd inherit—far more money than Dave and I would make in the next 20 years, even if he somehow became police chief and I got a full-time teaching job.

Dave cleared his throat. "This pretty much guts my theory."

"Unless you try to pin it on me," I said with a laugh.

"That's not funny, dear." Mrs. B seized my hand. "Sometimes your humor is just a shade too dark for my taste."

"Sorry. I should have said he'd try to pin it on Iz. I know for a fact she covets your chunky gold watch. And then there's Bernina."

Mrs. B raised her eyebrows. "But I didn't make a bequest to Bernina."

"Right. But if you, uh, took up residence, um, in the great beyond, she might make another run at setting stricter pet limits or bouncing Cheese Puff and Lola."

"If ever there was a reason to live," Dave observed, "seeing those two aren't evicted is it."

If I'd made that comment, Mrs. B would have delivered a mini-lecture about sarcasm being unattractive, but Dave skated.

"And then there's Jake," I said.

Her eyebrows shot up. "After all the aggravation he's caused, why would Jake think I'd leave him as much as a dime?"

"Jake's mind works in mysterious ways. When it works at all."

"But he's in jail."

"He has friends who aren't. But he knows his days on earth would be numbered in single digits if he was responsible for harming you." Dave stood and carried his empty bowl and mug to the counter. "I think we've just about run out of track for this train of thought."

"Except for Glorree Morning," I said. "She'd benefit if Mrs. B went to jail—or worse."

"I can't believe Glorree would do such a thing. Or that she could." Mrs. B tapped her forefinger against her chin. "Glorree had a way of losing her nerve in a pinch. She'd practice daring steps, but in the end she'd play it safe."

"And you didn't?" I asked.

Mrs. B twinkled a smile. "Never while Glorree was watching. Not that I was reckless, you understand, but Aunt Tildy used to say sometimes you can't get to the top of a mountain unless you set your feet on the toughest path. And I wanted to be on top of the mountain."

She patted Lola, gathered Cheese Puff in her arms, grabbed her cellphone, and headed for the door. "And now there's another mountain."

When she'd closed the door and lowered the canvas curtain, Dave let out a low whistle. "I knew she had money, but

I had no idea how much. Will you expect me to treat you like royalty now?"

"A little royal treatment would be nice, but I hope inheriting is a long way off." I carried my mug—emblazoned with a cartoon of the rotund President Taft in his jumbo bathtub—to the dishwasher. "What I'd really like is for you to check up on Glorree Morning. Mrs. B knew what she was like years ago, but as you always tell me, 'that day isn't this day.' Maybe she was close to Big Shiny. Maybe she knew he was living at the River Rise Inn."

"And killed him to frame Mrs. B and have a better shot at winning?" Dave scratched his chin. "I hate to use the word 'reach' because you're so fond of it, but—"

"This is about more than winning the competition and prize money. It's about beating the unbeatable Muriel Ballantine. It's about doing what she couldn't when they were young."

"Almost half a century ago," Dave scoffed

"To her that might seem like yesterday." I hooked a thumb toward the deck and the sound of tapping. "For Mrs. B, too."

Dave frowned.

"Please. Just check on where she was when it was lights out for Big Shiny."

"Lights out." Dave groaned and headed for the door. "Worst example of dark humor ever. I'll check on Glorree Morning if you promise you won't subject me to that again."

In all the excitement of loading the dishwasher and mopping the counter, I neglected to make that promise. Guaranteed groaners weren't always easy to come by. And, hey, the guy *was* killed with a lamp.

I'd taken Lola out on an excursion to the trash bins and was back at work on the dresser drawers when Gertrude Suttle called. "I know this is the last place you want to be on a day when you're not subbing, but what are the chances you could come in and have lunch?"

Eeek.

After the way Gertrude stormed out of the teachers' room, I had a feeling the invitation was about trying to win me to her side.

"I ordered pizza. Not from Ronzo's Royal Rounds. From that place with the crust you're always raving about."

Definitely an attempt to sway me. My fat cells were already caving. I had to nip this in the bud while there was still a bud to nip. "Thanks for the of—"

"Everybody will be here. Doug, Brenda, Aston, and Ardie. And Tremaine Scott says he'll drop by. And if Big Chill can—"

"Wait! Ardie will be there?"

"She's the reason we're celebrating."

"Celebrating what?"

"Guess you'll have to come and find out."

Gertrude clicked off and my fat cells clicked on, calling up visions of pizza crust thin and crisp in the center and thick and chewy on the edges. The cerebral movie shifted to toppings—mushrooms, olives, artichoke hearts, pesto, roasted garlic, sun dried toma—

"Enough!" I said. "I'm going!"

Lola raised her head and whined.

"Just talking to my fat cells, girl. It's okay."

Without questioning my mental health, Lola sneezed and resumed her nap, snugged against the wall beneath the window.

I finished off the dresser and slipped on a pair of jeans with more give in the waist. If Gertrude was buying, I'd be gorging.

Chapter 27

When I arrived at the teachers' room I found plenty to gorge on. Three huge pizza boxes lined the center of the cheery yellow tablecloth. The aroma escaping from beneath the lids made me salivate like one of Pavlov's pups.

Plates, forks, and knives marked six places at the table. Not paper plates. Not mismatched plates scavenged from other teachers' rooms. These were matching plates, simple, white, and without a chip or crack. And beside them were actual matching metal knives and forks. Not a bent tine in the bunch.

"Wow!"

Gertrude smiled. "Plastic tumblers, though. And lemon-lime cola that won't stain Doug's clothing too much. Although Ardie had a talk with Aston and he promised to be on his best behavior."

"Whatever that looks like." I hooked my purse on my usual chair.

"I hope it doesn't look like what we've seen before." Gertrude placed a tub of grated parmesan and a shaker of red pepper flakes between the boxes. "Ardie thinks if we raise the bar he might try to clear it."

That was twice in the last minute she'd quoted Ardie.

"The woman's a gem." Gertrude ducked her head and adjusted the position of the center box. "I was a total— Well, you know what I was. And I was sorry about it right away. But I felt worse this morning when I found out what she did."

"Which was?"

"I'll leave that for Ardie to tell." Gertrude raised her head. "I'm truly sorry you got caught up in my hissy fit. Can you forgive me?"

"Hmmm. Does one of those pizzas have artichoke hearts and feta cheese and chopped spinach and red onion?"

"Yes. Pesto and black olives, too."

Jackpot.

"As long as that particular pizza ends up closest to my seat, you're forgiven."

Gertrude shuffled two boxes, then produced a knife and sliced through the hinge of each lid for easy lifting when the magic moment arrived.

A few seconds later a bell rang and sounds of scuffling, shuffling, shoving, and shouting filled the hallway. The door opened and Doug shot through. "Whew." He patted his head and arms as if checking that everything was attached. "That was like crossing a river packed with crocodiles."

"Crocodiles with colds," Gertrude said. "Be sure to wash your hands before you eat."

"Aston's the one who should hear that advice." Doug shot me a grin and headed for the sink. "Although I bet his natural dirt and germs could fight off any infection a teenager threw at him."

"We're all washing from now on," Gertrude said in a steely voice. "And cleaning up after ourselves. Ardie went to a lot of trouble to freshen up this room. We need to respect her efforts—and each other."

"I'm all about that." Doug lathered his hands. "But some of us get the concept of respect to a greater degree than others."

"I hope there's meat on one of those pizzas." Aston burst in wearing a gray shirt with a torn cuff and a greenish stain shaped like Florida on the pocket. "A man needs more than a mess of namby-pamby vegetables and goat cheese."

"So much for respect," Doug muttered as he dried his hands on a paper towel.

Someone, I noted as I took my place at the sink, had filled the towel dispenser. That meant Ardie had found a way to open it, or perhaps discovered the key missing since Susan went to jail.

"As a matter of fact, I did order one with meat," Gertrude said, "but it wouldn't kill you to have a meatless meal. It might improve your digestion."

"Which would benefit the rest of us," Brenda added, signaling that their relationship was still off.

"This respect thing is working well," Doug observed. "I hope Ardie's a realist. And I hope she's tough. This group will test her patience *and* her sanity."

"She worked at the juvenile jail," I told him. "I can't vouch for her sanity, but she's long on patience. And I doubt they come much tougher."

"And here she is," Gertrude announced. "The woman of the hour."

Ardie rocketed in, all elbows and knees, moving at her usual pace—like a jagged bolt of black lightning. The only color in her outfit was the silver buckle on her black jeans and a hint of a gold filling when she smiled.

"Everyone," Gertrude said, "this is Ardette Johnson. She's a classroom aide. She started here on Monday, and last night she caught the thief who's been stealing from the Family Support Room."

Doug led a round of applause. Ardie damped it down with both hands.

"You use a trap?" Aston asked. "Or lie in wait and drop a noose?"

"Jumped through the door and asked why he needed to steal when supplies were his for the asking." Ardie aimed a finger at Aston like a gun. "You must be the guy who likes to wear leather. With fringe."

Brenda snickered and headed for the sink.

"It's historically accurate. I wear it for reenactments," Aston said in a tight voice.

"And other times," Brenda snarked. "Don't shake hands with him, Ardie, unless you've had your shots."

"And don't eat what she cooks unless you own a stomach pump in good working order," Aston shot back.

"Noted." Ardie grinned and nodded toward the sink. "Now if you'll wash up, we can get this party started."

Aston studied his hands. "Killing off natural bacteria leads to—"

"Getting a seat at the table," Gertrude said. "Wash. Or leave with your natural bacteria and the grime it's living in."

Aston eyed the pizza boxes. I raised the lid on the one in the center, releasing the aroma of sausage and pepperoni. Aston swallowed and shuffled to the sink. Ardie followed, rolling up the sleeves of her black blouse. Doug gave her a thumb up and headed for his usual seat.

"I rearranged the order a bit," Gertrude said. "I thought we all needed fresh perspective." She pointed to Aston's usual place. "You're over there, Doug. I made place cards."

"Did you sanitize the chair?"

"Better than that. Every chair in here is new. Well, new to us." Gertrude cupped her hands around her mouth and continued in a low voice. "I swapped ours to the teachers' rooms in the opposite wing."

"Those snobs deserve grungy chairs," Brenda huffed as she found her place card at the spot beside Doug. "Not one of them would sample the kumquat fruitcake with arugula icing I brought for the potluck last December."

Doug and I exchanged sidelong glances. Under duress, and the glint in Brenda's watchful eyes, we'd each taken a slice. We'd wrapped those slices in our napkins and disposed of them later.

"You're right there, Aston." Gertrude pointed at the chair closest to the sink. "And Ardie is beside you."

"Where I can keep an eye on those natural bacteria colonies." Ardie grinned, pulled out his chair, and bowed. "Barbara's on your other side. And just so you know, I've done some research on the availability of clear plastic panels. If we have to buy a couple because of your table manners, you'll get the bill."

"It's not always me," Aston grumped as he unfolded a napkin on his lap.

"It's you often enough," Doug said. "Own it like a man and move on."

"Good advice." I retrieved my purse and moved to the chair formerly Gertrude's while she popped the lids from the pizza boxes.

Aston grabbed two slices thick with meat and shiny with grease. As he reached for a third, Ardie clicked her tongue. He drew his hand back as if he'd encountered a snake, and went for pepper flakes and cheese instead.

So far, so good. But changing Aston's behavior wouldn't be a quick fix.

Fat cells humming a symphony of joy, I bit into my slice.

"Glad to see you all waited for me like one pig waits for another," Tremaine Scott boomed from the doorway.

Gertrude stood. "There isn't room for another place at the table. Take my chair. I'll sit at a desk."

Scott waved that aside. "I'll stand. Been sitting half the morning. Wilhelmina's on the phone to the central office. She'll come up later. And I can't stay more than a minute—have a couple of kids waiting for me to show them the light. But I have time for a slice." He reached past Doug and snagged a paper napkin and a triangle of the meat-laden pie. "What is it we're celebrating?"

"That's your cue," Gertrude told Ardie. "Explain how you discovered who was stealing from the Family Support Room."

Ardie set her slice of pizza—chicken, fresh tomatoes, broccoli, and onions—aside and patted her lips with a napkin. "First, it was nothing special. Anyone could have done it. Although, I have a certain knack for stillness."

Aston cocked his head and peered at her with interest.

"I checked the custodians' schedules," Ardie went on, "and figured appropriations from the Family Support Room happened on Tuesday evenings when they're shorthanded."

"Because Al is taking classes," Tremaine Scott said. "And they clean that area of the building last."

"Exactly." Ardie shot him a grin. "And once I checked with Big Chill about the history of the room, I knew how the 'appropriator' was getting in. See, six or seven years ago the student government kids used the room to store stuff they need for assemblies and proms. Before that it was old textbooks. Before that, sports uniforms."

"And no one changed the lock?" Brenda asked.

"I bet no one thought it was necessary," Gertrude said. "It's not like we're storing plutonium."

"Right," Ardie agreed. "And the key is also the same as the one used for what became the choir room five years ago. And it's a match for the office that used to be attendance and is now the registrar's."

Scott shook his head and mumbled something around a mouthful of pizza—something I won't print here.

"It's an old building," Gertrude said. "Classrooms get changed around all the time. Who knows how many keys fit other doors?"

"Or how many keys were lost over the years," I said. "Or misplaced, or abandoned in desk drawers."

Ardie pulled a key from her pocket and laid it on the table. "A kid found this one at the rear of a cabinet in the choir room."

Scott scowled. "Which kid?"

"Don't know," Ardie said. "Anyway, he traded it to another kid who traded it on. Eventually it got to the appropriator."

Scott's scowl became a glower. "And his name is?"

"I'd like to keep that confidential," Ardie said in a firm tone. She lifted her chin to show she wasn't intimidated by his expression. "Gertrude and I discussed the situation and decided meting out punishment for supplies meant to be free might be excessive, as well as self-defeating."

"And you didn't think I should be the judge of that?" The furrows in Scott's forehead deepened and his eyes practically shot fire. If I'd been the focus of his wrath, I would have taken cover beneath the table. Ardie, however, seemed unflustered.

"After you hear the rest of the story—if you still insist—we'll give you the name."

Scott kept his gaze locked on her as he reached for another slice of meaty pizza. "I'm listening."

"I hid around the corner." Ardie pulled a small mirror from the pocket that had contained the key and held it aloft. "I used this to view of the corridor. The rest was just a matter of waiting."

"You coulda had a long wait." Ignoring Gertrude's glare, Aston snatched a third slice of pizza.

"I figured the appropriator had to act while the custodians were elsewhere, and before after-school activities ended and a student roaming the halls would raise red flags." Her gaze swept the table. "And I was motivated. I had to do something big to prove I was more than an outsider who thought she could waltz in and take Susan's place."

Gertrude flushed. "Most of us don't like change we don't have a say in. We get set in our ways."

"Some of you are set like cement," Brenda said. "I'm more adventurous. *I'm* always ready to try new things. Take the fermented cabbage recipe, for example."

"You take it," Aston said. "Take it to Timbuktu. Just don't bring it here."

Scott made a slicing motion across his neck. "Back on topic."

I hid a grin behind a second slice of pizza. A topic was like a springboard for this group, a jumping-off point for flights of fancy.

Watching Aston devour his third slice, I wondered about his political plans. Was he still searching for a campaign trail? Or had he come to the conclusion that he should study issues and build a platform before tossing his coonskin cap in the ring?

"Anyway," Ardie said, "it wasn't long before I saw a young man jiggling the key in the lock. I gave him two minutes inside. Then I scared him to the middle of next week."

She rose, raised her arms, held her fingers like claws, and let out a rumbling growl. If I'd heard it on an isolated stretch of the river trail, I would have set a new personal best for the 100-yard dash.

(For the record, my previous personal best was so slow my high school gym teacher asked if I was clear on the difference between walking and running.)

"The kid dropped a sack of rice and fell to his knees," Ardie continued.

"He didn't try to run?" Aston asked.

"He confessed, said he was sorry, and understood we'd have to throw him out of school for stealing." Ardie sat and picked up her slice of pizza. "Said if he didn't get sent to jail, he'd get a job and pay for what he took."

"He didn't know it was all free?" I asked.

"He knew there was no cost for enrolled students and their immediate families," Gertrude said. "But he was taking supplies for his cousin and her baby. They're refugees from Guatemala." She raised her chin and aimed the next words at Scott. "Refugees from gang violence that killed her husband. Undocumented refugees."

"Ah." The furrows in his brow smoothed out. "Have you dealt with situations like this before?"

"A few," Gertrude said. "On my own time."

"I didn't ask that." Scott reached for his wallet and opened it. Bills fluttered to the table. "That's all I have on me at the moment." He turned toward the door. "Keep me posted. Let me know what I can do. Thanks for lunch."

Gertrude and Ardie gave each other a high-five followed by a long hug. Doug reached for his wallet. I reached for my purse. Aston reached for another slice of pizza. Brenda reached across the table and slapped his hand.

Life in the teachers' room was back to normal.

Chapter 28

As I drove home I thought about the boy willing to take such a risk for his cousin. Family bonds could be a powerful cohesive force. But if those bonds fractured and fell apart, individuals were often left adrift.

I thought of my parents, undoing the bonds when Iz and I were young. I thought of Mrs. B, leaving parents who put pride before her well-being. I thought of the "family" she and I had now. Mrs. Ballantine was my anchor, a font of wisdom, a woman I admired and trusted. And I was . . . well, along with being a source of amusement, I was her work in progress.

What kinds of risks would I take for my cobbled-together family? What kind of sacrifices would I make?

Would I steal?

If we were cold and hungry, sure.

Would I kill?

If my family was threatened and I felt I had no choice, possibly.

But I wouldn't steal money I was able to live without. And I certainly wouldn't commit murder because an opportunity presented itself and I bet I wouldn't be caught.

My mind drifted to Glorree Morning. Had she ever had children? Had she ever "adopted" a family?

I recalled Peabody Fontaine's blog. I'd bookmarked it in my computer but hadn't had time to return to it. Now the afternoon stretched before me.

So, after taking Lola out for a squat, I got a cola, shoved a stack of bills to one side of the desk, and settled in my office chair. Five minutes later I was immersed in the world of feathers, soaring headdresses, glittering costumes made from mere scraps of fabric, and long, shapely legs. Despite catty comments about a few specific competitors and performances, Peabody was over the moon about *Still Got That Strut*. He waxed poetic about flexibility, supple strength, and smooth skin. He went into enormous detail about shoes, beads, rhinestones, chains, chokers, and fringe.

He interviewed contestants, dishing details of their days onstage and the years since. He rehashed rumors, and shared diet, exercise, and beauty tips. And he illustrated his words with photographs, many from his personal archives. There was Mrs. Ballantine, wearing a few square inches of jeweled fabric, high-kicking her way across a stage in spindly heels. And there was Glorree Morning, strutting in a cloud of ostrich feathers and not much else.

She appeared to be several inches taller than Mrs. B. Her hair was blond and shining, her lipstick and mascara dramatic and applied with precision. Her smile beamed wide and her eyes sparkled. But I felt something was missing.

I found another photograph of her from that time and had the same feeling.

Was it me?

Was everything I knew about Glorree Morning undermining my objectivity?

Maybe.

I tried to blank my mind.

As you probably guessed, that worked as well as attempting to cancel out the dietary damage of pecan pie by eating a second slice to make my digestive system work harder and burn more calories.

(For the record, I never believed the strategy might work. I did, however, know a girl in college who insisted the theory was sound. She never passed on dessert. She also never went near a scale. Or a mirror. I admired that about her.)

I got up, walked down the hall, stretched, returned, and peered at the pictures again. Still something missing.

What I needed was a fresh set of eyes—eyes that weren't my own. I thought of Verna and Sybil and other members of the Cheese Puff Care and Comfort Committee. Sybil was flighty and apt to focus on feathers instead of facial features. Verna would want to know why she should waste her time.

Penelope was still off on the high-paying job in Olympia. And my sister would deliver a lecture on female exploitation.

That left Paulette and Lana.

I copied the photo, pasted it in an e-mail and zipped it off. To keep from tipping the judgment scales, I didn't identify the showgirl. I asked for their impressions of the picture and the woman. On a whim, I sent a copy to Allison.

Then I surfed to Peabody Fontaine's blog and the post about the upcoming competition between Glorree Morning and Mrs. B—or "The Marvelous Muriel" as she was known then. She'd declined to be interviewed until she arrived in Las Vegas, but Glorree had invited Peabody to her home and they'd "chatted over a bottle of bubbly." A photo showed them clinking glasses. She wore a flowing, floor-length red dress with a nipped-in waist. He wore a maroon velvet jacket too tight around his ample middle.

I scanned the text and found she'd worked as a hostess at a number of clubs—places where slinky dresses and sparkly jewelry were the uniform. She hinted at liaisons and dalliances, spoke of trips to exotic locations, and displayed a diamond as large as any I'd seen Mrs. B wear. But she refused to name the men she'd been involved with. And she adamantly denied rumors she'd had a child.

Despite her denials, Peabody shared salacious details of those rumors. A late-life baby girl had supposedly been born in a private clinic not far from Las Vegas one winter when Glorree claimed to be vacationing in the Caribbean. Gossip held the child had been adopted or perhaps fostered by a family in Arizona or possibly New Mexico or even in Nevada.

Hmmm.

All of this was juicy stuff, but rumors raised more questions. Who was the father? Did he know his sperm had found an egg? Was the child fostered or adopted? Did Glorree contribute to the child's upkeep? Did the father? Were there records? Could I get my hands on them?

I swiveled my chair and swung my feet to the corner of the desk. Adopted children often tried to find their biological parents. And searching had become easier thanks to open records and the Internet. Had Glorree's daughter found her? Had they established a relationship?

Grabbing a pencil, I did a little rudimentary math on the back of a bill from the power company. Glorree was maybe a little older than Mrs. B whose exact age, as I've mentioned before, has never been revealed. I guesstimated it at 70, felt guilty, and lowered it to 69. No, 68.

Now, how late could a late-life baby arrive?

I put the question to the Internet. It delivered a wide range of ages and articles. For absolutely no reason, I picked 43. That would make Glorree's child around 27, give or take.

So what did that have to do with anything?

Not much. Except, if the bonds of family were strong, Glorree might do anything to help her child—like framing her chief competitor to win a pot of money and provide a secure future. Or, conversely, Glorree's child might—

My phone rang, derailing my train of thought.

"I hope she got the dental work she needed," Lana said. "And found something that worked for foot and back pain."

"Huh?"

"The woman in the picture you sent." She raised her voice above the scrape of metal on metal. "Can you hear me okay? Jim's cleaning the grill."

"I hear you fine. My mind was drifting."

Lana laughed. "You're not in a classroom, are you?"

"No, I'm home today."

"Good thing, otherwise who knows what kids might get up to while you're distracted."

No kidding. The last time I lost focus for more than a few seconds, a kid clambered up on a table with the intention of demonstrating an aerial somersault.

"Anyway, I'm no expert, but I've seen a lot of faces over the years and it looks like her lower jaw is too small for her teeth. And arching her spine to compensate for those high heels probably took a toll. She may have sciatic nerve issues or plantar fasciitis or bunions."

Lana, who'd waited tables for many years, was an expert on foot problems.

I scrolled to the picture of Glorree Morning in her feathers and frills. "I can't see her lower teeth."

"I bet they're crooked. That's why she's smiling with just the upper row."

Interesting.

I'd have to ask Mrs. B if she ever noticed Glorree's teeth.

"If you're alone and there's no one to ask what you're doing," Lana said, "put yourself in that pose. See what your body says."

I studied Glorree Morning's posture, then stood on tiptoe and imitated her pose. In a few seconds the tendons in my legs screamed for mercy, my toes threatened to secede from my feet, and a muscle in my lower back did that twinge and pull thing indicating a spasm wasn't far off.

"My body says I shouldn't do that."

But Glorree Morning, if she wanted to keep her job, had to do it every day, for hours at a time. And, while Mrs. B married a man who took her away from all that, Glorree kept working. I scrolled to the shot of her toasting Peabody Fontaine. Her smile revealed just about all the teeth in her mouth. Somewhere along the line she'd had dental surgery.

"And there's that headdress," Lana said. "It must weigh a dozen pounds or more. That adds up to a pain in the neck."

No wonder Mrs. Ballantine had a bag of frozen veggies on the back of her neck the other day. I glanced around, spotted a dictionary, and decided to see what it felt like to tote weight on my skull while trying to balance in high heels. Up until now, although I hadn't scoffed at what was involved in being a showgirl, I certainly hadn't appreciated the strength and conditioning and coordination necessary to simply walk across the stage in full regalia. And Mrs. B and Glorree Morning had not only walked, but danced and twirled and kicked as well.

"Gotta run," Lana said. "We're testing sandwiches. From the way Jim's cursing, I think one flunked."

"Thanks for the help."

I clicked off, balanced the dictionary on my head, stood on tiptoe, and headed down the hallway. Two steps later the book hit the floor. Good thing I'd chosen a career where I could wear flats and didn't wear anything on my head except an occasional hair clip.

Returning to the office, I parked the dictionary on the desk and studied the picture of Glorree Morning again. Something about her was familiar. I held my hand over the screen and moved it up and down, alternately blocking out and revealing Glorree's facial features.

Not the eyes.

Not the nose.

But that chin.

That chin reminded me of someone.

I ran through a mental list of friends and got nothing. They were all in the square- or rounded-lower-jaw camp. Not a pointy chin among them. Even petite Paulette had a rounded chin—dainty, but still rounded.

I was about to take advantage of my alone time by napping and painting my toenails, when my cellphone rang.

"That's Glorree Morning," Allison said in a hollow voice with a trailing echo. "Didn't you know? Mrs. B showed me a picture of her like way last year."

Mrs. B hadn't agreed to participate in *Still Got That Strut* until a few months ago, but I didn't question Allison's last sentence for three reasons. First, Allison loved to page through Mrs. B's scrapbooks and photo albums and it's possible she knew who Glorree Morning was before Mrs. B learned they'd be matched as competitors. Second, questioning Allison often led to a yes/no discussion that gave me a headache. And third, a larger issue loomed, one triggered by a glance at my watch. "Where are you calling from? Why aren't you in history class?"

"The girls' room. History is boorrring. And you said this was important."

That last was a pants-on-fire statement if I ever heard one. But, as I pointed out earlier, my goal was to avoid a headache-inducing discussion, so I said nothing.

Allison apparently took my silence as permission to unload her impressions. "She looks like she's pretending she's happy, but she's really in a bad mood only she can't show it or she might get in trouble. And she looks stiff and like her ankles are about to wobble."

"Thanks," I said. "Now you bet—"

"I'm not finished. And someone should have told her not to hold her head so high because it makes her chin look pointier. It's a witchy chin, like that pushy-pushy Jackie has. Okay, now I'm done."

Before she disconnected, I heard her launch into a discussion of lipstick shades with another girl killing time in the restroom. I hoped she hadn't told her history teacher I needed to talk with her. No way did I want to be used as an excuse to skip out of class—even if it was possible Allison's teacher, a no-nonsense woman counting down to retirement—might be relieved to have her gone for a few minutes. Not that Allison was a troublemaker—at least not a major-league troublemaker. But her inability to focus and her lack of desire to do more than the minimum could be contagious.

However, she'd certainly focused on the photo of Glorree Morning. And she'd come up with Jackie DeWill.

Chapter 29

I trotted to the office, brought up Jackie's picture on my phone, and compared it to the shot of Glorree on the computer screen. Jackie was shorter, and more bony than buxom, but the pointy chins were identical. So were the thin, arched eyebrows.

I told myself two facial characteristics meant absolutely nothing. But my brain busily estimated Jackie's age, did the math, and came up with the possibility she could be Glorree's daughter.

If there was substance to the rumors of a child. *If* the child was a daughter. *If* the daughter snagged a position with *Still Got That Strut*.

If all of the above was true, was landing a job with the program more than coincidence? Did Jackie know the identity of her mother? Had she wormed her way into a position with the show to tip the balance in favor of Glorree Morning? Was that why she was so insistent on seeing Mrs. B's routine and costumes?

And if all of that was true, how far would she go to make certain her mother won?

My mind jumped to conclusions with the speed and agility of an Olympic hurdler. I imagined Jackie making off with a lamp from Mrs. B's room and using it to bludgeon Big Shiny.

But wait!

Why Big Shiny?

I slumped in my chair, tapping the phone against my chin.

The man had been living in seclusion for years. He was so far off the radar he might as well be at the bottom of a mineshaft. He—

But wait!

What if Glorree Morning had been involved with him? What if that involvement resulted in a baby? What if Big Shiny left Glorree in the lurch and refused to acknowledge the child? Or, what if she didn't want acknowledgement or an on-going relationship with him? What if she'd settled for cash? And what if she'd kept track of him over the years? What if Jackie learned who he was and where he was? What if she blamed him for her life with a foster family? What if she realized she could kill him, get revenge for her mother, and frame Mrs. B at the same time?

Question marks hooked each other, forming a chain in my brain.

I stood and turned in a tight circle.

I had to tell Mrs. B.

I had to tell Dave.

I had—

I had not one shred of evidence.

All my suppositions hung on pointy chins and arching brows.

And wouldn't Detective Charles Atwell howl with laughter when I explained how I took those facial features and came up with not one, but two motives for murder?

As for Dave, while he might not howl, he'd undoubtedly insinuate that I should leave the detecting to trained professionals.

Dizzy from pacing circles, I left the office and paced the hall.

It was obvious—at least to me—those professionals wouldn't consider my theory. They wouldn't check the baby rumors or Jackie's background. They wouldn't check whether Jackie had hopped a plane the day Big Shiny was killed. They wouldn't compare her image to video from the River Rise Inn. They wouldn't get her DNA. And they most definitely wouldn't bring her in for questioning.

Meanwhile, Mrs. B would remain the prime suspect. She'd become more drained and defeated, more depressed and discouraged.

Well, not on my watch!

I'd nail Jackie DeWill. And I'd uncover the truth. I'd find out if this chin stuff was coincidental or biological. If it turned out she was Glorree's daughter I'd—

Okay, I didn't know *what* I'd do.

But I knew someone who always had an idea.

And I knew someone else who wasn't overly picky about whether he colored outside the legal lines.

An hour later, Paulette and I hunched over my computer screen. I'd enlarged the shot of Jackie and placed it beside the photo of young Glorree Morning.

"Definitely the same chin," Paulette said. "And the bone structures under those brows appear to match. But . . ."

"I know. The rest is a leap."

"A world-record leap."

We sighed in unison and leaned back in our chairs. Paulette, being in Dave's chair with the loose wheel and sprung springs, didn't lean too far.

"Whatever we do, we can't tell Mrs. Ballantine," I said. "If I'm wrong she'll be wound up for no reason, and won't be able to focus on her routine."

"And if you're right, she'll be wound up for a good reason, and still won't focus on her routine."

We sighed again.

Paulette smoothed already perfect hair. "Maybe you should run it past Dave."

"You think?"

"No," she said after a moment. "Odds are he'll laugh. And even if he doesn't, he'll tell you to stay out of it while they do things by the book."

(For the record, I have no problem with doing things by the book. *If* the book in question is an abridged version, or a fast read, or supports my theories and plans. Otherwise . . .)

"And if things go sideways, Dave won't be happy." Paulette flipped her hand, displaying perfectly manicured nails painted lime green and black to match her sweater and slacks. "And Detective Atwell will be livid."

"He kind of starts at livid."

"Well, he'll be a human volcano if we solve the case." Paulette did the finger flip thing again. "Yet another reason to get Dario involved. He makes a great shield."

"Plus, he can get Jackie up here so they can arrest her without a bunch of red tape or jurisdiction questions or whatever."

"*If* she's guilty," Paulette reminded me.

"Right." I massaged my temples. "If."

242

You wouldn't think such a tiny word would be so vital. But "if" was a hinge for a door that swung both ways. If we accused Jackie and she was innocent, there would be repercussions.

"We have to be careful about what we say. We have to be subtle," Paulette mused. "We need a well-thought-out plan. And a script."

Not our strengths. Especially the well-thought-out and subtle parts. "Let's call Dario. He might have ideas."

I dialed.

"Is Muriel all right?" he asked in a strained voice pitched higher than his usual rumble. "They haven't hauled her to jail, have they?"

"No. She's fine. Well, not really fine," I babbled. "Tired, but okay."

"If she wants to pull out of the show, tell her I'm okay with that."

"She knows. Right now she intends to stick it out." I switched the phone to speaker mode. "Paulette's here. We have something to run by you. Are you alone?"

"For the next five minutes. Then I have a meeting."

"Five it is." I zipped him an e-mail with the side-by-side pictures attached. "I'm sending you pictures of Glorree Morning and Jackie DeWill. Paulette and I see a family resemblance. But we've been wrong before."

"Although not often," Paulette insisted.

"Hang on," Dario said. "Gotta get my cheaters."

Paulette and I waited—me gnawing at my thumbnail, Paulette fishing a tissue from the box at the edge of the desk and using it to dust the monitor and keyboard. Have I mentioned we're not from the same end of the gene pool?

"Huh," Dario said. "I wouldn't want to make book on it, but it's possible. I heard talk Glorree had a kid."

"Was there talk about who the father was?" Paulette asked.

"Nothing specific. Glorree ran with a lot of guys. She was always looking to trade up, especially after Muriel took off with Marco. And later, when the years piled on."

Drat.

"Where are you going with this?" Dario asked.

I hauled in a deep breath and spun my theory about Jackie murdering the mobster and framing Mrs. B to help Glorree triumph on *Still Got That Strut*. To keep things short and less complicated I left out the possibility that Big Shiny was Jackie's father.

"Huh. What does Dave say? And that detective? What's he think?"

"Um, I haven't, uh, shared this with them. It seems a little, uh, thin."

"Flimsy's what it is," Dario said. "Almost transparent. But I'd bet more on one of your gut feelings than on what a computer spits out. You got a plan?"

Paulette smiled and nudged me. "That's also flimsy."

"The one thing we're sure about is that we shouldn't tell Mrs. Ballantine what we're up to. She's under enough stress."

"She won't hear it from me. What do you need?"

"We need to get Jackie up here," Paulette said.

"And we need to put pressure on her, shake her up," I added. "Although I have no idea how."

"I might," Dario said. "Got a meeting. I'll call back."

I knew enough about meetings to realize they sometimes took on a life of their own, so I hunkered down in the office with a mug of decaf and Peabody Fontaine's blog. Paulette, meanwhile, rearranged the notice sheet and photos on the bulletin board beside the door to the parking lot. The board had been set up by members of the Cheese Puff Care and Comfort Committee—all of whom had keys to my condo—as a way of communicating with each other. In the early days of the CPCCC, they shared information about Cheese Puff's walks and snacks so he didn't get overtired or overfed. But postings soon expanded to include snapshots of outings and restaurant reviews.

I seldom passed the board without suffering pangs of envy. The dog got out and about more than I did. Wearing a tiny cape, he'd gone to the opera. Clad in plaid, he'd attended the Highland games. Outfitted with a wide leather belt and a rubber hatchet, he traveled to a timber carnival. And don't get me started on the restaurants he'd dined at and the gourmet meals he'd tasted.

There was a time I'd thought about restricting Cheese Puff's outings and his consumption of high-calorie "human" treats. But when I realized how tiny those treats were and how much he meant to the Committee, I canned the idea. If he showed signs of illness, I'd revisit my concerns.

As for that jealousy thing—if I really wanted a richer and more varied lifestyle, I could have one. Of course, it would involve wearing something besides T-shirts and jeans, and getting Dave to do likewise. Since neither of us owned much else, we'd need to shop. Then we'd have to bust the budget for tickets and meals at trendy restaurants.

Since Dave and I were more walk-along-the-river types, dressing up and dining out had limited appeal. And when it came to food, tiny dollops of special sauce or crisscrossing drizzles of toppings on small portions prompted Dave to suggest we go out later for a real meal. It wasn't that he was all about volume, but he preferred to leave the table satisfied, not tantalized.

As I turned my attention to Peabody's discussion of the correct methods of cleaning and mending showgirl costumes, Paulette moved along the hallway, straightening pictures. In a few minutes I heard her making "tsk" sounds. Those were followed a request that Lola move so she could reposition the sofa. Lola apparently shifted, because I heard a couple of grunts, followed by whacking sounds I assumed were efforts to beat cushions into shape. Those were followed by exclamations.

"I can't believe it! I can't believe no one noticed this!"

Hoping what I hadn't noticed wouldn't involve a massive expenditure for repairing, reupholstering, or replacing, I trudged to the living room.

Holding a seat cushion upright, Paulette stood beside the sofa. "I can't believe it," she repeated. "How could you not notice?"

Chapter 30

Paulette pointed to what lay beneath the cushion—a dozen cat toys. Squeaky mice crowded against plastic balls containing bells and those crowded against catnip-stuffed felt birds with tufts of dyed feathers.

She tossed the cushion to the floor and lifted the next one, revealing even more cat toys. The third cushion went up, uncovering another trove. "Not one of you noticed the lumps?"

I winced. "Um, well, we all noticed."

"But no one lifted the cushions?"

The answer was apparent, so I said nothing, not even that I'd wondered if stuffing got old and lumpy. Let's face it, when it comes to housekeeping, I'm not in Paulette's league. I wouldn't even be allowed to wash sweaty towels in her league. So what I said was, "Mrs. Ballantine wondered where all the cat toys went. Cheese Puff must have stolen them and stuffed them under the cushions."

I got a paper bag from the pantry and plunged on. "I bet he thought if he made off with enough toys, Mrs. B might decide having the cat around was too expensive. Then he'd have her all to himself."

Paulette pitched in and helped me load toys in the bag. "Seriously? You're giving him credit for complex thinking *and* knowledge of finance. My guess is he was motivated by jealousy. He took them to spite Apricot."

Jealousy was a powerful motive. I agreed with that. But I wasn't sure I bought Paulette's statement about the limits of Cheese Puff's thought processes. In the year and a half he'd owned me, I'd seen him snub my ex, save my life, and irritate a drug dealer into rash and stupid behavior. Okay, so his decision to try to trounce a rogue duck wasn't the smartest, but still, the spoiled little mutt was crafty. Not to mention sneaky.

I carried the bag to the door and listened. Mrs. B was tapping away, and carrying on a one-sided conversation with someone. Since the curtained deck area was off limits to humans, I assumed she was directing her comments to Cheese Puff. I hoped he at least appeared to be attentive. Wouldn't want her to write him out of the will.

Not that I thought she would. They had a bond. And learning the little darling had stolen a few dozen cat toys wouldn't break it. In fact, it would give her a laugh—a laugh she badly needed.

I was about to request permission to enter the tent when the phone rang.

"Dario." Paulette sprinted for the office in her kitten heels, moving faster than I did in shoes specifically designed for dashing.

"Here's what I got," Dario said. "I tell Jackie cops are making zero progress and we better plan to shoot in an alternative location. I say Muriel's attorney can arrange for her to travel up to 25 miles, so we gotta look at close-in venues. First on my list will give us free publicity and social media buzz."

He paused long enough for me to think of, and eliminate, at least half a dozen venues in the area. From the way Paulette's eyes tracked back and forth, I imagined she was doing the same. "Where?" she asked.

"The River Rise Inn."

"You're a genius," I blurted. "If Jackie killed Big Shiny, being sent to the scene of the crime should shake her up."

"Unless she has nerves of steel," Paulette said.

"Titanium, tungsten, whatever," Dario said with a chuckle. "My money says you two can rub those nerves raw. Meet Jackie at the airport in the morning and drive her to the inn."

"We're on it." Paulette gave me a high-five.

"I'll tell Farley to see you get anything you need. He's called every day to apologize for not knowing about Big Shiny. He'll turn himself inside out to help you."

"Wait a minute," I said. "You're not coming?"

"Can't get away."

Rats.

When you looked up "intimidating" in the dictionary, there was a picture of Dario. I'd been counting on having him in the background.

Fortunately, I knew someone who could intimidate almost as well. Someone who was between jobs and desperate for funds. Someone able to fray nerves faster than Paulette and I could, even working together after a full breakfast and three cups of coffee.

I hung up and uttered the name.

"No!" Paulette shrieked.

"Think about it," I urged.

"No."

"Come on."

"No." She leaped to her feet and trotted to the dining room.

249

I followed, not exactly begging, but heavily into beseech mode. "You're the one who's always telling me to have an open mind."

"No. No. No. No. No. Never." She seized her purse and headed for the door. "Involving your sister is a recipe for disaster."

I planted my feet and flung out my arms, blocking the narrow hallway.

Paulette came to a halt inches away. "It will be a calamity. A catastrophe. A full-fledged fiasco."

"True. Exactly why she'll be perfect for what I have in mind."

"If what you have in mind is a meltdown."

I abandoned beseeching in favor of commanding. "Don't be the kind of closed-minded pinhead you despise. Don't reject this without hearing me out. If you come up with a better plan, I'll listen to every tiny detail."

Paulette clamped her teeth on her lower lip, then turned and sulked her way to the sofa where she fluffed the cushions, restored them to their correct positions, and sat. "I'm listening. What do you intend to have Iz do, sit on Jackie and squeeze out a confession?"

"No." That idea had merit—but only as a final resort. "Although my plan does make use of a few of her major attributes."

"Bad attitude and general scariness?" Paulette asked.

"Exactly."

Plopping in Cheese Puff's favorite chair, I delivered a rough verbal sketch of my plan.

Paulette balked only once more.

Given her love of fashion, I couldn't blame her.

Late in the afternoon, with schemes made, contingencies considered, and Farley Dole alerted, Paulette took off to round up the necessary costumes. Her exit was not without much muttering about mice and men and plans going south, north, or even sideways.

I gritted my teeth, girded my loins, and called my sister. Dispensing with social niceties, I got right to it. "I need you to do something with me tomorrow."

"Does it pay?"

For a moment I flirted with the idea of asking Iz to do it for the sake of family. Then I did a reality check. "Yes."

"How much?"

I pulled a number from the air. "Two hundred dollars."

"Hmmph."

"And lunch." Letting Iz loose, even on a lunch menu, might cost me another 40 bucks. But, after all, I was an heiress now. Never mind that I hoped I wouldn't collect on that inheritance for decades.

"I guess that's better than nothing," she grumped. "What is it we're doing?"

"Saving the day."

"Right. Have you been drinking?"

"No. Paulette will fill you in when she picks you up."

"I hope she won't be driving that soup-can-sized car. Why small people can't be bothered to consider the comfort of those of us who—"

"See you tomorrow."

Cutting my sister off in mid rant felt good. As I hung up, I vowed to do it more often.

Dave trudged through the bedroom door shortly before 11:00. He looked like Frankenstein's monster would if he'd been dragged behind a hay wagon across a hundred miles of ant

251

hills, delivered to the gate of Count Dracula's castle wearing a sign that read BLOOD DONOR, scraped up the next morning by a bulldozer, and driven home through a demolition derby.

"Tough day?" I asked with a relatively straight face.

He opened his mouth, then shook his head and fell forward, landing beside me. Cheese Puff yipped and bolted for cover beneath the bed. Lola raised her head, sneezed, and went back to sleep.

I slid from beneath the covers and tugged at the knotted laces of his running shoes. "No progress, huh?"

He didn't answer. I took that to mean "No," and pulled off his shoes and socks. Holding my nose, I carried those to the clothes hamper. The scent almost made me long for the Captain Meriwether gym.

Flopping to his back, Dave unbuckled and unzipped. Grasping the hems and alternating right leg and left, I pulled off jeans stained with grease, catsup, and substances I decided not to ask about. By the time I tossed them on top of the socks and closed the lid on the hamper in the fond hope it might contain some of the odor, he had removed his T-shirt and burrowed beneath the sheet.

I turned out my light and massaged his neck. "No leads on the person who came to Mrs. B's room with fresh light bulbs and got her to handle the lamp?"

"Nobody saw her."

"Are you and Detective Atwell certain that jealousy couldn't be a motive—or part of a motive—for Big Shiny's murder?"

He snorted.

"I mean that maybe someone was jealous of Mrs. Ballantine."

"We went through this, remember? I checked on Glorree Morning. She hasn't been out of Las Vegas for months. She's been practicing. She thinks she'll win."

"That's what she has to say. And maybe she believes it." I went from massaging to squeezing gently. "Let's suppose someone decided to lend her a hand. Someone close to her. Very close. Let's suppose maybe she knew, but maybe she didn't. Let's sup—"

"Let's suppose," Dave said in a voice that tightened with every word, "that I have to be at the River Rise Inn first thing in the morning and question everyone on the staff again. Let's suppose I need to sleep. Let's suppose you let me do that."

Grasping a pillow, he anchored it over his head.

I shrugged.

You can't say I didn't try to share my theory.

I guess he could tell me what he thought after it all played out tomorrow. If it played out.

The next morning, as I inched along behind a dozen other vehicles cycling through the arrival area at the Portland Airport, I reminded myself that our plan—such as it was—required me to be vague. My job was to run off at the mouth, hint there were plenty of beans to be spilled about the investigation, and try to rattle Jackie. Apply pressure. Let up on it. Rinse, and repeat.

Jackie flung herself from a revolving door carrying a light jacket and a purse the size of the average backpack lugged around Captain Meriwether. Her hair was even darker, shorter, and spikier than the last time I saw her. She wore jeans and a T-shirt with the show's logo—the silhouette of a showgirl kicking high. Frowning, she scanned the area. I ducked my head for the count of 30, then tooted the horn and waved.

"I could have rented a car," she informed me after I unlatched the passenger door from the inside and issued instructions about lifting while pulling. Her emphasis on the word "car" made it clear mine didn't meet her definition. "I don't understand why Dario insisted on this arrangement."

253

"I guess he thought you might need help finding the venues on the list. And taking all the measurements and stuff." I flashed a bright and—hopefully—innocent smile.

"I don't." She set her purse on the floor and snapped her seatbelt. "I know how to read a map. And I'm good at my job."

"Oh, I'm certain you're very good at what you do." I pulled away from the curb and did the accelerate-brake thing for a few hundred yards. "But, just in case, I'll be right by your side all day."

Jackie's scowl told me that was the last place she wanted to find me. I flashed another smile and stomped the accelerator. After a few seconds of chugging and lugging, my car responded with a burst of speed. We closed on the pickup ahead.

"Watch out." Jackie braced herself against the dash.

I made the brakes squeal.

"Is this the way you usually drive?"

"Of course not. Usually I'm the queen of caution, but Dario said you'd be in a hurry. He said you're almost always in a hurry."

"Did he? Well, unlike *some people*, I don't like to waste time."

"Right." I swung to the right lane, hit the gas, and cut close in front of the pickup. "I totally understand. I'll get you to the River Rise as fast as I can. Then we'll head over to Portland and check out the second venue. Although, now that there's a private detective on the job, I think this is a wasted trip. Mrs. Ballantine will be cleared to go to Las Vegas in no time."

Give Jackie credit, she waited almost half a minute before scratching her curiosity itch. "I thought the case against her was solid."

"Between you and me, it's as solid as Swiss cheese. And Angus Drummond III is an expert on sliding clients through holes in the evidence. If the private detective—she's really aggressive—can make a few of those holes bigger by, you know, casting suspicion on someone else, I bet the prosecutor won't even take this to trial."

"That's the way it goes," Jackie snarked, "when you have the bucks to pay people to pull off the blindfold and tip the scales of justice."

"Huh?" I played dumb—really dumb. "Mrs. Ballantine isn't paying a sculptor to make a new statue of that justice lady."

"It was a metaphor," Jackie said from between gritted teeth.

"Okaaaaay."

"I thought you were an English teacher."

"I'm still a substitute," I said in a tone implying that identifying metaphors was a rite of passage to a permanent position. If, indeed, Jackie's image was actually a metaphor.

We bucketed across the bridge and swung off on the ramp to Highway 14, then east into the Columbia Gorge on the north side of the river. When the highway burrowed through thick stands of trees and gained elevation in a series of turns, I did a few more gas/brake rotations. Sneaking peeks from the corners of my eyes, I checked Jackie's reaction. When she was green around the gills and swallowing hard, I settled to a steady 45.

C h a p te r 3 1

Even though I'd memorized directions and distances, the turnoff appeared before I expected it. I stomped the brake, spun the wheel, and leaned to my left in a futile attempt to help the car along.

Jackie squealed louder than the tires. "You're a maniac. They should yank your license."

"Sorry."

We made the turn and I over-compensated to the right. Jackie bounced against the door.

"Sorry again."

Not.

While she was still rocking in her seat, I planted a few mental seeds. "I guess I wasn't paying attention. I was thinking about the private detective, you know, the one I told you about. Ivy Zinnia. She goes by Iz. No wonder. I mean, what kind of a name is Ivy Zinnia? Maybe that's why she's so tough. Because of her name."

Jackie, who had both feet and both hands braced, said nothing.

"Anyway, she's closed a few major cases where the cops were stumped. Cold cases. Hot cases. It doesn't matter to Iz.

She's at the River Rise Inn right now, interviewing everyone on the staff."

I paused to take another turn, this one to the right, and babbled on. "They say it's almost like she's a human lie detector. They say all someone has to do is say 'Hello' and she knows if they'll tell the truth. But enough about her. Tell me about you and your job. Where did you grow up? Are you excited to be working on *Still Got That Strut*? Did you have to go to college to get a job like yours? Have you met Glorree Morning? What's she like? Is her routine spectacular?"

Jackie described her job with a few terse sentences, and then added that she grew up in Nevada and took a few college theater classes. She said Glorree Morning was "professional" and "a pleasure to work with." She dodged my question about Glorree's routine by saying she couldn't discuss a performance.

I navigated a few more twists and turns, prattling about what different lives Mrs. B and Glorree Morning had and how maybe that gave Glorree an advantage because she hadn't been retired as long and was more motivated by the financial prize.

Jackie's body language—clenched hands and clamped jaw—indicated she longed to give me significantly more than her two cents. But she held her silence.

I yanked the car through another turn as the road twisted into deep shadows along a stream. Steep slopes rose on either side, slopes thick with fir and spruce, fallen branches and looming stumps. Ferns and blackberry bushes crowded the pavement. Fronds and canes seemed to reach for us as we approached and wave farewell as we passed. Moss grew thick on gravel shoulders no wider than my hand and, in places, crept onto the road itself.

The scenery reminded me of Longfellow's description of the forest primeval at the beginning of *Evangeline*. I felt confined and claustrophobic, and hoped Jackie felt the same.

Slowing, I gave us a few more minutes of Pacific Northwest atmosphere, tossing out stories about hikers wandering from trails never to be seen again, and speculating that Bigfoot would find this area ideal.

Sunlight sliced through trees ahead and the road threaded between a pair of stacked stone columns holding back the forest. The pavement widened and became a broad parking area before the River Rise Inn. The weathered log and rock façade of the main building drew attention away from the more ordinary extensions that angled behind it. The inn welcomed visitors with shallow stone steps leading to a wide plank porch and a pair of massive doors twice my height with iron handles as long as my arm. A dozen tall windows flanked the doors. Through the set on the left I glimpsed small chandeliers and tables covered with white cloths. Dining room—according to what I'd researched on the Internet. The registration area and lobby would be to the right as we entered. And the ballroom would be beyond.

As I parked in one of a hundred vacant spaces, I spotted Detective Atwell's car and, nearby, Paulette's sporty model. Good. Everything should be in place. If we got past Dave and Atwell, and if Iz played her part without too much embellishment, we might get results.

I shut down the engine and tossed my car key in the console. Then I went all clumsy getting out, bracing my hand on the radio, pushing in the knob that turned it on, and rotating it clockwise.

"You're leaving your key?" Jackie asked.

"Sure." I pointed at Paulette's car. "Who would steal this wreck when there are better choices? Besides, the top of the key broke, so it won't stay on the ring. It snags in my pocket, and it gets lost in my purse."

After a shake of the head and a brief bout of wrestling with the passenger door, Jackie got out.

"Leave it ajar," I advised. "It's not going to rain."

She shook her head again, retrieved her purse, and checked through gear including a laptop, giant tape measure and sound and light meters.

"Crud. My shoe's untied." I bent beside the front tire on the driver's side and put the next phase of the plan into action.

That completed, I took two steps, claimed the other lace was loose, and squatted by the rear tire.

Mission accomplished without Jackie noticing, I caught up with her and did more to set the scene as we trekked along the stone walkway bisecting an expanse of grass that could double as a football field. "Kind of spooky up here, don't you think? I mean, the place is so far from anything. There's nothing else for miles and there's only one way in and out. The person who killed that mobster couldn't just walk out the door and get lost in a crowd."

Jackie didn't respond.

Like a mosquito buzzing around her head, I kept up the chatter as we climbed the steps. "Wow. Someone needs to put fresh cement around these stones. And look at all the moss. I bet if you stood still for a few hours it would grow over your shoes. I'd hate to be the guy who has to clean it off. Except maybe there isn't a guy, or there wouldn't be so much moss and some of the stones wouldn't be loose. I guess not a lot of people stay here. And now that there was a murder and there's a killer on the loose—"

"The killer is under house arrest." Jackie reached for the door handle on the right.

"Not the *real* killer." I grabbed the other handle. "I know Mrs. Ballantine didn't do it."

"Despite the evidence piling up against her?"

"It's a pretty small pile." I swung my door wide. "And as far as I know, nothing fresh has been added to the heap."

"That fool's paradise you live in must be a charming place," Jackie muttered.

I pretended I hadn't heard and stepped into an open area that appeared to have been decorated by Paul Bunyan. Pillars of rough-hewn log supported a ceiling high above us. A staircase ten feet wide rose straight ahead. Each step had been crafted from a log sawn lengthwise. The railings were saplings stripped of their bark. The carpet was the color of moss on a dark day.

To my relief, there was no sign of Dave. Or of Detective Atwell.

As the doors closed behind us, Paulette emerged from the lobby wearing a pair of black slacks and a black and white striped blouse with a badge that proclaimed her to be the assistant manager. Her hair was brushed back in a severe do, her makeup was minimal, and her nails were short and without polish. Despite yesterday's griping, she'd dressed the part.

"Barbara Reed?" she enquired in a haughty voice. "We were expecting you half an hour ago."

Jackie shot me a glance that indicated I was as competent as a trout in a typing class. "I'm Jackie DeWill. Sorry we're late. I hope we haven't upset your schedule."

"There isn't much of a schedule today." Paulette nodded toward the dining area. "Between the police interviewing the staff again in the executive dining area and a private detective lurking around and doing the same, Mr. Dole and I have given up on order and organization. Would you like a cup of coffee before you begin?"

"Sure," I said. "Coffee would be—"

"A waste of valuable time." Jackie waved her tape measure. "I need to see the stage and begin measuring."

"I understand. I'll have coffee brought to you." Paulette shot me a wink Jackie couldn't see, and launched the next phase of the plan. "You've been here before, Ms. DeWill, haven't you?"

"No," Jackie replied.

"Hmmm." Paulette cocked her head. "I could swear I saw you recently, perhaps early last week. Are you pos—?"

"Of course I'm positive." Jackie drew in a sharp breath. "I'd remember a place that resembled a wood products showroom."

Paulette studied her for another few seconds. "If you say so. Now if you'll come this way."

She headed across half an acre of carpet, passing chairs constructed of woven branches and tables crafted from slabs of polished wood. A balding man with a few tufts of gingery hair on his freckled scalp stood behind a tall registration desk paneled with caramel-colored wood heavy on knots and nicks. "That's Mr. Dole," Paulette said. "The owner and manager."

Farley Dole didn't look up from the sheaf of papers he was paging through, but my sister emerged from the entrance to the ballroom and strode to intercept us. She wore a trench coat and a menacing scowl. "Who are *these* people?" she asked in a gruff voice. "Do they work here?"

"No," Paulette said. "They're scouting locations for *Still Got That Strut*."

"*I'm* scouting," Jackie corrected.

"I'm in charge of transportation," I added.

Jackie snorted.

"This is the private investigator," Paulette said. "Ivy Zinnia."

"Call me Iz." My sister shot me a glare that said the bill would come due later for the Ivy Zinnia alias. She pried a wrinkled notebook and pencil from a sagging pocket. "Names."

"Why do you need our names?" I asked. "We don't work here. And we certainly weren't here when that mobster was killed."

"Maybe *you* weren't." Iz turned, loomed over Jackie, and hooked a thumb toward Paulette. "But she saw *you* here last week."

"She *thought* she saw me," Jackie insisted. "She was mistaken."

"Were you?" Iz asked Paulette.

Paulette canted her head and studied Jackie who stood as if cast in bronze. If, that is, bronze could sweat. A line of moisture glistened on Jackie's upper lip. Another traced her hairline. A blood vessel throbbed in her left temple. And, was it my imagination, or did I sniff the faint odor of fear?

"I suppose I must have been mistaken," Paulette said slowly, "since she denies ever being here."

"Could be she's lying." Iz flipped pages in her notebook and licked the tip of her pencil. Facing Jackie, she raised her voice. "Are you lying?"

"Why would I lie?" Jackie's scornful voice didn't waver in the slightest.

"You tell me," Iz said.

Jackie folded her arms across her chest. "This is ridiculous. I refuse to waste time being terrorized by this towering heap of excess flesh. I have a job to do."

And things might have stuck right there.

Except Farley Dole glanced up from the paperwork spread across the registration desk.

Chapter 32

Dole squinted through a pair of black-rimmed glasses, and tapped the desktop call bell twice. "Did you bring that invoice?"

Iz peered over her shoulder. I did the same. There was no one else in the registration area.

Paulette raised her eyebrows. This wasn't in our script.

"For the termite inspection." Farley Dole aimed his pen at Jackie. "I'm talking to you. You with the spiky hair. You didn't e-mail me your report, either. Or leave a card."

Jackie executed a full range of puzzled and confused expressions, but more sweat popped out on her forehead and another blood vessel throbbed above her right eye. "What are you talking about?"

"Tuesday. Last week. You turned up in white coveralls and a hat with a bug on it. Your hair was blond and you looked like a man, but your voice—"

Jackie threw her giant tape measure at Dole's head and took off as if her feet were on fire.

Iz, perhaps seeking revenge for the comment about excess flesh, trundled after her. Paulette and I brought up the rear, me sliding on the thick carpet as I made a hard left for the double doors.

"I'll get Dave." Paulette raced for the dining room.

I came out of my skid and hurtled through the open doors and across the porch. Jackie, lean as a whippet, was closing on my car. Iz, hefty as a hippo, was several yards behind and losing ground fast.

Heedless of moss and uneven stones, I charged down the steps and along the walk.

Feet pounded behind me. "Get inside," Dave shouted. "She might be armed."

Something I hadn't considered. The purse slung over Jackie's shoulder was large enough to contain several guns and a few hundred rounds of ammunition. Not to mention knives, throwing stars, grenades, and pepper spray.

But if I went inside, I'd miss Jackie's capture.

Or her escape.

Compromising, I slowed my pace.

Dave sprinted past yelling, "Stop! Police!"

Jackie glanced over her shoulder, yanked her laptop from her bag, and flung it at my sister. Iz ducked, stumbled, and thudded to the asphalt. The laptop sailed past and bounced along the walkway.

"Halt," Detective Atwell shouted from the porch.

Jackie put on a burst of speed, reached my car, wrenched the passenger door wide, and dove inside.

"Police. Stop!" Dave leaped over the laptop and darted past my moaning sister. He ran in a crouch, raising his cast like a shield.

My car, generally difficult to start and given to more than an occasional stall, apparently had failed to listen when I shared the plan on the way to the airport. The engine fired with a roar. Rap music blasted from the station I'd set the radio to earlier.

With a squeal and thud of rubber, Jackie took off.

Hampered by two flat tires, the car slewed hard to the left.

With a slower start, and at a lower speed, she might have controlled the vehicle's veer and drift. She might have made it between the stacked stone columns.

But she didn't.

The grinding collision sheared off the right front fender and took out the front tire with a whomp of air.

Screaming in frustration and defiance, Jackie threw herself from the car and plunged into the forest.

She didn't get far.

On the walk back, she admitted everything.

"What if she'd had a gun? Or a knife?" Dave paced a circle on the moss-green carpet while Paulette, Iz, and I sat like those three monkeys that refused to hear, see, or discuss evil.

I was the monkey that longed to slap hands over its ears. I'd had lectures like this before. Dave wasn't breaking new ground.

Paulette hadn't covered her eyes, but stared off into the distance. She drew air patterns with her fingers in a way that made me suspect she was mentally decorating a room.

And, although she hadn't placed her hands over her mouth, my sister kept it shut. Her out-of-character behavior had the effect of confusing and even spooking Dave. The path he paced veered sharply just before he reached Iz. And when he paced away from her, he kept his head partially turned as if he expected to be tackled from behind.

"You're not bulletproof. You don't have nine lives," Dave raged at me as he passed. "You ought to know better. What if Chuck and I hadn't been here? Why didn't you tell me your theory before you hatched this scheme?"

Duh.

The answer was "I did." But Dave was in rant overdrive. Reminding him would be a waste of breath. Besides, Jackie DeWill was in custody and, except for a sore shoulder Iz would no doubt complain about for weeks, there had been no injuries.

Unless you counted my car.

The words "total loss" sprang to mind when I reached it. Well, total loss except for the radio. It was still broadcasting the rhymed grievances of a guy who got no respect from society in general and the police in particular.

"Promise you won't allow loyalty to trump good sense." Paulette had told me as she patted my arm. "Don't even think about having it towed to Start 'er Up so Larry can take a look."

"But—"

"It's toast." She'd gripped my wrist and towed me to the hotel. "Mrs. Ballantine will be so thrilled we caught the killer, she'll buy you a new car."

"I don't want a new car," I'd argued. "I'd be anxious all the time in a new car. And suppose Allison got her license and wanted to drive it?"

"Good point," Paulette had conceded. "Maybe you should get a tank. A used tank."

I snapped back from that memory and saw Dave directing his comments at Paulette. "*One* of you should have demonstrated adult thinking. *One* of you should have put a halt to this hare-brained scheme. What if she'd had a gun? Or a—"

"This is where I came in." Iz levered herself from the sofa. "I'll be in the dining room when someone is ready to take my statement. I hope the food here has more appeal than the furniture."

Paulette giggled and bounced from her cushion. "I hear they make very tasty seafood bisque."

"Bisque. Schmisque. I want real food. Something I can chew."

Without a glance at me or Dave, they strolled past the reception desk.

"I think I have a knack for this detecting stuff," Iz said.

"You're a natural," Paulette assured her.

Dave shuddered.

I held in a laugh, folded my hands in my lap, tipped my chin, and made with wide-eyed expectation. "Go on," I urged him. "I'm listening."

"That will be the day." He flopped to the cushion Paulette had abandoned. "I was the one who should have listened. You were on the money about Jackie and her relationship to Glorree Morning. You have good instincts. No respect for process, but good instincts."

He flung an arm around my shoulders and pulled me against him. "But, seriously, you could have been hurt. Or worse. And . . . I . . ."

His voice fractured and he hauled in a breath. "It sounds trite and stupid and simplistic, but I don't know what I'd do without you."

Although I secretly suspected he'd get on with his life after a few months of misery—a good measure of that caused by dealing with Cheese Puff and the Committee—I murmured that I was sorry. Then I promised I'd be more careful next time, and we settled in for some serious snuggling.

Saturday night Mrs. B threw a dinner party under the canopy on the deck and invited all the usual suspects. She'd let Allison loose to decorate with strings of twinkling lights and hollowed out pumpkins filled with autumn leaves and fall flowers. The menu featured grilled steak and shrimp and a dozen side dishes. The general conversation featured more details about Jackie DeWill and a host of other topics.

For example, my ex-husband Jake.

After all his efforts to find character witnesses for his defense, Jake didn't need a single one. His trial was cancelled when the district attorney agreed to a plea bargain giving Jake credit for time served and sentencing him to a few hundred hours of community service. Within moments of his release, Jake called members of the Committee, asking about volunteer opportunities where he could demonstrate his financial, business, and computer skills. Given that the last demonstration of those computer skills was the cat-bashing blog he'd started for Cheese Puff, no one volunteered any ideas.

"And we made it clear to Bernina," Jim told me, "that if any of us spotted Jake on the premises, we'd shut down her decorating extravaganza so fast she'd have whiplash."

"And I made it clear," Verna said, "that we didn't want or need his advice about running the restaurant."

"And he'll get no free meals," Lana added. "I was married to a handsome liar. I know one when I see one."

Another topic: Dick McBain.

"Fired from his new job already," Dave crowed. "Farley Dole got the legal bill for the keep-away routine with the lobby-cam video and raised a major stink with the security company. Apparently that stink wasn't the first. When it came to annoying clients, Dick was a busy boy. But now he's in an employment timeout."

And another topic: my sister.

Still wearing the thrift-store trench coat Paulette had purchased for our performance at the River Rise Inn, she was regaling Sybil with her version of events and proclaiming her intention to get a private investigator's license. "How hard can it be? If Barb can bumble her way to catching crooks, I can, too. Only without the bumbling."

Penelope, carrying a bowl of water out for Lola, caught my eye and winked. She was home and happy to find Iz out of the dumps and interested in something. We both suspected Iz would rail about the process of getting licensed and soon head off on a tangent. But perhaps the tangent would lead to her next career.

For yet another topic: Glorree Morning.

"She called me this morning and we had a nice, long chat," Mrs. B confided as she mixed a pitcher of frothy drinks. "She apologized for what Jackie did, and said she'd drop out of the competition."

"And you responded?"

"That she'd certainly do nothing of the sort." Mrs. B plunked bright red cherries in stemmed glasses and poured. "Glorree was jealous and competitive in those distant days. She complained that things weren't fair, but she never cheated. If she knew what Jackie was up to, she would have put a stop to it. Besides, think of all the publicity this generated. Ratings will skyrocket."

That caused Dario to flash a huge shark-like smile. I suspected he was anticipating Mrs. B's performance the way a kid looks forward to Christmas, Halloween, or the last day of school.

And for yet another topic: Big Shiny.

"You came up with an interesting theory about the biological relationship," Detective Charles Atwell informed me. "But he wasn't Jackie DeWill's father. Glorree Morning swears he never got to first base with her. I expect the DNA will confirm her story."

I nodded but said nothing. Atwell had a way of twisting my words, so I'd gotten in the habit of handing out darn few for him to mangle. Paulette, however, asked the question in my mind. "Who was Jackie's father?"

Atwell brushed the question aside with a flip of his hand. "Don't know. Doesn't matter."

"If it wasn't Big Shiny," Paulette persisted, "then why did she kill him?"

"Because he was there and it was easy." Atwell took a swig of beer. "She went to the River Rise disguised as a termite inspector to get a look at Muriel Ballantine's routine."

"To help her mother win the competition," Paulette said.

Atwell frowned. He hated interruptions. "To make the disguise convincing, she had to go through the motions of checking the rooms. Apparently Big Shiny resented having his nap interrupted and teed off on her the way he did on the staff. She decided to make the world a better place while framing Mrs. Ballantine. She got a smock and a shower cap and a pack of light bulbs from the supply closet and—"

"Zipped to Mrs. B's room and got her to handle the lamps," Paulette finished.

Atwell did an about-face and headed for a table loaded with appetizers. Like I said, he hated to be interrupted.

Paulette smothered a giggle and raised her glass. "To a productive week. Oh, and you might want to dash out tonight and buy the early edition of the Sunday paper."

"The pool story?"

"Story, sidebars, accusations, shocked reactions. The whole nine yards." She raised her glass again. "Smart money says we'll never have to listen to Cheryl again."

Mrs. B tucked Cheese Puff under one arm, tapped a knife against the rim of a water glass, and called us to the long table angled across the deck. "Find your places and fill your plates."

"Yum." Allison led the attack on the buffet. Josh, always polite, hung back with Luke while Verna, Sybil, Lana, and Paulette got in line. I waited for Dave who, to no avail, was glowering at his daughter and muttering about a lack of manners.

Her plate piled high, Allison flounced to her seat. "I was so afraid I wouldn't get to Las Vegas."

"Well, now the way is clear." Mrs. B beamed at me. "Thanks to my friends."

"What airline are we flying?" Allison chewed a jumbo shrimp as she talked. "Are we sitting in first class? When do I get my ticket?"

"Oh, you won't need a ticket, dear. I intend to charter a plane. That will be much more comfortable for everyone, especially the dogs."

Allison gaped. "The dogs are going?"

"Of course. The change in climate might help Lola's allergies." Mrs. B cradled Cheese Puff and nuzzled his head. "And as for the little prince, why he's part of my act."

Also by Carolyn J. Rose

No Substitute for Murder
No Substitute for Money
No Substitute for Maturity
No Substitute for Myth
No Substitute for Mistakes
Hemlock Lake
Through a Yellow Wood
The Devil's Tombstone
An Uncertain Refuge
Sea of Regret
A Place of Forgetting

With Michael A. Nettleton

Death at Devil's Harbor
Deception at Devil's Harbor
The Hard Karma Shuffle
The Crushed Velvet Miasma
Drum Warrior
Sucker Punches

Carolyn J. Rose grew up in New York's Catskill Mountains, graduated from the University of Arizona, logged two years in Arkansas with Volunteers in Service to America, and spent 25 years as a television news researcher, writer, producer, and assignment editor in Arkansas, New Mexico, Oregon, and Washington. She's now a substitute teacher in Vancouver, Washington. Her interests are reading, swimming, walking, gardening, and NOT cooking.

www.deadlyduomysteries.com